CHAPTER 1

Immortality ends tonight.

Standing on the ledge of a mountainous cliff, Perdita gazed over the majestic storm raging beneath her. Mountainous swells thrust foamy claws into the sky. Black, slick as ink, spewed from angry heavens. Lightning hurled white-hot forks toward Erden, while thunder announced the doom of all in the tempest's path.

Perdita had been waiting endlessly for such a violent squall. Mayhap this would be the night. Mayhap this would be the moment the unbearable pain in her heart would end. Oh, let it be so! What would it be like to die, to finally close her eyes forever? To know naught but darkness and emptiness. Nothingness. Part of her feared it. Most of her yearned for it. At least her agony would be no more. The pain, the loneliness gripping her heart would finally cease.

Tears spilled from her eyes but the wind stole them away. Even her tears were not her own. After tonight, she would cry no more. Finally, her three hundred-year nightmare would come to an end.

Wind whipped around her naked body, forcing her against the cliff wall. Jagged rock slashed her skin as the tempest roared madly in her ears—berating voices from a thousand rejections, a thousand unkept promises, a thousand abandonments. She jammed her hands over her ears, but the voices taunted her mercilessly … reminding her that no matter how hard she tried, she failed to obtain the one thing she desperately craved, the one thing that continually eluded her, the one thing—the only thing—that could liberate her from infinite torment.

She trembled. Rain pelted her like rocks from a cruel god. Welts rose on her skin. Ignoring the pain, she drew a deep breath and fought through the wind to the edge of the cliff. It wrenched around her, punching her, pulling her hair, beating her for being so worthless, so useless. Then lifting her arms above her, she closed her eyes, and leaned over the precipice. At first, like a benevolent friend unwilling to let her go, the wind held her back, buffeting her in place. But soon even the gale couldn't hold her up, and she felt herself tumbling down … down … down …

She shattered the surface. Seawater engulfed her, ramming into her from all sides. Deeper and deeper she descended. The jolts mutated to gentle caresses and the sounds of the storm muffled to mere whispers. Her legs melded together. Awkward kicks transformed into one efficient, powerful stroke. Tingling skittered over her body, molding skin into scale.

Perdita released her breath. Bubbles rose. She gulped. Water flooded her lungs—always uncomfortable at first, but then as her skin breathed in the sea, more natural than she cared to admit. More normal to her than breathing air. As normal as the grief that ripped through her every time she dove in the water and became a creature she loathed.

Slipping with ease through the dark sea toward her destination, she soared upward and punched through the surface into the storm once again. Wind spit salty foam in her face. A massive wave carried her high into the night sky like a princess on her chariot. Scanning the turbulent scene, she spotted the monstrous rock—the one they called Hades' Gate—just half a mile away, aptly named for the number of sailors who had died upon its barbed spikes. Sharp, craggy spears stuck out in every direction as if Natas himself crouched in the sea with a thousand claws extended.

Natas or not, Perdita hoped *she* would be the next victim.

If only she could position herself just right so the next colossal wave would smash her against the rock with such force, such ferocity, that her body would be completely shredded.

If only ...

It *had* to work. 'Twas her last idea. She'd tried everything else: poison, pistol shot, starvation, stabbing, even leaping into a fire. Each time she'd suffered terribly, but she had always healed. The last time, when she'd jumped off a cliff into a deep ravine, it had taken much longer to recover, and she realized that there was a point past which her body, immortal or not, would not be able to mend itself and would hopefully drift into that peaceful state that was the reward of all mankind. Death.

Ah, sweet, sweet death! To at last find the rest her soul craved. To be free of the tormenting bitterness and despair that plagued her by day and the perpetual hopelessness that assaulted her dreams by night. She *must* be free—now!

Leaping off the crest of a wave, she dove into the trough and swam to just the right position. Then, arms by her side and tail strong and taut, she swooped up inside the next undulating surge, allowing the force of sea and wind to lift her to the top. Water caressed her body and gurgled and sloshed past her ears in a magnificent orchestra that would put great composers to shame.

Bursting through the foamy cap, she glanced at Hades' Gate. In perfect position. Daggers of lightning scored the sky. Thunder bellowed its displeasure. No matter. She only needed to ride this swell until it hurled her onto the barbed rock that would set her free.

Some people said if you spoke King Abbas's name, he would hear your plea and answer. Perdita had always thought them fools. How could he hear anything from here in Erden when he lived far across the chasm? She wasn't even sure he existed, for no one had ever seen him. Still, mayhap 'twas worth a try. "King Abbas, help me this night, I beg you. Help me find peace."

Facing forward, she started to close her eyes, wanting to enjoy her last moments as the wave carried her along, but a flicker in the distance snagged her attention. A flash of light, then darkness. Wiping water from her face, she focused on the spot. There it was again. A burst of light. Then black.

She adjusted her body and flapped her tail to keep up with the wave. Foam spun around her. The sea roared its fury. Whatever the flickering light was, what did it matter to her? She would be gone soon enough.

A shout battled for preeminence over thunder. A scream echoed over waves. Against her will, she stared into the darkness for its source. A ship appeared, tottering on the churning swells like a child's toy in a rushing creek. One of its two masts lay on its side, half in the water, half on deck. Sails and rigging tangled on the ship like a fisherman's net. The vessel dove into a trough and disappeared from sight. Wails ricocheted around her—wails of impending death. She knew them well.

Had envied them for so long.

The ship appeared again, spinning on a coiling whitecap. Men clung to yards and railings while others scrambled across the deck in a frenzy. Three men raised axes to chop lines in an effort to free the broken mast that threatened to drag them to the deep. One of them crawled precariously out upon the wood, hacking at the rigging with a desperation inherent only to mortals who dreaded their lives cut short.

He fell. One minute he was there, chopping the ropes, the next gone, swallowed up by a raging sea that showed no mercy—except to Perdita.

"Zost!" She swore, glancing back at Hades' Gate. So close ... just moments away. She faced the ship again, drifting farther and farther from the man, who was now but a nob of flailing arms atop liquid coal. What did one more life matter? This was *her* moment, her time to find freedom. Many sailors fell into the sea with no one to save them. Who was she to disturb the natural course of life and death?

A giant swell grabbed the man and tossed him in the air, then smothered him with raging foam. He disappeared below. One glance behind her told her she had but one more minute and she'd slam into Hades' Gate. One more minute and the man would drown. Life was precious. All life but hers. She could not leave him.

"Zost!" She groaned and dove into the agitated foam.

Savion pounded his fist on the binnacle, ignoring the pain, then raked sodden hair from his face.

"What should we do, Captain?" His first mate, Petrok, stared at the dark clouds that had appeared out of nowhere and now cloaked sky and sea in an ominous black shroud.

The ship canted to larboard. Both men gripped the binnacle, rapidly adjusting boots on the slippery deck as a bold wave washed over the ship, upending sailors before sloshing back to sea through the scuppers. Lightning severed the charcoal sky, flickering a ghostly gray over the scene and drawing the harried gazes of even the most hardened sailors toward the black monster stampeding toward them.

After spotting a shadow on the horizon early that morning, Savion had set a course twenty degrees north by northwest toward the coast of a nearby island where they could seek shelter. They should have made it. Even with a hold full of goods Savion promised to deliver for Governor Grigson. Then why was the tempest now upon them, growling and spitting like a ravenous dragon from some mythical tale? Or worse, perhaps it was Natas's doing, though Savion didn't believe the evil warlord had the power over wind and wave.

"Orders, Captain?" Petrok shouted over the increasing wind that whipped his dark hair wildly about his head like a sea urchin.

"We have no choice. We run before the wind as best we can." Savion was always amazed at the confidence he found in Petrok's dark squinty eyes. "All hands about ship. Lower mizzen, tops, and stays. Raise the main."

Petrok gave him a nod and started to turn away. Savion gripped his arm. "Have Nuto secure the guns, and tell Bart and Tund to man the pumps."

"Aye, aye, Captain," Petrok shouted as a wave crashed over them. The crusty sailor shook water from his leathery face, then turned to yell orders to the crew.

Sailors scrambled across the deck, some grabbing lines, others dropping below, while others flung themselves into the ratlines and raced above. Savion had chosen his crew well. Seasoned sailors, devoid of fear in both battle and storm. Hona, his quartermaster and the youngest of the crew looked up at Savion. Admiration beamed from the lad's eyes as his blond hair thrashed about him. Savion gave him a reassuring nod. Honorable men, loyal men, all. Men who laughed in the face of death and risked everything to defend the Kingdom of Erden. Men who had been by his side for over two years as he scoured the Ancient

Seas defending the weak, helping the poor, and crushing the rebellion started by Natas.

Thunder bellowed. The ship pitched. Savion gripped the railing, allowing the wind to slap his face. He deserved it, he supposed, for his failure as a son. All he'd ever wanted was to be like his father. But how does one rise to the standards of a man who is pure goodness, wisdom, love, honesty, grace, mercy, justice ...? Savion could go on endlessly.

The truth is, he'd failed miserably.

His punishment—though his father had not called it such—was to be sent across the gulf to the Ancient Seas on a mission to save someone or something. Savion was not told. Only that he would "know" when the time was right. In the meantime, he must help the people of the realm and attack the enemy's strongholds wherever he found them.

But if Savion was honest, he was frustrated. He'd been following his father's orders for two years, yet he still had no idea what his precise assignment was. He longed to go home to Nevaeh and be with his family and friends again, but he was stranded on Erden until his mission was complete.

A blast of wind clawed the scarf from his head and nearly tore off his shirt. His hair lashed his cheek as the ship lunged over a wave. Savion gripped the quarterdeck railing, groaning. He could fight an enemy in battle, but how could he fight a tempest? Especially one that only grew more violent. Raindrops stung his face like grape shot. The mainsail billowed and snapped in a frantic effort to capture the wind. With just the one sail raised, he hoped to scud before the gale and miss the worst of the storm.

Sailors dropped to the deck from the shrouds and attempted to grab lines to secure the yards, but the ropes flailed in the wind like evil whips, striking one of the men. He cried out and dropped to the deck.

Rushing to assist him, Savion leapt down the quarter-deck ladder. The ship bucked, and he toppled to the heaving deck. The sky above, dark and thick, hung low enough to touch, twisting and turning as if it was alive. As if it were Natas himself trying to swipe Savion from the seas. But Savion refused to give up.

Gripping the capstan, he pulled himself up. White light flashed across his vision. Heat surrounded him. A loud snap, a crack, and the sound of wood splintering sizzled over his ears. The smell of electricity and charred wood stung his nose. A wall of water rose and seized him, hurling him to the deck. He grabbed, clutched, gasped for air as he tumbled across the sodden planks. Finally, he hooked onto a hatch grating. The deck leveled. He opened his eyes. The mainmast dangled in the wind like a noodle hanging from a fork.

"Look out below!" a sailor shouted, scattering men like rats right before the eighty-foot mast toppled to the deck.

Thuwnk! A staggering tremble jolted the ship—jarred all of Savion's bones. Wood groaned. Like a teeter-totter, the deck tilted to starboard. Sailors rolled over the wooden planks, reaching for anything to keep them from plunging into the sea.

Fighting wind and rain, Savion shoved his way to the capstan and grabbed an ax, one thought in his mind: free the mast, lest it haul the ship to a watery grave. If he could not, this would be the last fateful voyage of the *Scepter*.

And he would have failed his father once again.

Nuto and Petrok joined him, furiously sawing and chopping away at shifting lines the size of sailor's arms, yet thick and hard and coated in tar.

Savion's boots slipped on the slick wood. He lost control. He would have fallen if not for Petrok's firm grasp on his arm. Nodding his thanks, Savion spit water from his mouth as unfamiliar terror clenched his gut. Was this to be his end? Though he'd rather die in battle, he supposed dying at sea wasn't so bad. Better than facing his father and admitting he'd failed his mission.

"No!" The wind stole his growl. He wasn't done with life yet. He would discover who or what his father wished him to save. He would continue to help others and battle Natas's rebellion. He would make his father proud and return to Nevaeh a victor. Raising his ax, he slashed at the lines again and again, anger fueling his dwindling strength.

The ship jerked and mounted another swell. Sailors flopped over the deck. Savion clung to a line and closed his eyes. A torrent of seawater pounded him like a thousand fists. His feet floundered beneath him. Water filled his mouth. His hand slipped from the rope. *No!* He heard Petrok call his name in a muffled desperate cry before the wave launched him into the sea.

The roar of the storm faded under the heavy water. He searched for air, thrusting arms and legs through what felt like molasses. Deeper and deeper he sank. Down to the depths where there was no pain. The sea embraced him like a long-lost friend, refusing to let go, refusing to let him fight to the surface. It rocked him back and forth as if trying to lull him to sleep.

His final sleep.

He kicked with all his might, unsure whether he headed toward air or farther into the deep. The current grew stronger, hauling him in its mighty grip. He broke the surface and gulped for air. A wave closed a fist around him and carried him forward as if he were a puppet. A heavy, dark object loomed up ahead. A giant rock—perhaps the throne of Natas himself. Fear strangled him. Sharp spires pointed toward him. He frantically tried to swim away, but the wave cruelly thrust him toward them.

Pain. Excruciating pain as if he'd been stabbed a hundred times.

Something touched him. Someone grabbed his arms and pulled him through the sea. Fast! So fast the water sped by him in an ethereal swoosh. His pain faded, and the world became no more.

Chapter 2

With her arms straining and tail churning up foam, Perdita lifted the human male out of the water and heaved him onto the rocky ledge. Backing away, she spit out the sea as air convulsed in her lungs. The man coughed. Water spewed from his mouth before he collapsed back into unconsciousness. Blood trickled down the rock and dripped into the water filling the cave that had been Perdita's home for centuries.

Drip, drip, drip. Life spilled from the man, echoing an eerie cadence off the rock walls. She must do something or he would die. Swimming to the edge of the pool, she lifted herself upon the rocky sand that formed a ridge around the water and swung her tail up, waiting for its transformation. She ran her fingers over the smooth circular scales of turquoise edged in silvery glitter that spanned from her waist down to her tail in a lustrous mirage of turquoise, maroon, and green, shimmering like an abalone shell.

How could she hate something so beautiful?

That beauty began to fade. Melt would be a better word. An agonizing itch gripped her waist and traversed down her legs, spanning to her tail. She shifted uncomfortably, resisting the urge to scratch as scales melted away like ice before the sun. Bit by bit, the pearly skin of her legs appeared until finally her tail separated and transformed into feet. She wiggled her toes. Two beautiful feet.

Leaping up on those beautiful feet, she lit a lantern, made her way to a chest she'd salvaged from a shipwreck two hundred years ago, and began rummaging through the mementos that reminded her of home, of being human, of friendships and love and life: engraved silverware from a captain's cabin, a golden locket, a hairbrush and mirror, a porcelain tea service, King Urdon of Tidor's leather shoes—she smiled as she remembered stealing them from beneath his bed—tomes from an ancient library, and the hilt of a knight's broken sword. She caressed the pouch containing Sir Ivan's livery collar—the one he'd given her as a promise of his love. After three hundred years in a salty, moist cave, the velvet had shredded and flashes of the gold medallion winked at her from within its folds.

Sir Ivan of Morehead. She sighed. Her first love. The man who'd started it all, back when she had been human and so very young. Odd, she could hardly remember what he looked like. Only that he was deliciously handsome. The first one hurt the most. But what did it matter? He was long dead. And she was alone.

Still.

Beside the pouch, another larger sack bulged with precious tokens from other Ivans: Ivan two, Ivan three, Ivan four, and so on until the last one, Ivan twenty-nine. What was his name? Thankfully, the past ten years had wiped away the memory. It mattered naught. Ivan twenty-nine would be the final Ivan.

Thunder bellowed outside the cave, shaking the rocks, jarring her from her thoughts. The human male moaned. Shoving aside the sack, she grabbed some bandages, blankets, and a soft down pillow from the bottom of the chest—things she kept for such an emergency, for she had no use for these things herself. Holding them to her face, she snuggled her cheek into the soft fabric and sighed as vague memories of sleeping dry and cuddled in blankets teased her.

Slipping an oversized shirt over her head in case the human male awoke, she added a jar of seaweed balm to her stack and made her way back to him. She would keep him warm and dry and tend his wounds. The same thing she'd done for hundreds before him. 'Twas the only thing that had kept her sane these past three hundred years—saving the lives of shipwrecked sailors. At least it had given her purpose, a reason to leave her cave, though recently even that had become meaningless.

After making a bed in the sand beside him, Perdita dragged him on top of the soft blankets, then removed his shirt, scarf, and boots. Cuts and scrapes marred his chest and arms. A deep hole bled from his shoulder. But it was the puncture on his head that worried her most. She pressed a cloth to it, hoping to stay the blood saturating her pillow. She would have to stitch the hole and hope infection didn't set in. So frail, this human condition, she envied it. Still, she would not let him die. Nay, she would use her powers to heal him as she'd done with so many others, even though it meant she'd suffer the worst torture imaginable, along with the loss of all her strength for at least an hour.

Thank the stars the man had not struck Hades' Gate head on, its barbed spikes only clipping him in passing. Though the evil rock had done plenty of damage, she shuddered to think what condition he'd be in otherwise.

The condition *she* would have been in if she hadn't been so rudely interrupted—the sweet sleep of death.

She knew his type. Proud sailors with no respect for the power of the wind and wave—so bloated with their arrogance they actually believed they could outwit and conquer the sea. Perdita had rescued countless pompous imbeciles who had tried over the years, always depositing them safely ashore before they regained full consciousness, their minds assailed with vague memories of a mermaid who rescued them. Myths and fables from fever-delusioned minds, or so those who heard the tales claimed.

All save Damien Gund and his minions. But that was another story.

The man groaned and his lips twitched. Dabbing a cloth into the pool, Perdita began cleaning his wounds, then quickly stitched and bandaged him up as best she could. She hadn't much time left before the curse would force her back into the water.

Finally done, she sat back to examine her patient. Light-brown hair streaked in gold tumbled about an angular face, strong bristly jaw, and aquiline nose. Sculpted muscles bulged on his arms and legs and rippled across his stomach. Aside from his powerful physique, he wasn't a particularly attractive man—rather average-looking, if she had to admit. A typical sailor among so many.

She ran her fingers over a tattoo of a lion on his right bicep and huffed at the symbol of power and virility. Obviously her assessment had been correct. He was simply another man suffering from an overinflated ego.

She tugged on a rope around his neck and pulled a medallion from his hair. 'Twas heavy and thick, no doubt made of solid gold. The figure of a dove was etched on one side and a lamb on the other. A dove and lamb? Interesting symbols worn by a man with a lion tattoo. The word Nevaeh was carved in fancy letters above both gentle animals. Very curious. 'Twas the royal city that existed on the other side of the gulf.

She hadn't time to ponder the meaning when pain seared from her toes up through her legs, growing in intensity as scales began to form on her skin. Her feet melded together. Her lungs collapsed. Gasping for air, she quickly covered the man with a blanket and dove into the pool.

Four hours later when she emerged again, the human was feverish, and just as she feared, his wound was turning green. She knew all too well what would happen next if she delayed. Laying her hands atop the cut, she closed her eyes and concentrated on the man, his torn flesh, his lifeblood draining. Scales formed on her hands, inviting the pain in, drawing out the agony, pulling the infection, from the man into her. Blood spilled from the gills at her side—*his* blood. Spasms of torment racked through her. Biting her lip, she tried not to cry out. The pain increased until she could hardly breathe. Every muscle, every cell screamed for release. Her arms trembled. Her legs shook. Her insides burned like fire. If she would only die! But then the pain subsided, like the retreating of a storm, slow at first but then draining from her until she collapsed and dragged herself back into the water.

Hours later, after she regained her strength and health, she pulled herself onto the ledge. He was well! At least the wound on his head was healed. But he was still hot and remained unconscious. Perdita yanked her tail from the water and waited for her feet to form. Now, she must keep him cool and ensure he drank water. A difficult feat when she could only emerge from the sea for twenty minutes every four hours. Yet during the next day, she spent every one of those precious minutes patting him down with moist cloths and dribbling fresh water into his mouth.

Now, as she sat beside the human, his skin blotchy and sweat-laden, watching him breathe heavily and fidget uncomfortably, she decided mayhap a song would soothe him. 'Twas said a mermaid's song could send a man into a deep sleep of peace and comfort, even lure him beneath the water to his death. Such evil was not for Perdita. She leaned toward the man and sang softly.

"How fare thee, oh sailor boy

How fare thee on the sea
Doest thou want my beauty, boy
Doest thou have a plea
Whene'er the ships teeter so
Whene'er the waters rise
Thou wilt find me in the deep
Where thou wilt see me with thine eyes"

The tune echoed off the moist walls, magnifying her voice and making it sound sweet and alluring. Much more than when on land where she could hardly carry a tune. Or mayhap singing was another charm that came with being a mermaid.

She was about to start another chorus when the man tossed his head and began mumbling in his delirium. "The lion. The lion."

Dipping a cloth in the cool seawater, Perdita dabbed his cheeks and neck, but it did naught to calm him.

"I'm sorry, Father," he mumbled.

"Shhh. 'Tis all right." Perdita drew close.

"The lion," he breathed out. "The lion breaks the curse."

What? What would this human know about a curse? Certainly he spoke not of *her* curse. Nay, he was feverish and rambled nonsensical as most humans did.

Her legs burned. Zost! She was running out of time. Grabbing the bowl of fresh water, she dipped the sponge in and gave him one last drink as scales formed on her legs. She had to leave. The human clutched her wrist. Tight. Pain sped up her arm. She struggled as her lungs collapsed, begging to be filled with water. She wouldn't die, of course, but the pain of suffocation would be unbearable.

Her feet joined and then spread into a tail.

The human's eyes shot open. He panted, turning to stare at her with the most golden eyes she'd ever seen. "Do not despair, the lamb will break Natas's curse!" he rasped then fell back onto the pillow, eyes shut.

Suffocating and confused, Perdita shook from his grip and slipped into the water.

CHAPTER 3

Something tickled Savion's hand. It crawled, stopped, then crawled again, moving up his arm and onto his neck as if someone played a keyboard on his skin. He weakly tried to swat the offender away, but his hand felt like an anchor. A breeze blew hair into his face as the thunder of waves pounded his ears.

The keyboard-player bit his cheek. "Ouch!" Savion batted at his face and pried his eyes open against what felt like cannonballs strapped to his lids. A tiny crab skittered away over the sand and dove into a hole. Beyond him, many of its friends did the same as a wave crashed ashore.

Ashore?

Indeed, he *was* ashore. Lying on a bed of palm fronds beneath the shade of a tree. His wet clothes clung to his skin as a searing ache drummed through his head. He rubbed it, but pain and the feel of stitches caused him to jerk back his hand. *What?* The last thing he remembered was hacking away at the mast lines, trying to save the ship.

The *Scepter*!

He painfully pushed his body up to rest on his elbows. After the dizziness cleared, he scanned the shore, where foamed-capped waters extended to the horizon. Where was his ship? How did he get here? And more importantly, did his crew survive the storm?

Terror prickled his skin. Planting his palms in the sand, he tried to rise. Twice he fell and had to wait to gather his strength. On the third attempt, he finally stood on wobbly legs, clutching onto the tree trunk. Memories swam through his mind. He'd fallen into the sea. The waters had covered him, forcing him below. Then fierce pain. The last thing he remembered was the pain.

Perhaps he'd managed to cling to a piece of wood. No, surely he would have woken in the waves—not lying on a bed of leaves.

Had his men rescued him and brought him here? Taking tentative steps, he made his way to the water's edge, scouring the shoreline and the jungle beyond for any sign that his crew had survived. *Father, please, surely they are alive and well.*

A flicker, a glimmer, a reflection of sunlight caught his gaze. Something stirred in the waves just offshore. A shadow. Shimmers. Then a foamy splash. He rubbed his eyes. He could have sworn he saw the tail of an enormous fish.

His legs gave out, and he sank to the sand. He was seeing things. Wind flapped his damp shirt, chilling him, and revealing deep gashes and dark bruises covering his chest. Whatever happened to him, he was lucky to be alive.

"Father, did you send Guardians to rescue me?" As expected, no answer came. His father wasn't here, though Savion often spoke to him as if he were. Which provided much fodder for taunting from his crew. Perhaps it made Savion feel closer to the man who was eons away . . . across the gulf. He gripped the amulet hanging about his neck, thankful for its comforting warmth.

A wave splashed over his toes, and a vision of a dark-haired beauty flickered through his mind. A dark-haired beauty with eyes the color of the sea. Now he *knew* he was dreaming, for he'd never get within twenty feet of a woman so beautiful. He'd been deceived by a lovely face once. Shamed by an alluring figure …

But never again.

Perdita popped her head above water and studied the man who was but a speck on the beach. He seemed well—well enough to stand and walk and remain conscious. Which was why she quickly deposited him on shore before he awoke and saw who tended his wounds. A slight pang struck her heart as she watched him struggle to rise and lumber down the beach. Why? She'd plucked a thousand sailors from Neptune's death grip, nursed them back to life, and she'd never given them another thought after returning them to land.

This human was different.

Dipping beneath the waves, she followed him along the shore, careful to dive out of sight when he glanced her way. This human had muttered constantly in his delirium, as most sailors did. But unlike most sailors, he did not speak of liquor or wenches or treasure or battles at sea. He did not utter a single curse nor spew angry words of revenge at some vile enemy. Nay, this man mumbled about purpose and a mission to defeat evil. His words were hopeful and eager. His face even lit with joy when he spoke of a father he missed and his longing for Nevaeh, the land beyond the gulf. That baffled her the most. Nevaeh was naught but a mythical place. No one had ever gone there. At least no one Perdita ever met.

No doubt too much sun and salt had driven the human mad. Still, his words carried such intensity, they stirred something deep within her.

Hope.

Zost! Hope was the opiate of fools. Which made this human naught but a fool. And she a bigger one for following him now. Yet, as he stumbled along, she found herself unusually curious about him: to know who he was and where he came from and why he seemed so different.

After an hour, the man found the small fishing town she knew he would stumble upon. Another hour passed in which he bartered his way on board a merchant vessel that was preparing to set sail.

She should leave now.

He could take care of himself, and Perdita had her death to plan. It was nearly the time of ephemeral redemption, and she couldn't bear to endure another torturous month.

The human male boarded the ship, and shouts from the captain to weigh anchor and raise sails echoed over the water. Perdita dove beneath the waves and swam to the bottom of the small harbor. Coral in every imaginable color blossomed like crystalline flowers from the seabed, plants swayed in the water like graceful dancers, starfish clung to living rock, and crabs skittered to and fro. Sunlight pierced the water—spears of rainbows from above—while colorful fish of all sizes scattered as she approached. She fanned her tail, propelling herself forward as the warm water slid over her body. This was her curse. Condemned to live in such splendor forever. Indeed, she had once thought it beautiful and peaceful. And in many ways, it was more pleasing than land. But the beauty only reminded her that she had no one to share it with—no family, no friends, no lover. Paradise, no matter how dazzling, when experienced alone was worse than hell.

A fish slid beside her, matching her pace, and she reached over and touched its slick skin. Nay, not completely alone, she supposed. Mayhap she would have gotten used to her underwater world if not for the forced ephemeral redemption—a chance every ten years to break the curse, a month's time in which she became human again. She welcomed it at first, even looked forward to it with great anticipation. But as each month sped past in failure and she was plunged back in the sea to wait another ten years—another long, miserable, lonely ten years—she dreaded the chance to hope yet again, only to have her hopes inevitably crushed.

What a cruel twist of fate Forwin had pronounced upon her.

The yellow tang rubbed against her and swam off, and Perdita flipped onto her back and admired the surface of the water rippling in the sunlight. There. The keel of the fishing ship slid through the bay out to sea, its hull casting a shadow over the otherwise luminescent scene.

The human male was on that ship. Sailing out of her life as they all did. Then why did she feel so distraught? Swooshing her tail, she sped upward and broke the surface just behind the stern of the ship. In moments, she spotted the man high in the rigging of the mizzen mast, working along with other top men to unfurl sail. He shouldn't be up there! Not with a head wound that had nearly caused his death. Dizziness could overcome him, and he could find himself once again in the sea.

Then all her efforts, her pain, would have been for naught.

Nay. She could not allow that to happen. She would ensure he arrived at his destination safely, and then she would leave him be. Diving back beneath the waves, she sped after the ship.

CHAPTER 4

Savion stood at the main deck railing and gazed over the ebony sea. He stretched his sore back, rubbing muscles stiff from hard work and skin tanned from the sun. Though a captain's responsibilities were many, Savion would do well to remember how difficult a long day's work in the sun could be, so he would be more understanding of his crew.

If he found them again. Yet all he could do now was hope they survived and go to the meeting place they'd agreed upon should they get separated.

Above him myriad stars sprinkled light atop foamy waves, like diamond necklaces draped over black satin. He never ceased to marvel at the beauty of creation, the love put into every detail. He would have missed this scene if he'd been sleeping below deck. As he should be if he expected to endure another day of hard work. Yet ever since he'd boarded this ship, his sleep had been fitful and full of strange dreams. All his life his dreams had been pleasant and peaceful, but the ones that recently plagued him were filled with strange sea creatures and frightening scenes of blood and battles.

"Father," he spoke aloud, "what is happening to me? I even dreamt of Lorelei, and she has not invaded my dreams in years."

He'd been happy for the reprieve since she was the reason he was sailing upon the Ancient Seas and not at home with his father. Though he'd long since forgiven the temptress, just the thought of her made his skin crawl. If only he hadn't been such a fool. If only he hadn't fallen for her wiles. But he'd been young and impressionable. And she'd been so beautiful. So very beautiful. In his naivety he'd equated beauty with goodness. But he'd learned the hard way that appearance had nothing to do with the heart. In fact, he'd discovered that beauty often corrupted the heart. He had so desperately wanted a bride—to choose a lady who would make his father proud. Instead, he'd brought shame to the entire family.

And banishment to himself.

"Father, haven't I learned my lesson?"

A shriek and a splash drew his attention below, and he peered over the railing just in time to see a large fish disappear beneath the foam curling off the hull.

Growing tired of keeping up with the ship, Perdita found a comfortable grip on a strake lining the hull. She'd spotted the man as soon as he'd leaned on the railing, hands clasped, staring out to sea.

Being by himself, she hadn't expected him to speak, but then his voice—distinctive in its richness—filtered down to her, and she angled her ear upward, desperate to hear him over the rustle of water. He had called out to his father, then mentioned a woman named Lorelei. Odd. Why would a grown man talk to a father who wasn't there? He spoke again, softer this time, and she pulled herself up the hull blocks, straining to hear. Her hand slipped and before she knew it, she'd tumbled backward into the water.

The sounds of the sea gurgled in her ears as she recovered and sped to catch up to the ship. Easing as close to the hull as she could, she grabbed ahold and popped her head above water once again.

This time two voices met her ears.

"I thought I saw something," the man said.

"Just a fish. Dolphin perhaps. They like to follow the ship sometimes, Mr. … Mr. …"

"Ryne. Savion Ryne."

Savion Ryne. A strong name.

"But I could have sworn I saw … never mind. It sure didn't look like a dolphin's tail."

"Moonlight plays tricks on ye sometimes, Mr. Ryne." The man slapped Savion on the back.

"Call me Savion."

A few minutes passed in silence before the sailor spoke. "Yer that fellow who saved me sister, ain't ye? I thought I recognized ye."

"I wouldn't know. Who might your sister be?"

"I'm sure ye remember her. She's quite unforgettable. The lady with flamin' red hair and ten kids. Ye saved her life an' her little ones, if what she told me was true."

"I don't recall."

"She an' her wee ones was stuck in Ardenton when Natas's raiders invaded last month. Accordin' t' her, ye fought off several o' them scalawags at great risk t' yerself an' brought her t' safety."

"Ah yes," Savion said. "Kind woman. Loves her children. A bit … *enthusiastic,* if I remember."

The sailor chuckled. "If that's what ye call it. We who knows her call her neurotic. Har har! But aye, she be a good mother. She said ye go around savin' people where'er ye find them, all the whiles fightin' Natas's hordes. Like some hero, a savior o' sorts."

"Naw." Savion gave an embarrassed huff. "I do what any man would do in the face of evil."

"Aye, she said ye were humble too. Seems she didn't 'xaggerate on that account."

Minutes passed in silence.

"Well, I jist wanted t' thank ye, Mr. Ry … Savion. Keep up the fight against Natas. That vermin be a liar an' the worst sort o' thief."

"You are a good judge of character, my friend. But remember you can fight against him too."

"If the occasion presents itself, I will do jist that, Savion. Now ye best be gettin' some rest. The captain 'xpects us up early t' man the sails."

Perdita heard the sailor clomp away. After a few minutes, Savion, too, shoved from the railing and disappeared.

Incredible—a rescuer, a savior, a man who put others before himself. In all her years, she'd never met anyone like that. And she'd been alive a long time.

Had she found *the one*? The one who could finally break the curse?

The next few days passed by like a sea turtle slogging through mud. Savion made no further appearances at the railing, though Perdita spotted him often in the tops. Sometimes she swam alongside the ship. Sometimes she grabbed hold of the hull strake and rested. All the time she did her best to keep out of sight. Mermaids carried a high price, not only to Damien Gund but to anyone with the craftiness to catch one. Of course she knew of no others of her kind in the Ancient Seas. She'd spent the first ten years of her time searching from shore to shore for any companionship, finally concluding that if there'd ever been other mermaids, they'd long since been caught or dead. Probably both.

Finally, the ship sailed into the harbor of Hoffnung, a well-known port famous for its nightly entertainments, good food, and haven for all sorts of ruffians. Perdita knew it well. 'Twas where she'd met two of her Ivans.

Two of the worst ones.

She should leave. Go back to her cave and plot her demise. It wasn't safe for her so close to so many humans. Yet first, she must ensure the man—Savion—got ashore safely. She hadn't followed him all this way to abandon him now. Keeping her distance, she frolicked among the waves, hid among the shoals, and watched as he thanked the captain and crew then was finally rowed ashore.

When he disappeared in the maze of buildings cluttering the town, an odd sorrow shrouded Perdita. If the story that sailor had told was true, here was a human worth pursuing. Here was a man who fought evil and helped others—even at risk to himself. Which was the key, after all. In his delirium, hadn't he spoken of breaking a curse? Could it all be a sign? Or some cruel trick of Natas's to resurrect her hope?

Hope. There was that nasty little word again. She should leave. But still Perdita remained—embroiled in a battle between *that* hope and her normal despair. Despair was winning. As it always did. In years past, it had become her only friend and the one thing keeping her from embarking on another quest that would surely pound her crumbling heart to dust.

Perdita found a bed of sea grass shielded by a coral wall and settled down to rest, to think, to plan. What did it matter if she stayed here or returned to her cave? Neither place offered her solace. After a while, the gentle sway of the sea lulled her to sleep.

As she slept, the nightmare replayed itself in vivid color. Forwin strutted before her, his long crimson robes flowing behind him like waves of blood. "Even in light of Sir Ivan's rejection!" he bellowed. "Even after he walked away and proved me right, you still will not have me!"

But Perdita barely heard the words. Her legs gave out and she sank to the large boulder in the middle of what was now a soggy riverbed and numbly stared down the wooded path where she'd last seen Sir Ivan—the chinks of his armor glinting in the sunlight as he ran away. *Ran.* Not strutted or marched as he usually did.

But ran like a coward.

Water dripped from boulders and low-hanging branches along the river that had been overflowing only moments before—overflowing and raging in a mad dash of water that rose higher and grew more violent with each passing second. It had splashed and clawed at Perdita perched on a rock in the center as she begged her knight to save her.

Of course he would save her. He had sworn his fealty, his love to her. Forever, he had said. *I will love thee with all that I am until the end of time and beyond. I pledge to thee my life, my loyalty, my love, and will gladly give my life to protect thee.*

But as soon as he'd seen the rampaging river and the improbability of reaching her before the water swept her away—the risk to *himself* of being swept away—the desperation in his eyes turned to sorrow and finally to shame.

And she knew.

His love went only so deep. Not even as deep as this river. He could have at least tried! He could have at least gathered downed tree trunks and attempted to form a bridge before the rising waters overwhelmed him. Instead, he had fled, leaving her to die.

Forwin emerged from his hiding spot, grinning like a satiated lion. With one wave of his jeweled hand, the waters fled.

And her heart along with them.

She could not—*would* not—marry the warlock, Forwin of Rabbah. No matter her bargain. Numbly she remained on the rock, watching him pace before the riverbed, stroking his pointed beard, fuming and casting her seething looks.

A squirrel entered the clearing, but with a snap of his fingers the creature became a puff of smoke. If only he would do that to Perdita. For she felt like naught but a vapor, all save her heart, which surely had a thousand pins stuck in it.

Forwin halted and glared at her. He had decided her fate.

Swallowing, Perdita returned his stare.

"Where is your champion now? I have proven to you there is no such thing as true love. None save that which *I* offer. Come with me, and I will make you a queen."

"I would rather die," she spat, then braced herself, waiting for him to turn her into a wisp as he'd done with the squirrel. Or mayhap a bat or a frog.

She was not to be so lucky.

His face reddened and grew taut as if someone had stretched it across a frame. "Very well." He drew a deep breath. "Since you enjoy the water so much, I will doom you to it." He pulled a pouch from his pocket, poured powder into his palm, and blew it into the wind. It spun and twisted and danced in the sunlight ... a kaleidoscope of glittering colors so beautiful, her fears subsided. Mesmerized, she watched it until it showered over her like mist.

Something stabbed her toes. It twisted like a knife through her feet and then up her legs. Pain consumed her. She screamed. "What have you done?"

"You are cursed to wander the seas half-fish, half-woman, lonely and unloved for all eternity."

Her skirts melted away. Her legs slammed together. Her feet became one. She struggled to separate them. The pain burned a trail up her thighs to her hips.

Panic sent her blood racing. “You cannot do this to me!”

“Ah, but I can.” He grinned. “You see, my beauty, the second you made a bargain with me, you opened the door to my powers.”

She could no longer move her legs. Her bodice shriveled and dissipated into the wind. She covered her bare breasts as scales formed over her skin—like flowers blooming, luminous and sparkling in the sunlight. Horrified, she tried to yell, to shout for help, but her lungs began to collapse. Gasping, sobbing, she begged the warlock, “Not forever! Not forever!”

Forwin propped a boot atop a rock and leaned one arm on his knee, examining his nails. “Only one thing will break the curse. And one thing alone. Every ten years you will become human again for a month. All you must do is find a man who will die for you, then you will be free.” He shrugged. “Since you seem to believe true love exists, that should be an easy task.”

He grinned, lifted his hands to the sky, and closed his eyes. A roar thundered. The ground shook. No longer able to breathe, speak, or even scream, Perdita could only stare as a wall of foamy water at least twenty feet high tumbled toward her. It struck her with the force of a thousand stampeding horses, twisting and turning, tossing her against rocks, plummeting her to the raging creek bed, then thrusting her to the raging surface.

“You should have loved me!” Forwin shouted.

Pain ripped through her like none she’d ever felt. Her lungs filled with water. Good. She would die soon.

But she didn’t. Bruised, battered, and heartbroken, the river spit her into the sea like so much refuse.

And in the sea she had remained.

For three hundred years.

Itching jarred her awake. She opened her eyes to a world transformed from one of color and beauty to one of muted shades of gray and black. Her tail prickled. Irritation crawled up her legs. "Zost! Not now!" She had forgotten the time of ephemeral redemption was nigh.

If she didn't emerge onto land by the time her legs formed and her lungs sought air, she would lose all control and be swept out to sea—a slave to wind and wave for the entire month. And she had no intention of doing that again. Once, when she had given up hope of ever finding love, she'd stayed in the sea, thinking that mayhap when she turned human again, she would simply drown. Instead, her muscles atrophied and she'd floated aimlessly, pummeled by waves and tossed against reefs that sliced and battered her. But the worst part was the excruciating pain in her legs—the kind of pain that makes the most devout religious zealot renounce their faith.

It lasted the entire month.

Pushing from her bed of sea grass, she swam and broke the surface. The port town had transformed into flickering dots of light that reflected on the bay, where ships had dropped both sails and anchors for the night. Tavern ballads, a fiddle, and laughter tumbled on the evening breeze.

The gills on her side began to close. With heavy heart, she flapped her tail and started for the shore. It wasn't as if she didn't take some pleasure in her months on land. She loved the feel of dirt beneath her feet. She loved being dry—especially her hair—and wearing fancy attire. She adored the taste of good food and sleeping in a bed. But most of all, she craved being around people, talking and laughing, and sharing experiences.

Ten years was a long time to be alone.

But these short months as a human had become an unbearable torment. Every minute, every second, was one less chime on the cruel clock of time in which she had a chance to find true love before she was forced to enter the sea again for another ten agonizing years. Like a prisoner under a life sentence who was released for a day, the taunting pleasures of freedom became naught but a cruel whip of fate.

She wasn't fool enough to hope that this time would be any different. Still, she might as well try to win the heart of this Savion Ryne. Getting a man's attention had never been a problem. Getting them to swear their undying love was easy. But finding a man willing to die for her … that, she had discovered, was nigh impossible. 'Twas what made the curse so formidable.

She'd never be able to break it.

For there was no such thing as true love. She had once naïvely believed there was. But now she knew Forwin had been right all along.

Still, if she had to be on land with a man who possessed a passion for self-sacrificing, she might as well do her best to divert his passion to her. After she failed, she would go back to her cave and pursue the quest to end her life.

Her feet separated. Then her legs. The ease with which she sped through the water grew clumsy and difficult. The ocean spewed from her lungs. And still she swam. Finally she struck the soft sand and allowed the waves to carry her in. Time had not permitted her to seek out a more private landing, so she headed toward the shadows at the far end of the beach. Gasping for air, she rose from the water on shaky legs unaccustomed to standing. Waves struck her back as she plodded ashore, then fell into a heap on the sand. The transformation always drained her of strength.

She lay there, relishing in the breath flowing in and out of her lungs, when shuffling sounds met her ears and she looked up to see two shadows emerge from the trees.

"Why lookie here, fellas. If it ain't a naked lady!"

CHAPTER 5

"We knew you weren't dead." Petrok took a sip of ale and smiled at Savion.

"Good thing." Savion nodded at the barmaid as she brought another round for his men. "Otherwise you wouldn't have waited here for me as I instructed, and I'd be without a ship and a crew."

A gust blew into the tavern, stirring dust on the floor and swaying lanterns hanging from hooks on the wooden ceiling. Someone banged a tune on a harpsichord in the corner while patrons drank, sang, played cards, and flirted with the tavern wenches.

"Well." Hona thumbed toward the master gunner. "Nuto thought you were dead. He wanted to turn the ship into a fishing vessel. Fishing, us?" The young lad chuckled, and Nuto shot him an angry glance.

"I just wanted to keep busy until we knew for sure, Captain." He shrugged. "I'm mighty glad to see you."

"As I am you, Nuto." Savion glanced over his men sitting round the table, eating, drinking, and enjoying their time ashore. "I'm happy to see all of you." As they nodded to him in return, he spotted Verrad standing at the bar talking to a woman.

"We would have waited for you forever, Captain." Petrok smiled. "We knew no one as good as you could ever be defeated. Not by Natas and especially not by a summer squall."

Hona pointed to the wound on Savion's forehead. "What happened to your head?"

Savion sipped his drink. "I can't remember. I fell into the sea, and when I awoke, I was ashore on some island."

"You don't recollect getting stitches?" Nuto asked.

"No." Savion touched the nearly-healed wound, but for all his trying, he couldn't remember who had cared for him. All he had were flashes: a dark-haired woman, a rock wall, water everywhere—its gentle lapping easing his nerves. Or was it a song, a beautiful melody, that had settled him?

"Praise King Abbas you are alive and here with us again." Petrok raised his mug in salute. "We kept the ship in good shape, Captain, and she's ready to sail when you are."

"Good. I'm anxious to be back to task."

Two men in black uniforms with red insignias and curved swords at their hips walked in, glanced over the mob, and headed for the far corner. Lanterns flickered in their wake. Along with a sudden chill that slithered over Savion.

"Malum—Natas's minions." Petrok spit on the floor, and clutched the hilt of his sword.

The men looked to Savion who shook his head. "No, we don't fight them now."

"How dare you?" A shriek blared from the bar, where the woman Verrad had been speaking to slapped him across the face and stomped away. Verrad shrugged at the chuckling bystanders, then headed toward the table and plopped in a chair beside Savion.

"Excellent work, Verrad." Hona snickered. "It's difficult to insult a barmaid."

The dark-haired man lifted his drink. "I'm misunderstood is all."

Hona cocked a brow. "Your good looks only go so far, Verrad."

He grinned. "Usually far enough."

Nuto turned to Savion. "Where are we headed next, Captain?"

"Wherever we are needed." Savion scanned the tavern, sensing unease. "I will know soon enough. In the meantime, we should inquire of the merchants if there are goods in need of transport. We are short on funds."

"How is it you always know when someone is in trouble?" Hona leaned forward.

"A gift, I guess. A sense." Reaching inside his shirt, Savion pulled out his amulet and held it tight.

In the back corner, two men argued drunkenly over spilt rum. One of the Malum warriors pushed back his chair and approached the men, a scowl on his face. His cohort followed, plucking a knife from his belt.

Petrok growled. "Should we put them in their place, Captain?"

"It's their job to cause trouble, Petrok. But only for those who seek it. Let these be." Savion shifted in his seat and glanced out the window. "Something else is afoot this night."

The sensation began when he'd first awoke on the island. It had grown stronger on the ship. He thought it would surely disappear once he arrived at Hoffnung, but it had only increased. The amulet warmed.

Nuto's brows drew together. "What is it, Captain?"

One of the Malum slugged the man while the other held a knife to his friend. The table fell with a *thunk,* sending mugs crashing to the floor.

"Let's go." Savion stood. His men shoved their drinks aside and rose with him. Outside the tavern, he ordered all but Hona and Petrok to return to the ship as his uneasiness grew—a urging within that tugged and pulled until he obeyed. He never knew when these senses would hit or where they would take him. Perhaps into a battle with a horde of Malum, or maybe feeding a small child abandoned in the street.

Night dropped an inky curtain on the scene as he walked down the sandy street, focusing inward for direction. Upon the bay, mist slithered across the dark water, twisting and turning beneath the milky light of a moon.

A woman screamed.

If there was one thing about being human Perdita hated, it was being helpless. Especially against lecherous swine like the two men skulking her way. In the sea, she was as strong as a crustacean, as powerful as a whale, and as sleek as a dolphin. She could leap twenty feet in the air and then plunge to the seabed within seconds. All the creatures of the sea bowed to her. All save the sharks, and even those she had defeated. These particular *land sharks,* however, were another story. Though she was immortal, or mayhap because of it, she felt pain—intensely. In fact, all her feelings were heightened during her month on land.

Grabbing a palm frond from the sand, she covered herself as the two men sauntered toward her.

"Come 'ere, little missy. We won't do ye no harm," one of them slurred, his rum-putrefied breath wafting toward her.

"Back off, gentlemen. I have a dagger." She hoped they were too drunk to wonder where she could possibly have hid it.

The other man's belch preceded a disbelieving snort.

Wind whipped sand up to sting her bare legs as the thundering crash of waves surely would drown out her screams.

"Now, don't play 'ard to get, missy. Ain't no other reason fer ye to be in sich condition, save that ye saw us handsome gents and wanted to play."

Perdita couldn't help her nervous laugh. Casting a glance over her shoulder to the copse of trees, she retreated a step. "Perchance rum has distorted your vision, you salacious prigs, for I doubt even a dog in heat would find you appealing."

She knew she shouldn't have insulted them, but once again, her tongue overstepped its bounds. Both men pounced on her. Dropping the palm frond, she elbowed one in the gut while twisting the other man's arm. The first bent over, groaning, while the other yelped in pain. Perdita made a dash for the jungle. Grunts and curses followed her. Fingers clamped her ankle, and she slammed face-first into the sand. Pain smashed through her head and across her chest. Her vision swam.

The man dragged her backward. Sand ground into her face and crawled up her nose. The man flipped her over. She jerked her feet from his grip, shoved one in his groin, then leapt up and snatched the frond. While the other man was laughing at his friend, she plucked the sword from his scabbard.

"Huh?" He spun to face her. This time to the point of a blade. The moon broke through a cloud, and despite his predicament, the man licked his lips as his gaze scoured over her. Spitting sand from her mouth, she shoved the tip of the sword harder into his chest.

Boots shuffled. Dark forms approached. Zost! How many men must she fight off tonight?

"What goes on here?" The tallest of the men burst into view, the chime of his sword being drawn ringing across the shore. The two men with him followed his lead.

Still groaning, the man Perdita had kicked straightened and faced the intruders. The other one pulled back and spat into the sand. "What's it to ye? Begone. We saw 'er first."

Perdita stepped into the shadows. She still had the sword, but mayhap she wouldn't have to use it. When these wolves began their dance for dominance, 'twould be easy to slip away.

"Saw her first, did you?" The tall man mocked. "Which gives you what claim on her?"

That voice. So familiar.

One of his friends stepped forward and gestured toward the sword in Perdita's hand. "Seems the lady has things well in hand, Savion." He chuckled.

Savion! Perdita smiled at her good fortune.

"She was playin' 'ard to get is all." The man she'd kicked drew a pistol and pointed it at the intruders. "Now git. Go find yer own entertainment."

Savion cocked his head. "Are you going to shoot all three of us with but one shot?"

"No." He wiped his mouth on his sleeve, then swung his pistol toward Perdita. "Just her."

Silence, save the crash of waves, thickened the air. The shot would hurt. She'd found that out the hard way. It would bore into her flesh and cause her agony for days.

Oddly, only silence answered the fiend. An intimidating silence.

The pistol wavered in the man's hand. "If'n ye care so much 'bout this wench, leave us be, an' I promise ye can have 'er next."

"How kind of you." Savion replied with calm assurance. Moonlight glinted off steel as he swung his sword and knocked the pistol from the man's grip, shoving him to the sand, and then swept the blade to the other man's neck. Startled, the drunk tumbled backward to join his friend.

Both of them scrambled to rise and darted into the darkness.

While Savion sheathed his sword, his two friends approached her. "Are you all right, miss?"

They halted, eyes widening. She leveled her sword at them as one of them gulped and looked away and the other grinned.

"She's naked," the grinning, dark-haired one said, never taking his eyes from her.

"Then turn your backs!" Savion commanded. They obeyed as he cautiously approached her, took one glance, then turned aside. "You have no need of your weapon. You are safe with us. Are you harmed?"

Abbas's luck be hers! So it *was* true. Here was a man willing to risk his life for others—even strangers. She gave a breathless sigh, adding a tremble to her voice. "I am unharmed, thanks to you, kind sir."

Keeping his eyes averted, he removed his cloak and flung it over her shoulders. She dropped the sword to the ground and clutched the edges of the robe together, staring at him and wondering how any man could possess such self-control. Even his two friends both risked peeks from the distance. Normally, she found the attention flattering, but when she glanced back at Savion, unusual shame settled on her. What he must think of her!

"Those sailors stole my attire. I shudder to consider what they would have done if you hadn't come along."

"Is there somewhere safe we can escort you?" Savion asked.

Clouds parted, freeing a shaft of moonlight upon his face and glinting off the medallion hanging around his neck. Yes. 'Twas him. Same strong jaw, same regal light-brown hair and golden eyes. Though she hadn't realized how tall he was, nor how much his presence affected her, now that he was conscious.

She didn't want to hope. She hated hope. But somehow … somewhere deep within her, she couldn't help wondering if Savion was the one she'd waited for all these years.

"I have nowhere to go," she finally said. "But 'tis none of your concern. I thank you for your kindness." Kneeling to retrieve the sword, Perdita turned to leave.

"Wait." His command spun her around.

"I can hardly leave you alone in such a dangerous town, miss. Surely you have lodging nearby? How did you end up on this beach alone and without your …"

Was that a blush creeping up his neck? How fascinating. "Clothing?" She rescued him. "I told you, those men stole it. But 'tis a long story, and one I shan't bore you with."

He gave her an assuring smile. "I will pay for your lodging. And if you are in need of employment, I know the proprietor at the milliner's shop."

Nay! This would not do. How could she make the man fall in love with her if she were in some stuffy shop making hats and he was out at sea?

"How very kind of you," she replied sweetly.

"Then, it's settled. Come. The innkeeper's wife can find you some decent attire as well." He waved her forward, but when she didn't move, he gently took her elbow.

Desperate, she did the only thing she could think to do. She pretended to faint.

CHAPTER 6

Though her voice bore no trembling, the poor lady had no doubt been overcome by fear. What lady wouldn't in the threat of such a brutal attack? Breaking her fall, Savion hoisted her in his arms, ensuring the cloak she wore remained closed. Now, what to do with her? He couldn't very well leave her unconscious in an inn. Such an unprotected beauty would not go unnoticed. And she was a beauty, undeniable now that he carried her into the full moonlight. Waves of raven hair spiraled across her shoulder to her waist. Plump coral-colored lips, lashes full and lush fanning across creamy cheeks. Great. Just what he needed.

On board his ship, he laid her on the bed in his cabin. She moaned.

"Are we going to keep her, Captain?" Hona asked, excited as a child receiving a new toy.

"Wonder where she came from." Petrok drew close to examine her.

"She stays only until she recovers." Savion laid a blanket over her just in case the cloak slipped open. "Call Haddeus to examine her." The aged man was the closest thing to a surgeon Savion had, but perhaps he could revive her. The sooner the better, for then Savion could return her to town.

Beauty had fooled him once. It would not do so again.

Though he had to admit, he was a bit more than curious about this particular beauty. After ordering Petrok and Hona to their duties, Savion took a seat beside Haddeus as he checked the lady's vitals. There was something familiar about her—flashes in his mind of dark hair, excruciating pain, and her comely face hovering over him. *No.* He rubbed his tired eyes. Surely he would have remembered meeting such a woman.

Haddeus packed his medical bag and rose. "I see nothin' wrong with her, Captain. I'd let her sleep if I was you. Sometimes shock does this to a person, knocks 'em out for a while."

Thanking him, Savion saw him to the door. Then raking back his hair, he faced the lady.

"Father, what am I to do? Is this some sort of test?"

He had hoped he was done with tests and trials. He had hoped that he had saved enough people, regained enough enemy territory to be called home again. Ah … Nevaeh. He sighed. How he dreamt of its crystalline streams and flowered fields—painted in colors so vivid they made even the turquoise sea pale by comparison—its ivory castles and majestic halls, its regal ceremonies and lavish festivals. And the people: honorable, kind, good. So different from the Kingdom of Erden—the land of the Ancient Seas, where Savion now lived.

His father would call him home when Savion was ready—when he had rescued the person or thing he'd been sent to save. In the meantime, Savion would further the kingdom and do all he could to quell the rebellion.

And he would not fail again by trusting a beautiful woman.

Pulling up a chair, he made himself as comfortable as possible and tried to sleep. His two years in Erden had taught him to trust no one, and he refused to leave this woman alone in a cabin filled with valuables for the taking.

Yet instead of stealing, she tossed and turned and mumbled in her sleep. Names such as Forwin and Ivan and a host of others spoken with such heartache and pain, they formed a lump in Savion's throat. He reached for her more than once, wanting to offer comfort, but always halted for fear of frightening her.

By the time sunlight broke through the stained glass of the stern windows, exhaustion weighed heavy on Savion. He rubbed his eyes and glanced at the woman, her hair a tangle of wild black around her head, her cheeks pink, her breathing heavy and deep.

At least one of them had gotten some sleep.

Rising, he tugged on the bell pull to ring for coffee, a drink he'd grown quite fond of since he'd been living in Erden. Within minutes, Bart entered with a tray of the hot liquid, along with fresh biscuits.

The short, bull-like sailor peeked at the woman before setting the tray on Savion's desk. "Have a pleasant evening?" His tone taunted.

"Actually, I hardly slept." Savion poured coffee into his pewter mug, then at Bart's teasing grin, he added hastily, "Not for the reason you're thinking." He sipped the coffee. Black, strong, and bitter, just the way he liked it. No cream or sugar, though he saw Bart had included them on the tray for the lady.

"You think of everything, Bart. Thank you."

The man's smile revealed two missing teeth. "Can I get you anything else, Captain?"

"I do have an odd request." The woman stirred, drawing Savion's gaze. "A gown, a bodice, underthings. Whatever it is women wear these days."

Bart scratched his thick graying hair. "Women's clothes, eh? I'll do my best."

"I know you will. And be quick about it. I want to put her ashore as soon as possible."

The delicious smell of coffee lured Perdita from her sleep. The sound of male voices kept her eyes shut, but the last statement from Savion sent her heart racing. What sort of man wants to get rid of a beautiful unclad woman? None she had ever encountered. She needed to act. And act fast. After the servant left, she let out a tiny moan and began to stretch. She moved her body as alluringly as possible—knowing the man was no doubt gaping at her.

Ready to continue her seduction, she opened her eyes.

He was staring out the window, sipping his coffee.

Frustrated, she moaned again and propped herself up on one elbow, allowing the blanket to slip over her bare shoulder. "Oh my!" She feigned a fearful tone. "Who are you? What am I doing here?"

Savion turned, set down his coffee, and approached slowly. "Never fear, miss. You are safe. No one will harm you here."

Perdita intended to continue her fearful theatrics, if only to lure the man closer, but the sight of him basked in sunlight held her tongue. *Handsome* wasn't a word she'd use to describe him, though he had a strong jaw and a well-shaped nose. Thick hair the color of bronze threaded with gold fell to shoulders that spanned wide and strong on a tall sturdy body clad in leather and linen. *Powerful, commanding, masculine* ... those were words she would use to describe him. With a presence that was both unsettling and peaceful at the same time. She actually might be frightened save for the look in his eyes—the golden color of a warm fire, yet filled with such kindness and wisdom, she felt herself drawn into them.

Glancing down, she gasped. "What have you done with my clothes? Zost! What have you done with *me*?" Feigning horror, she clutched the cloak, leapt from the bed, and backed away from him.

He made no move toward her, merely stared at her with enough assurance to calm a raging storm. "Nothing, I promise. We rescued you from those ruffians on the beach. Don't you remember?"

She glanced around the cabin, spacious for a ship, its dark mahogany furniture regal and masculine like its captain. She hadn't realized he was the captain of the ship when she'd nursed him back to health. "Vaguely, yes," she replied. "Thank you for your rescue. 'Twas beyond terrifying." She pressed the back of her hand to her forehead and allowed the cloak to slip once again off her shoulder.

He turned away and gestured to a tray on his desk. "My man is fetching you some proper attire. In the meantime, help yourself to coffee and biscuits, miss … miss …."

"Perdita. Perdita Mulier."

"Miss Mulier." He smiled, faced her, saw her bare shoulder, and turned away again. "I shall leave you for now. When you are properly attired, I will escort you ashore." He started for the door.

She knew she should try to stop him, but her eyes fastened on the food. Hurrying toward it, she shoved a sweet biscuit into her mouth and poured herself some coffee, plopping in chunks of sugar—several in fact. "Mmm." She bit off a piece of the biscuit and allowed it to roll about her mouth. "Have you ever tasted anything so delicious?" A sip of rich, sweet coffee nearly sent her into ecstasy.

Savion halted and was staring at her oddly.

"Forgive me. I don't often get such fine fare." She set down the cup but slipped the rest of the biscuit into her mouth.

He chuckled and rubbed the back of his neck. "I will agree that our ship's cook is better than most, but I've never heard his coffee and biscuits called fine before."

Perdita quickly finished the food in her mouth and smiled. "I was rather hungry. But did you say you were taking me ashore?"

"Of course." He turned to leave.

"Please, I beg you. You cannot return me to town."

Her insistent tone caused his eyes to narrow. "I assure you, I can."

She forced a shudder and lowered her gaze. "Then you sign my death warrant. There are men after me. To kill me."

He shifted boots over the wooden deck. "And why would they want to do that?"

"Jealousy, Captain. A jealous powerful man whose proposal I refused." She turned her back to him and sniffed, lifting a hand to her nose. "But I can see you do not believe me." She allowed the cloak to slide down her bare back.

"Woman," he huffed. "I find you naked on a beach. What do you expect me to believe?"

She released a shuddering sob. "This same man longs to humiliate me, to punish me. He knocked me unconscious, dropped me on the beach, and hired those men to steal my clothing, hoping I'd be beaten, ravished, or worse." She glanced at him over her shoulder.

The look of concern in his eyes pricked her guilt. She hated lying, but how else could she convince him to allow her to stay?

"I will give you enough coin to live for a week and procure a position for you at the milliners. But the *Scepter* is no place for a woman."

The *Scepter*, eh? Mayhap that was the man's flaw. He thought himself a king and his ship an implement of his power. She dashed toward him and laid a hand on his arm. "Please, I beg you, at least take me to Kadon. I have friends there who will help me." The ship rolled over a wavelet. She stumbled, and Savion took her elbow and led her to a chair. Sinking into the soft leather, she allowed the cloak to slip from one leg. "I promise I'll behave."

As expected, his gaze lowered to her shapely calf. He swallowed and turned away, staring out the windows.

Perdita smiled. Surely, she had him now. No man had ever been able to resist either her body or her helpless female routine. And never when she combined the two.

Oddly, instead of kneeling before her and begging for liberties, he plucked a sword from his desk and slipped it into his scabbard. "Very well, I will take you as far as Kadon." He headed for the door. "If you will do two things for me."

Here it came, the proposition. Somehow she found herself disappointed. She smiled sweetly, waiting.

But not a speck of desire rode on his expression. "One, that when your clothes arrive, you get dressed and remain that way; and two, that you stay away from my crew."

Then without waiting for her answer, he left, closing the door behind him.

Perdita sank back into the chair, perplexed. She glanced at her leg thinking mayhap there was mud on it. Nay. Mayhap a wart had grown on her shoulder? Nay. She was as lovely as always. *Stay dressed?* 'Twas the one thing no man had ever asked of her.

Wouldn't it be just her luck to choose a man who preferred men over women? Nay. She'd seen the way he looked at her. Mayhap he was merely unschooled in the art of love-making. Then what luck for him that he now had a great teacher on board. She smiled.

Mark her words, by the end of the three-day journey to Kadon, Savion would be groveling at her feet, swearing his love, and begging for her favors like a lovesick porpoise.

CHAPTER 7

Two days later, Perdita stood at the main deck railing, admiring the familiar span of foam-capped azure sea and cursing herself for not staying on land. At least she could be enjoying the feel of solid ground beneath her feet instead of the incessant roll of waves she'd endured for decades at a time. At least she could be enjoying tasteful delicacies instead of hard tack and bitter fish stew. Fish for dinner! Ugg. Could she never escape it? The man, this Savion Ryne, as he was called, had done naught but avoid her. Nay, worse than avoid—he acted as though she didn't exist.

Even now as she glanced at him standing on the quarterdeck commanding his men, he wouldn't look her way. Not even a peek! And here she was squeezed into the undersized gown his man had brought her—squeezed so that every inch of her curves were evident to all. At least some of his crew stole glances her way. One man in particular stole more than glances. He plundered every inch of her with his brazen stare. With black hair slicked back and bound in a tie, dark eyebrows flattened above deep sinister eyes, he was quite handsome. Forsooth! At least she hadn't completely lost her charm.

Or—as she had first feared—grown old and saggy in her transformation from fish to human.

But when she'd glanced in the looking glass in Savion's cabin, she found herself even more beautiful than ever. 'Twas the only part of the curse she enjoyed. Forwin had not only allowed her to keep her beauty, but ensured she would be the most gorgeous woman on Erden. "To help you find your 'true love'," he had mocked with his usual twisted grin.

It had definitely been an advantage in drawing any male attention she sought.

Until now.

Perdita had waited for nearly two days in Savion's cabin for him to dine with her or check on her well-being or share tea with her at night. Instead, he had sent his man Bart, a bullish-shaped, crusty old sailor who tended to her needs and refused to answer her questions.

How was she supposed to win Savion's love when he wouldn't even give her a moment of his time?

So, against his express wishes, she'd finally come on deck and sashayed to the railing, feigning stumbles on the heaving ship, which caused several of the crew to rush to her aid with red faces and gaping mouths. But not Savion.

A gust blasted over her, rumbling through the sails and flapping the flag hung from the mainmast. She glanced upward at the ensign: a fierce lion with a king's scepter in his hand. Meant to scare off pirates and other nefarious sorts, she supposed, though it only proved the arrogance of the man who brandished it.

Closing her eyes, she allowed the breeze to swirl through her hair, relishing in the feel of her dry curls. Beneath the waves, they weighed her down like seaweed. On land they felt like silk against her skin.

Zost! This wasn't going well. She'd already wasted three days with this prudish saint. Another day and he'd leave her at Kadon, where she'd have to start all over with another man.

The ship leapt over a wave and she gripped the railing, feeling hope drain from her and slide into the sea.

"Good day to you, miss." A tall, lanky man with sun-streaked shaggy hair and barely a bristle on his chin smiled her way.

"Good day."

"Hona, the *Scepter*'s quartermaster." He held out his hand.

Perdita gripped it. "Perdita Mulier. A pleasure."

"I figured you might be lonely."

"Why, because your captain is avoiding me?" she replied sarcastically.

"Avoiding? No. He's just busy. Has a lot on his mind."

"Mayhap he believes me to be beneath him. He did find me stripped bare on the beach, after all."

"Mayhap?" Hona looked confused.

Another sailor slid on her other side, this one with dark curly hair and a gruff face. "The captain don't judge people like that. I'm Petrok, first mate."

"Perdita." She smiled then glanced over her shoulder at Savion. "I see no other reason for his dismissal."

Hona leaned back against the railing. "He's not had the best of luck with women, you see."

"At least that's what we guess," Petrok added. The wind tossed his hair about like palm fronds in a storm. "He won't talk much about it," Petrok continued. "But never fear, miss. He'll treat you kindly and deliver you safe to Kadon. You can count on that."

She didn't want to count on that. That he *was* a gentleman, she had no doubt. But with only a month's time, a gentleman is not what she needed. Her glance shifted between the two men, sizing them up as possibilities. The light-haired one was far too young and innocent. The other—though she saw the way he admired her curves—seemed too intense, too distracted to be lured by a female. Over her shoulder the dark, handsome man continued to blatantly stare her way. Nay, not him either. She knew that look. It bespoke of a selfishness that would never sacrifice for another.

"Petrok!" Savion's voice thundered across the deck, causing the man to stiffen and look up at his captain.

"Twenty degrees south by southwest! We must away to Skivia!" Savion shouted.

"What of delivering the lady to Kadon?"

The captain lowered the spyglass, his eyes finally landing on Perdita. "She'll have to wait."

Petrok began spouting orders to the crew. Men leapt into the ratlines and climbed up shrouds to adjust sail as the helmsman turned the tiller.

Hona started to leave, but Perdita stayed him with a touch. "We aren't going to Kadon?" Her voice came out more excited than she anticipated, but the young lad didn't seem to notice.

"Savion must'a had one of his senses."

Sails thundered overhead as they caught the wind. "Whatever do you mean?"

Hona shrugged. "He senses when someone needs his help, when there is trouble."

Perdita scanned the horizon. Nary a cloud nor sail in sight. "How does he know?"

"He just does. How d'ye think we found you?" He winked and darted away.

Savion barreled into his cabin and made his way to the cabinet where he stored his weapons. He could feel the woman's eyes following his every move. Beautiful sea-green eyes. Eyes he had avoided rather successfully for two days. Along with her alluring figure. Savion no longer had trouble avoiding beautiful women, thanks to that seductress Lorelei. Her deception and betrayal cured any desire to appease his eyes and reinforced his determination to obey his good sense. Though he desperately wanted a bride and longed for the companionship and love of a woman, he sought a pure heart above all else—a kind, unselfish, honorable heart. A woman who would never trick him, lie to him, or deceive him.

A woman who would love him as truly as he would love her.

Opening his cabinet, he turned his back to Perdita while he chose his weapons—a short sword, two pistols, three grenades, and a knife—and stuffed them in his baldric. Still, this woman, this Perdita Mulier, was different somehow. Despite her stunning appearance, Savion found himself drawn to her, thinking of her as he commanded his ship, dreaming of her at night. What was wrong with him? Though Bart reported that she'd treated him kindly, and Petrok and Hona seemed to enjoy her company today, Savion hardly knew her. What he *did* know should make him run as far away from her as possible. Besides, she'd done nothing but try to seduce him. Even now, he could hear her breathing, feel her watching his every move, and wanted more than anything to turn around and spend hours getting to know her.

"Pray, what is happening, Savion? Why the need for so many weapons?" Her voice softened him.

"There is a disturbance in Skivia." He spun to face her, swallowing at the sight of her sitting in a chair, her legs drawn up beside her, her skirts draped over her knees like a lavender waterfall, her black hair tumbling over a bodice that was far too tight. Not her fault, of course, yet it did nothing to aid his efforts to ignore her.

"A disturbance?" She blinked, looking more like an innocent maiden than the vixen he'd met two nights ago.

"A sickness that weakens the town, and Natas's warriors are on the way."

She rose, her skirts falling in a swish of silk. "How do you know such things?"

She smelled of the sea, not a briny scent but more of a sweet saltiness. "I'm sorry for the delay. I'll take you to Kadon after I deal with this problem. In the meantime, I order you to stay on board, where you'll be safe."

Perdita considered telling him he had no right ordering her about, but then remembered most men liked to control women. It made them feel manly, she supposed. Mayhap she should pretend to faint, so he would be forced to carry her to the bed as he had that first night. But how many times could she use that ploy? Finally, she simply put on her sweetest smile and bid him be safe. This seemed to have the desired effect, as he stared at her with more interest than he'd shown of yet. Then his eyes narrowed, and he let out a huff before storming out the door.

Zost! She took up a pace and bit her nails. Stay on board, indeed. She had no intention of remaining on this ship if the object of her quest was elsewhere. She would go ashore to this village of Skivia and see what mischief was afoot. If anything, she'd enjoy walking on land again, mayhap get some decent food. And if the place suited her and had other prospective lovers, she might stay and give up her pursuit of this cocksure snod.

An hour later, footsteps pounded above her as commands were issued to lower sail. The ship halted, and the mighty anchor splashed into the harbor. Boats were lowered, then filled with men, and Perdita watched from the stern windows as they rowed ashore. The moon slid behind dark clouds, and after ten yards she lost them in the shadows of night. In the distance, the flicker of lanterns revealed the town's location, along with a flaming blaze too large to be a normal fire. Musket shot drummed the sky, followed by screams.

A disturbance, indeed. More like a war. Making her way up the companionway and onto the main deck, Perdita had no trouble sneaking by the two sailors on watch. Both were drinking from a jug. One strummed a tune on a mandolin while the other whittled a piece of wood. She slipped over the side, happy to see a small dingy left behind. She could swim of course. Unlike the myths, she did not turn back into a mermaid during the ephemeral redemption. Instead, after a few minutes in the water, the pain would become excruciating, and she would lose all muscle control and be subject to wind and wave. Not a pleasant prospect and one that made the ache spanning her shoulders and perspiration beading on her skin worth the effort of rowing.

After hiding the dingy beneath some fronds and seaweed, Perdita gathered her skirts and headed toward the sound of mayhem. First order of business: see what Savion and his men were about. After that, she'd search for any male prospects worthy enough to compel her to stay. Though shadows cloaked the island, she could tell it was large and lush, and the city she now approached was no small fishing port. If Savion Ryne did not find her appealing, she could find dozens who would.

But there was fighting in the streets. And sickness. The acrid scent of gunpowder and fear floated atop the putrid odor of disease. Keeping to the shadows, Perdita crept down the narrow byways on the outskirts of town. Candles flickered in the windows of wooden homes from which coughing and moaning arose. Citizens fled in wagons filled with their children and belongings. Up ahead, two men crossed swords. One was Malum. She could tell by the insignia of Natas on the dark uniform. The other man wore the clothes of a farmer. He was no match for the warrior, and within seconds the Malum thrust his sword into the man's gut. The farmer's eyes popped, his jaw opened, and he slumped over with a painful moan.

A woman wailed in horror. Two more Malum entered the street beckoning to their friend, and without so much as a belch, the Malum pulled his blade from the man and rushed behind them. In a mad dash of brown calico, a woman emerged from the shadows and fell to her knees beside the farmer. Her sobs bled into the night.

Perdita's throat closed with emotion. Death no longer shocked or even repulsed her, for she'd seen enough of it to last a millennium. She'd even envied the fragility of humans. What she couldn't stand was the sorrow that overwhelmed those left behind.

Sorrow of loss was something she understood all too well.

As Perdita continued on her way, the woman looked up, agony twisting her features and tears pouring down her cheeks. "Please save us. Please, miss, save us."

"I cannot save you," Perdita answered, her heart sinking. "I cannot even save myself." Yet as she stared at the wounded man, she saw his chest rise and fall. Kneeling, she placed two fingers on his throat. The throb of a weak pulse drummed on her fingers. There was still time.

A child no more than four crept out from a nearby building and dashed toward the wounded man crying, "Papa! Papa!", but her mother scooped her up and held the little girl who thrashed and wailed in her arms.

Perdita glanced down the dark street. She dreaded the excruciating pain and the vulnerability that helping the farmer would cause her—especially amidst a war. Plus, 'twas possible Savion and his ship would leave without her while she was indisposed. But one look again at the distraught woman and her child made the choice an easy one.

She placed both hands on the man's wound. Warm blood gurgled between her fingers. He moaned, and the woman lunged forward in an attempt to push Perdita aside.

"I'm helping him," she said sternly then nodded in reassurance. "Trust me." Then closing her eyes, she pressed harder, bracing herself for the pain. It came slowly at first, in waves, a gentle lapping that grew stronger and stronger like a tempest upon the sea.

"Your hands. They glow!" the woman shouted, and Perdita pried her eyes open to see scales appear on her hands—bright luminous scales. Warmth spilled from the gills at her side. And still the pain increased. It consumed her, ripping at her flesh, piercing her organs, and tearing her limbs apart. She did everything to keep from crying out, clenching every muscle and nerve until she felt she would explode.

The woman gasped, the child cried, the man groaned—stronger now.

Torment, agony racked through Perdita like a thousand flaming spikes. Yet she could not pull her hands back. Not until she felt the life return to the man and the wound close.

Flesh grew beneath her fingers; blood halted in its trek. More spilled from her side. The pain mounted, reaching its crescendo of torture.

Perdita let out an ear-piercing wail.

Blood gushed from her side. She jerked her hands back and gasped for air. Sweat streamed down her neck and slid beneath her bodice. All her strength leeched onto the dirt. The man sat up, wide-eyed and heaving. The child tore from her mother and flew into his arms. The woman dropped beside Perdita.

A shot fired in the distance. Another one sounded closer.

"Thank you! Thank you!" she uttered over and over before the man grabbed her and dragged her off.

With her last ounce of strength, Perdita crawled into the shadows of the building and crumpled to the ground.

Sometime later—she had no idea when—she woke, drew a deep breath, and tried to get her bearings. Thank the stars she was in the same spot and no one had found her. 'Twas a risk she had taken, but one that was worth it as she remembered the look on the woman's face and the way the child had embraced her Papa.

Struggling to rise, Perdita ran a hand over the wet patch covering the right side of her gown. Blood. Not her own, but the man's. The blood, the scales on her hands, the pain—she had no idea how it all worked, only that it did.

She stumbled down the street toward the sound of battle. Her strength returned. Along the way, she plucked a pistol and a short sword off two dead men—just in case. She'd endured enough pain for one night and had no desire to suffer the agony of a wound that would not end in her death. And besides, mayhap she could help save a life.

Somewhere a child cried. The sandy streets gave way to cobblestones, wooden houses transformed to brick with red tile roofs and iron fences. Citizens, their backs loaded with goods and hands dragging children, raced through the cones of light flung by lanterns onto the street. Several carried sick loved ones on makeshift cots.

Pistol shots pummeled the air, along with horrified shrieks. A horse-drawn carriage flew by, nearly running over Perdita. A woman with a baby strapped to her chest darted up to her, her eyes filled with terror. "Dear, you should hide. They'll hurt a pretty young thing like you." Perdita blinked at the genuine concern in her eyes.

The baby started to cry, and the woman sped off.

Fear of death. Perdita could feel it in the air like an icy mist. 'Twas a plague that squeezed the life from people. Yet it was not a fear she knew. Rather, her greatest fear was loneliness, emptiness, and despair—the fear of being unloved forever. This fear of death surrounding her now was one she longed to know.

Ducking into the shadows of a small shop, she cringed at the sight before her. Men—some from the *Scepter*—fought against a horde of Malum. At least twenty. Some hand-to-hand, some with blades, others firing pistols from across the square. One Malum held a knife to a man's throat while his family begged for mercy. Farmers and merchants and fisherman fought bravely to defend their town. The dead and wounded littered the ground like horse droppings. Another group of Malum set fire to nearby buildings. Flames leapt into the night sky while smoke curled from the crumbing remains. A woman lay weeping beside a storefront.

Holding her sword out, Perdita scanned the mob. There. Savion entered the square parrying with two Malum. Both attacked him at once, yet, with a sword in each hand, he fought them off with more skill than Perdita had ever seen. His movements were so quick, graceful, slick, and measured—each hitting its mark and forcing his opponents back—that Perdita found herself mesmerized.

Flashing shapes of light caught her eye—large, distinct, positioned around the edges of the square. Glimmering forms of men, warriors fully armed. Yet no evil hovered about them—just power and hope. Then they vanished. She blinked.

But there was no time to ponder the odd sight as six more Malum dragged a group of terrified citizens into the square: women, children, and a few struggling old men.

Petrok and Hona, the two men she'd met on the *Scepter*, along with the comely man who'd been gaping at her, started for them, weapons drawn.

"Ryne!" the lead Malum yelled. "Call your men off, or we cut these people's throats." Grabbing one trembling man, the beast held a blade to his neck.

Quickly dispatching his two combatants, Savion approached this new threat, breath heaving and sweat gleaming over his neck and chest. "Warriors of Natas!" he bellowed. "You have no power here!"

"Aye, but we do, Prince of Abbas," the largest of the Malum spat. "*We* were invited. Were you?"

"Silence!" Savion shouted.

Prince of Abbas? Perdita hadn't time to consider what that meant when two men leapt in front of her, battling with knives as thick as fists. They paid her no mind as they continued their fight, and she slipped to a nearby vacant building and stood before its smashed window.

"We need no invitation." Savion leveled his sword before the warrior. "This land belongs to King Abbas. You are only here by the invitation of one ignorant fool, the man whom your infectious illness has already killed."

Perdita watched with great interest, her heart thrashing. How would Savion and his crew escape such a formidable force? Malum were expert fighters, strong, skilled, not to mention some of the ugliest beasts she'd ever seen—lusty, snarling fiends who smelled like rot and sulfur.

The tall one addressing Savion towered over the rest. "I'm Prince Skivian, the rightful ruler of this town!" The other Malum grunted cheers and waved their weapons in the air.

Savion wiped a sleeve over his brow. "You will never rule this town." He spoke the words with a confidence that belied the swarms of Malum now spilling into the square.

"You know in whose power I come," Savion proclaimed loudly.

Prince Skivian snorted arrogantly. "You will lose this war, and our king will reign."

"You serve no king, but a snake impersonating a king."

As if in agreement, the large Malum's eyes became slits. He pushed the blade deeper into the old man's throat, spilling a stream of his blood. Yet, oddly, the other Malum stopped rushing into the square, and the ones with victims dragged them backward as if frightened by Savion's words. Yet, Perdita saw no reinforcements, no warriors rising to Savion's aid. Clearly Savion and his men were outnumbered. Why, then, did the Malum tremble?

"*I* will fight you," Savion said. "For the lives of these people and this town. You and two of your best warriors."

"No, Cap'n!" Petrok shouted defiantly.

Ignoring him, Savion continued. "If I win, you will leave and never return to this town."

Prince Skivian chuckled. "And if you lose?"

Savion spread out his arms. "Then the town is yours."

"And yet, it is already ours." He shoved the quivering man he held to the ground then kicked him as he crawled away.

"Is it? Come and see." Savion motioned him forward with sword held high—regardless of the fact that he was outnumbered.

Perdita could only stare, dumbfounded. What baffled her even further was the terror burning in Prince Skivian's eyes while only courage brimmed from Savion's. Not from his crew, however. Fear gripped their expressions. Hona urged Savion not to fight. Petrok drew his sword and stood by his captain's side, while the handsome one slipped into the background. The others merely stood by watching their captain make a deal for his death.

Perdita's throat went dry. How could Savion ever win against three of Natas's best? And for what? Farmers, shopkeepers, and fisherman? The same people who Savion had said *invited* the Malum here, people Savion didn't even know!

She looked at him in awe. He was the bravest man she'd ever seen. A true savior. And just the type of man she needed to break her curse. Trouble was, the fool was about to get himself killed.

CHAPTER 8

"This is my fight, Petrok." Savion pushed his friend aside, then stepped toward his enemy. "Shall we?"

Prince Skivian gestured behind him. Two men of equal brawn stepped forward, both with equally-evil glints in their eyes.

Taking a deep breath, Savion sought the peace within, feeling the medallion warm on his chest. There. Flowing through his veins like a calm river—the peace of Nevaeh. The peace that assured him he was not alone. The peace that told him he followed the right path.

Prince Skivian and his men swooped down on Savion. Blades caught in the air with mighty clangs, joining distant screams and the crackle of fires. Savion pursued the sense, the flow of power, the movement that directed his hands. Tapping into it, his muscles, arms, hands, and feet became one, moved as one, joined in a graceful dance of strength and authority.

Focus! Focus! He swung his blades this way and that, allowing the peace and power to direct him—striking, thrusting. *Clank, Gong! Groan.* Cussing bit his ears. He swerved, dipped, hunched, and swung about, all in rhythm to the music within. A painful howl! Lifeblood tainted the breeze.

Sweat stung his eyes. He shook his head and blinked. A muscular forearm slammed into his neck, shoving him back while the tip of a blade reached for his side. He jumped to the left, kicked one Malum in the shin, and thrust his sword into the other one's gut. Before the first Malum knew what hit him, Savion tossed his blade in the air, caught it by the hilt, and pounded it on his jaw. Blood spurted from the Malum's mouth as he spun to the ground. Following the sense, Savion ducked just in time to avoid a pistol shot from Prince Skivian. Then dropping to one hand, he swung his legs at the brute's feet and knocked him to the dirt.

He landed with a *thunk* that shook the ground and sent a cloud of dust into the air. Turning away, Savion coughed. A flash of lavender caught his eyes. *Perdita!* The daft woman stood alone next to a battered shop, a pistol in one hand, sword in the other, staring at him as if he were some creature from the otherworld. Two Malum headed her way.

Foolish woman! She would be killed. He started for her, but Prince Skivian recovered and charged him. Savion swerved to meet his challenge. Blade on blade, he shoved the fiend back, all the while stealing glances at Perdita. The two Malum halted before her. Savion blocked an incoming slash, then searched for one of his men to aid her. The tip of a blade struck his shoulder. He leapt out of the way and whirled his sword through the air. He must focus! A hurried glance back revealed the two Malum dismissed her and proceeded into the store.

He could make no sense of it. Peace fled him.

Prince Skivian let out a threatening growl, his face a pulsing bulge of sweat and dirt. Raising his sword, he spit on the ground. Savion steadied himself, desperately seeking his lost focus. Too late. The savage must have followed Savion's concerned glance toward Perdita. A slow grin lifted Prince Skivian's scarred lips. One signal sent his Malum advancing toward her.

Brandishing his blade high, Savion swept it down upon the beast, but the monster met his thrust with an eerie *hiss* of grinding metal. Savion's heart thundered in his chest. He tightened his grip on his sword as the second man rose. Together, they came at Savion as one, pounding mercilessly on him, slash after slash, thrust after thrust.

He sought the power within, but his moves were clumsy, his peace gone. His eyes snapped to Perdita. With sword high and pistol drawn, she stood defiantly waiting for her attackers. Not running, not cowering, but ready to fight off the advancing Malum warriors! Was that blood on her bodice? Petrok and Hona finally spotted her, grabbed Nuto and Verrad, and rushed to her aid.

Relief filled Savion. He strained to latch onto the place where the power originated—the dance of the three. There. He felt it surge through his veins once again. Swords came at him. He swung his own to assuage the attack. Blades chimed. He stumbled. Pain sliced his side. Agony drained him of strength. The peace returned. The light remained. Ignoring the pain—or rather absorbing it—he fought back his attackers. Ducking, swooping, leaping, shifting, he grew weary of the exchange. One of the Malum drew a pistol. Savion kicked it from his grip. He whirled around, slicing deep into Prince Skivian's shoulder. Dropping one of his swords, Savion snatched up the gun and shot the other Malum, who barreled backward, gripping his arm.

Blood gurgled from Prince Skivian's shoulder as he crumpled to his knees. "You won this one, Savion." Hatred mangled his features.

"Leave town at once and never return," Savion commanded loudly, his breath heaving.

Glancing at his two fallen warriors, Prince Skivian struggled to rise, then gestured toward the townspeople. "If they invite us again, we have every right to come."

Savion nodded. The dark warrior was right. Hopefully, the people had learned their lesson. People who now crowded around him, cheering. One glance told him that his men had rescued Perdita and were standing guard around her. But there was no longer a need. The Malum were leaving—some marching defiantly, others limping, and some sneering at the cowering citizens as they left.

Savion shouted, "The town of Skivia now belongs to King Abbas! This defeated Malum is your prince no longer. You have been set free—do not give up your freedom again."

"You saved us!" one man yelled, clinging to Savion.

"Thank you, sir. Thank you!"

"Savion! Savion! Savion!" They began to chant, but he shook his head. Extricating himself from their clutches, he leapt onto a broken wall, wincing in pain, then lifted his hands until the cheers silenced. "They *will* come back if you invite them. They bring sickness and death. You know this!"

"But how did we invite them?" one old man asked.

"Your own magistrate agreed to trade with them. Struck a deal to purchase their stolen goods to make a profit for the town. But any of you could have made a deal with them. They are deceivers and liars. Do not be fools!"

Gasps filtered about. "Where is our faithful magistrate now?" one lady spoke with spite.

"He died o' the sickness," another answered. "Jist last night."

"Let this be a lesson," Savion said. "You can *never* deal with Malum. They always bring slavery, despair, and death."

Muttering sifted through the crowd over heads bobbing in agreement. Savion's eyes met Perdita's. She wore the oddest expression. Shock? Admiration? But, inexplicably absolutely *no fear*. Astonishing for a woman who'd entered a fierce battle and was nearly killed. He turned back to the murmuring crowd.

"Go back to your homes!" he said. "Bury your dead. Tend the injured. Those who are sick will soon get well now that the Malum are gone. Live your life in the peace of King Abbas."

But instead of honoring the King, they continued to cheer, "Savion! Savion! Savion!"

Ordering them to stop, he stepped down and slowly headed toward his waiting men. Petrok and Hona met him with wide grins, Nuto a knowing look, and Verrad proud eyes. The rest nodded his way, gathered their weapons, and stood awaiting orders.

They parted as he approached Perdita, eyes blazing. "For the love of Nevaeh, I told you to stay on board." Stains covered the side of her gown. "You're wounded!" He gently lifted her arm, studying the pool of blood, but saw no rip in her clothes.

"Not my blood," she replied calmly, but then gaped at him in shock. "How did you? How ...?"

He dropped her arm and snorted. "You could have been killed."

"I thought you might need help."

His crew chuckled.

Savion would love to banter with this woman, but the sky was spinning at the moment, and he was having trouble finding his breath. He pressed a hand on his side, and a moan escaped his lips.

"You're hurt!" Petrok rushed forward, the others following.

Moving Savion's arm aside, Hona opened the captain's coat. A stream of red soaked most of his shirt and dribbled down his breeches.

Perdita gasped.

Voices shouted. The world grew fuzzy and hands

grabbed Savion just before he toppled to the ground.

CHAPTER 9

Perdita remained in the shadows of Savion's cabin while the ship's doctor tended the captain's injury. The fact that his men hovered over him like a flock of nervous hens spoke volumes about the man's character. Not one of her Ivans—not even those who had professed their undying love—had ever cared for her that much. What that revealed about her, she didn't want to consider. All that mattered now was that this honorable, kind, fascinating man had been injured because of her. She hadn't meant to distract him—to break whatever powerful trance had come over him. Whether a trance, an inbred skill, or a supernatural power, 'twas like nothing she'd ever witnessed. And she'd seen numerous battles through the centuries. His was more like a dance than a battle, his movements fluid, assured, beautiful … and terrifying.

Who was this man? So much more than a mere sailor. No wonder these men followed him.

"He will live," Haddeus announced as he washed his hands in a bowl of bloody water. "Thank Abbas the wound wasn't too deep."

"Did you stitch him up?" Perdita asked, drawing the gaze of the five men in the room: Petrok and Hona, standing at their captain's bedside; the dark-haired man leaning against the bulkhead, whose look even now made her squirm; a lanky man with short red hair and a grumpy face who sat on Savion's desk; and the doctor himself.

"Aye, of course," Haddeus answered, as if insulted by the question.

"With the whisker of a sea lion? They provide the best comfort and strength."

They all merely gaped at her.

"And of course you poured rum on it?" she added.

The thick man's eyes narrowed. "I perceive you have some doctorin' skills, miss?"

More than all of them put together, she imagined. "Some."

The lithe redhead they called Nuto rose from the desk and pointed a finger at her. "You! You're the one who caused this. You shouldn't have been there. You should have listened to the captain!"

"That's not fair, Nuto." Petrok ran a hand through his springy brown hair. "I'm sure she didn't mean it."

Perdita took a step forward. "Indeed. I meant no harm."

"Still, after all the captain's done for you." Hona frowned.

Haddeus gathered his utensils and rags. "Holler if you need me. I've other wounds to mend." And off he went—leaving her with these men who stared at her with a mixture of curiosity and hatred.

Perdita took another tentative step forward, her mind spinning with questions. "How did he …?" She glanced at Savion, still unconscious from the pain. "How did he …?"

"Fight off three trained Malum warriors?" The one they called Verrad gave her a crooked smile. "He has"—his lips tightened as he studied his captain—"unusual powers. If only he'd use the full force of them, we could defeat Natas and his Malum forever."

Petrok snorted. "There will come a time for that. We will wait. We all know Savion is destined for greatness."

The ship creaked over a wavelet, and Perdita shifted her weight. "But why does he even bother to fight Natas's rebellion with only a ship full of men? Natas was the mightiest general in all of Erden before he betrayed King Abbas. Surely such battles are best left to the king's armies."

Hona slid onto a chair beside his captain. "He says it's everyone's duty to fight evil."

Nuto shook his head. "Yet it seems we make no progress. We are victorious in one city, and Natas attacks another. We rescue those he imprisons in one place, and he only captures more."

Verrad shrugged. "Maybe Savion hasn't enough power, after all."

Petrok swept fiery eyes his way. "Why stay with him then?"

Verrad huffed. "Not for the treasure, that's for sure."

"None of us signed up for treasure, Verrad. If that's what you want, you should leave!" Nuto snapped.

"For the honor." Hona lifted his chin. "We joined Savion for the honor, for the purpose, for all the good we do."

"And someday when he conquers Natas," Petrok added. "Perhaps King Abbas will make him ruler over the Ancient Seas and we will rule by his side." His eyes flashed above a wide grin.

"Rule? You?" Hona tossed a rag at him. "You can't even decide what to eat for breakfast!"

They all laughed, and even Perdita smiled.

Soon, the conversation lulled and the men grew weary. One by one, they rose and left, all except Hona, who sat by his captain's side, unwilling to trust anyone with his care—especially, it would seem, Perdita. But finally after much reassurance on her part and heavy eyes on his, he relented, but only so far as to move to the other side of the cabin, where he promptly lay on the deck and fell asleep.

Perdita sat in the empty chair beside Savion and took his hand in hers, remembering how she'd done the same a week ago in her cave. Haddeus had removed the stitches Perdita had sewn in Savion's forehead where the wound that would have killed him was now naught but a tiny pink scar. The sway of the ship sent lantern light oscillating over his strong stubbled jaw, the regal curve of his nose, and his sun-streaked hair, and she wondered how she'd ever thought him ordinary. In truth, after seeing the kind of man he was, she found him strikingly handsome.

His bare chest rose and fell with each breath, lifting the medallion he always wore. She couldn't help but stare at the taut muscles still twitching from battle, stretching over his chest and down his arms where the lion tattoo on his bicep seemed to roar at her. She rubbed her thumb over the calluses of his rough hand and thought of the strength in those hands. Where did his "special powers" come from? 'Twas like he hailed from another type of being.

He moaned and shifted under the blankets, his expression agitated. Perdita began to sing. Though her tone was not as pleasing when she was in human form, mayhap it would help soothe him.

"Destined to roam the waves and the sea
I will forever be lost to thee
Will thou love me enough to die
Sailor boy, don't make me cry ..."

She sang for several minutes until Savion settled into a peaceful sleep.

His crew was right about one thing. This was no ordinary man. This man was indeed destined for greatness. Yet despite his skill in battle and his inward premonitions of evil, he was still mortal. He *could* be wounded. And even die. Then why did he toss fear and good sense overboard and charge into a deadly battle as if he were merely attending a spring festival?

Risking his life for people he didn't even know!

A strange sensation caressed her heart, a gentle yearning, an uncontrollable pull. Admiration, attraction, respect, even care, all budded within her. *Nay!* She did not want to feel any of those things. She never wanted to feel them again. They only caused vulnerability and heartache.

Leaning back in the chair, still holding his hand, she closed her eyes and eventually succumbed to the gentle roll of the ship lulling her to sleep.

To a place where nightmares haunted … Duncan Mallory's blurry face came into clear focus as he leaned across the linen-clad table and caressed Perdita's hand, admiring the sparkling ruby he'd just slid onto her finger. Lifting her hand to his lips, he kissed it as his gray eyes remained on her, sparking with interest, with love, even a hint of desperation. "Do say you'll become my wife, Perdita. I shall go mad without you."

It was the year of King Abbas, 1523, and Duncan had ordered his servants to set up a table overlooking the falls of Credon—the most beautiful waterfalls ever to be found on the island of Jamak. Complete with white tablecloth, fine china, silver serving dishes, goblets of wine, and a golden candelabra, it was a scene right out of the myths of Nevaeh. His servants stood at a distance, offering them privacy but ready to come at a snap of Duncan's fingers.

Rich, powerful, handsome Duncan. Perdita could hardly believe her luck in finding him. And now after twenty-five wondrous days together, she knew he was the one. He loved her. He *truly* loved her! He'd already proven it by going against his father's wishes and offering Perdita his troth, even at the risk of losing his inheritance. The ten

Ivans before Duncan were like shadows, mists that were soon whisked away in light of this man's wisdom, charm, looks, and kindness. There was naught he wouldn't do for her. She had but to mention a craving and within a day he produced whatever she fancied.

The soothing melody of rushing water accompanied the laughter of leaves beneath a tropical breeze. "Yes! Yes! A thousand yesses!" Perdita smiled, and Duncan leapt from his chair and pulled her into his arms. Laying her cheek on the silk of his coat, she drew in his scent and felt a twinge of guilt at her plans for the morrow. But if all went well, no one would be harmed. Perchance the test was only in the *risking* of one's life, in the sincerity of the heart, not the actual sacrifice of life. Perchance true love would win in the end, and once Perdita was freed from the curse, she and Duncan would live together in loving bliss.

Oh, how she did love him! Mayhap even more than Sir Ivan of Morehead.

That one thought propelled her forward with her plans to lure him down to the docks of the city, down to the alley between the wharf and the fish market where the pirates she hired waited. Their instructions? To capture her and threaten Duncan with death if he attempted her rescue. They were also commanded to do him no harm and were paid well for their trouble. Duncan would come to her aid, of that she had no doubt. Otherwise, she wouldn't put herself—and him—in the hands of such ruffians.

No sooner had she and Duncan entered the alleyway, arm-in-arm, then the brigands grabbed her and held a knife to her throat—the drawing of her blood a little too realistic. Her heart soared as, when expected, Duncan fought off two of the pirates. She could almost feel herself becoming human again. Any minute now the tingling would begin, the itching like a thousand bugs crawling through her insides. Then the curse would be lifted, and she'd be free!

One of the pirates held a pistol to Duncan's head. "If ye don't stand down an' run along, I'll carve yer gizzard out an' fry 'em up fer supper."

Perdita frowned. Inexcusably dramatic. She would have to speak to them about that later.

Her rescuer, her champion, froze, his wild eyes darting toward her in the dim light of the alleyway.

Fight, my love. Fight! She urged him silently. *And we will both be free!*

Instead, sorrow breached his eyes, and his handsome face crumpled like dust. "I'm sorry, Perdita."

"Sorry?" She struggled against the pirate's grip. "But I gave myself to you."

The pirates chuckled. "How's about givin' us a bit o' that sweetness, darlin'?"

Ignoring them—along with the terror cinching her heart, she turned disbelieving eyes toward Duncan. "But we are betrothed. I am to be your wife."

"I don't want to die, Perdita. Forgive me. I'll get help." And before she could answer, he turned and fled into the darkness.

She suffered more than a broken heart that night. She suffered a battered, violated, and beaten body as the pirates reneged on their deal, took her back to their ship, and passed her around like an old blanket for two days. In the end, they tossed her into the sea, where she drifted in unbelievable pain for another day before she transformed back into a mermaid. Back in her cave, she nursed her wounds for a month, but there was naught to do for the gaping wound in her soul. She removed Duncan's ring and tossed it in her chest of treasures.

But she could not remove him from her heart.

She *had* loved him. Mayhap even more than all the others. And he'd promised to love her forever. Yet in the end, he hadn't loved her at all. His love went only as far as the happiness and pleasure she brought him. But was that love at all?

That's when she determined two things. One: never to fall in love again. And two: to learn how to fight.

Chapter 10

Familiar creaks and groans drew Savion out of his sleep. Pain in his side brought him fully conscious. But it was a tight grip on his hand that startled him. Opening his eyes, he blinked in the dim light of a waning lantern to find Perdita slumped in a chair beside him, chin on her chest and her fingers intertwined with his. The soft roll of wavelets told him they were still anchored at Skivia as memories crowded his mind of the events of the day.

He thought to pull his hand back, but for some reason, he liked the feel of her soft skin next to his. He liked it a lot. Too much. He also liked gazing at her when she wasn't looking. Hair like shimmering ink spilled from her pins down the front of her gown over a delicate frame that held enough curves to drive a man to distraction. And her unique smell. A scent he couldn't quite place—a sweetness that reminded him of the sea. Women like her knew they were beautiful and expected attention from men. He wouldn't give her that satisfaction.

She moaned and said something he couldn't make out, but her tone was so melancholy, so despairing. "Duncan, please. Please don't leave me. Why didn't you love me?"

Ah, one of her many lovers, no doubt. Savion yanked back his hand.

Jerking awake, she sat up and stared at him as if trying to remember where she was. "Savion, are you all right?" True concern shadowed her expression as she leaned toward him. "Does your wound pain you?"

Something in the measure of her voice, the way the lantern light flowed over her hair and sparkled on her skin, gave Savion a sense of having lived this moment before. Impossible. He closed his eyes, but still the images came in bursts: candlelight dancing over the slick walls of a cave, the sound of water dripping, and a black-haired beauty hovering over him. Just like this one was doing now. He also remembered songs, ballads, sung in the sweetest voice he'd ever heard.

Wait. Perdita had sung to him earlier in the night—her off-key voice even now etching uncomfortably down his spine. He'd pretended to fall asleep just to get her to stop. Nothing like his memory. Still …

"I've seen you before." He rubbed his eyes.

She shifted in her seat, bit her lip, then rose and strolled to his desk. "Of course you have, Savion. You rescued me nigh three nights ago."

"No, from somewhere else."

But she wasn't paying attention. She was filling the lamp with oil, pruning the wick, and chasing shadows from the room. She was hiding something. He could sense it. But what? His thoughts drifted to the recent battle in Skivia.

"You are either very brave or very foolish. I haven't decided which. Either way you disobeyed a direct order." He tried to sit, but the pain in his side prevented him.

"I am not one of your crew, Captain. Besides, I thought I could help." She kept her back to him and stared into the darkness outside the stern windows.

"I doubt that. After all, how much help could you be?"

At this, she spun around. "Because I'm a woman?"

The arch of one dainty brow made him chuckle. "Precisely. If you think you are any match for the Malum, you are as delusional as I first assumed."

"Delu—" She slammed her mouth shut. "You forget I had a pistol and a sword."

And a shrewish wit to match, he thought. "If you are so adept at protecting yourself, why did I find you stripped of your clothing and left on a beach at the mercy of two men?"

She moved closer, a coy lift to her lips. "I *said* I had a pistol and sword, not that I knew how to use them."

Behold, the seductress returned. Somehow, he preferred the shrew. Visions of that shrew being overlooked by the Malum as if she wasn't even there caused unease to ripple through him. "Why weren't the Malum interested in you?"

She lowered to a chair and fidgeted. "I don't know what you mean."

"There were two of them … heading straight toward you, but they passed you by and went into the store."

She shrugged, looking away. "Mayhap they didn't see me."

"They saw you."

She traced a finger over the intricate carving on the arm of the chair. "In good sooth, Malum never pay me any mind. I have no idea why." She gave him a sarcastic smile. "Mayhap because I'm a lowly woman, as you so aptly pointed out."

In good sooth. Who says that anymore? He narrowed his eyes. "Malum prey on the weak."

She huffed and waved a hand through the air. "They eventually came after me. You saw them."

"Only when their leader noticed my concer—me looking at you."

"Indeed?" She smiled again—one of those deliciously mischievous smiles. "A bit egocentric, aren't we?"

Infuriating woman! Savion made another attempt to rise, but his side caught on fire. His moan brought her rushing to him. She examined the bandage as if she knew what she was doing, then brought a glass of water to his lips.

"Enough of this nonsense. Stay still. You need your rest."

He drank the liquid, staring at her over the rim. The tenderness in her eyes swept away all thoughts of Malum. All thoughts of pretty much anything. For she *did* seem to care about his wellbeing. Snores drew his glance to Hona sound asleep in the corner. He smiled at his friend's loyalty, then shifted his gaze back to Perdita. The shadows beneath her eyes spoke of her exhaustion. Still, she had stayed awake to tend to him. Lorelei would have never sacrificed a moment's rest for his needs. Or anyone else's, for that matter.

He had determined never to trust beauty again, and this particular beauty wore many masks. Which one was the real Perdita? What was she up to? For he sensed a restlessness in her, a duplicity that pricked his nerves. *And* his good sense.

Despite his misgivings, during the next week, he found her to be a skilled nurse, almost saint-like in her ministrations.

Savion knew his crew cared for his welfare, but their talents did not include nursing the injured. More oft than not when he was ill, they left him alone in his cabin. One time when he'd been down with a fever, he'd had to drag his searing body up the companionway ladder just to ask for a drink of water.

But not this woman. She hovered over him as a mother would an only child, tending to his every need, allowing him the peace he needed to recover. Only once did Petrok enter the cabin and that was to get orders on where to set sail. "Kadon," Savion replied, keeping his promise to Perdita.

On the second day, when Savion's fever abated and he was able to sit, Perdita read to him from *The Chronicles of Maylon* with perfect pronunciation and faultless elocution of the archaic language in which it had been written nearly two hundred years ago. Not only that, her passion for the words, the story they told, was like none he'd seen during all his studies.

"You must have had the privilege of an education, Perdita."

She seemed surprised and looked down, her sweep of lashes fanning her cheeks. "Yes, my father insisted. He had only daughters and wanted us to have the same education he would have given a son." Sorrow lingered at the corners of her mouth.

Because she missed her family or because they had all departed this world? "Tell me of your childhood."

She would not look at him. The ship bucked over a wave, and a breeze from the porthole spun through a lock of her hair. "There is not much to tell."

Rising, she closed the book and moved to replace it on the shelf lining the bulkhead. "I was but a poor shepherd's daughter."

"Rich enough to afford an education, it would seem." His tone emerged with more sarcasm than he intended.

"You doubt me?" She faced him, indignant, her green skirts whirling about her legs. She'd found a gown somewhere—one without bloodstains. But unfortunately, this one was just as tight as the other. "Education was important to my mother. She hailed from privilege."

"Is that why you use expressions from our ancient tongue? 'Tis, 'twas, naught, mayhap, and forsooth—of all words? Because of your mother? Was she some sort of historian?"

Her jaw tightened. "Yes, if you must know." But then her shoulders slumped, and a look of longing replaced her anger.

"Forgive me." Savion chastised himself. Whether she was telling the truth or not, he had no right to belittle her.

"Your parents must have loved you very much to ensure you were properly taught."

She stared out the window. "My father wanted me to marry well. He always said with my beauty I could catch a prince." She gave a sad smile.

"Why haven't you then?"

For a moment she looked as though she would cry. But then she took a deep breath and faced him with a hint of a smile. "I suppose I haven't found my prince yet."

After a knock, Bart entered with a tray of food: pork stew, bowls of rice, sweet corn, buttered yams, a platter of salt fish, fried plantains, and coconut milk. Perdita's eyes lit up, as they normally did at the sight of food, and she rushed toward the desk where Bart laid the tray, thanking the man over and over.

Savion had never thought the crusty old sailor capable of blushing, but Savion could swear the red hue on Bart's face was not due to the heat.

After Bart left and they both settled down to eat, Savion continued the conversation. "What happened to your parents?"

"What do you mean?" She brought a spoonful of stew to her lips.

"Surely if they are alive, you'd be living with them, not wandering the Ancient Seas alone and with no support."

"My family still lives. But I cannot … I … I have business here before I can return home."

"Business?"

"Indeed. Business that is *my* business." She slid a spoonful of buttered yams into her mouth and closed her eyes as if in ecstasy.

Savion smiled. "I've never seen anyone enjoy their food so much."

"When you are deprived of it for so long, you appre—" She bit her lip and looked away.

"Ah, your impoverished upbringing, I take it?"

She nodded and slipped a plantain into her mouth, then glanced over the feast as if deciding what to eat next. Her hand wavered over the platter, hastily avoiding the salt fish.

Savion sipped his coconut milk. "Why such an aversion to fish? You never touch it."

"Fish is so bland, don't you think? I much prefer beef or pork. And cake!" Her eyes sparkled. "Cake is surely from Nevaeh!"

Savion couldn't help but chuckle at her childlike exuberance.

Fascinating, extraordinary woman! *Captivating* would be a better word, for he found himself completely enthralled with her, wanting to know more, longing to delve into her secrets. Even though he wasn't sure he could believe much of what she told him.

The next two days only added to his suspicions, for no shepherd's daughter could know of the things she spoke. As much as he tried not to, he found himself looking forward to their conversations and to her opinions on history, art, and literature. Not surprisingly, he hadn't found his intellectual equivalent among the crew, and he now realized how much he missed conversing with someone who had an in-depth understanding of important topics: Natas's rebellion, the Kalok wars, the rise of enlightened thought, governmental theory, as well as new scientific discoveries of air pressure, the human cell, and the magnetic properties of Erden. In addition, she possessed an extraordinary knowledge about wind and tides and the fish and mammals inhabiting the Ancient Seas, as well as geography, native superstitions, and the flora and fauna of nearby islands.

Savion was also amazed at how much they had in common. Their appreciation for the art of Flionna—the fluid lines, vivid colors, and expressions of pain he painted on his portraits. And Bettricheil's music—the intensity and passion in every note. They spent hours discussing such things and during that time, all her masks slipped off unnoticed, and she was just …

Perdita.

What he found even more astounding was her resolute defense of her own opinions, which were not easily altered—no matter Savion's arguments to the contrary. Though most of the time they agreed, her unwillingness to be convinced on certain points intrigued him. Only in Nevaeh had he found women possessing such freedom of individuality and thought. For a woman who seemed intent on seducing him most of the time, these moments in which she refused to give in to him on some point of history or political thought were moments he found himself utterly lost in her.

And he both hated it and loved it.

"How do you know so much?" he asked her on his sixth day of recovery after she'd brought him his noonday meal. Outside, dark clouds shielded the sun, and the ship teetered over a heavy swell.

"Do you believe a woman incapable of deep thought?"

He sat in a chair, a bandage wrapped tightly around his chest, his lunch of tea, turtle stew, and banana crisps beside him on a table. "I've met many intelligent women, some far wiser than me, but none of them *look* like you."

At first her brow crinkled. Then—and much to Savion's dismay—her lips curved and the seductress returned. "Beauty and brains cannot exist together?"

He stared at her, longing for the real Perdita, but instead she sashayed his way and leaned to pour his tea, offering him a view of the figure spilling from her bodice.

Disappointed, he took the pot from her. "I can do it. I'm recovered now and in no need of a nursemaid." He regretted his harsh tone.

Wind whistled outside the window as thunder rumbled in the distance.

Grabbing a few banana crisps, she moved away, not hiding her pain at his dismissal, and plopped them in her mouth. But there was nothing he could do about it. As much as he enjoyed this woman's company, he didn't trust her. And trust was everything to him.

The deck canted over a wave, and Perdita took advantage of her imbalance to throw herself in Savion's lap. She'd been wanting to get this close to him for days as he sat in the same chair, the muscles of his bare chest taunting her to touch them—to touch him and feel his warmth and strength. The more they talked and laughed, the more she wanted to crawl in his arms. And this was the perfect excuse. But no sooner had she pressed her curves against his rock-hard chest, than he pushed her off as if she had Gengees plague. Flustered as she'd never seen him, he grabbed a shirt, tossed it over his head—wincing from his wound—and led her to a chair.

"You'd better sit, Perdita. Seems we are in for a rough ride."

She slunk, more than sat, in the chair. Frustration ate at her hope. She'd enjoyed her time with Savion immensely, and she knew he felt the same. She'd sensed him softening toward her, seen the looks of longing in his eyes, but whenever she tried to charm him, he put her off.

Petrok poked his head in, a blast of rain-spiced wind barreling in behind him. "A storm, Captain. A pretty bad one. Are you up to taking command?"

Savion nodded, told her to stay put, and left.

A flash of lightning scored the dark sky outside the windows, and with it came a glorious idea—a frighteningly glorious idea. She knew exactly what she had to do.

CHAPTER 11

Damien Gund slammed the brandy to the back of his throat and tossed the empty glass to a passing wench. Surprisingly she caught it and glowered at him as she made her way to the bar. He focused his attention back on the slimy worm of a man pilfering drink after drink from him with a promise of forthcoming information.

"Do tell us, Mr. Menlend, about the woman you saw?" Damien glanced at his two men flanking the reprobate, both ready to pounce on him and use less than serendipitous means to extract the information should he renege on his promise.

Licking his lips, Menlend's glazed eyes scanned the drinks Damien had purchased for him lined up across the stained table: Rum, Brandy, Port, Gin, Whisper, and the finest Dray from Cassinaw.

After gulping down the third one, he whistled for a trollop lingering by the stairway. The buxom woman bounced over, plopped in his lap, and promptly held out her hand. Menlend's eyes met Damien's.

Fighting back his annoyance, Damien flipped the woman a coin. She expertly caught it—did women have special ability to catch things in taverns?—then began reaching inside the man's shirt to fondle his chest.

"The woman?" Damien demanded.

"Ah, yes." Menlend sipped his fourth drink and leaned toward Damien as if he were telling him some grand secret. "Naked as a beached porpoise, says I. Ne'er saw anything like it. Right there on the beach." He shook his head and whistled. "She be a looker too. Woooyee. I'll tell ye. Every curve in its place with lots to spare, if ye know what I mean."

Damien's friends lifted their brows, but Damien frowned. He could care less what the woman looked like. "You said she came from the water."

"Aye, right out o' the sea, she walked, all casual an' confident … like goin' fer an evenin' swim in the raw was as natural as strolling down Main Street."

The trollop dove her head into the man's neck and showered him with kisses.

"Then what happened?" Damien raised his voice, jerking the man from his revelry.

"Sailors attacked her, like I said, but then others came t' her rescue."

"Who?"

"Dunno. I knows he was a captain o' one of the ships in the bay. The *Scepter,* methinks. But they be gone now. Sailed away five days ago."

"And you are sure they took her on board?"

The man offered the woman one of his drinks and then downed his last one. "As far as I know."

Damien nodded at his friends, and they jerked the man and woman from the chair and shoved them on their way.

One of Damien's men took the vacated seat. "It's her."

"Aye, has to be. It's been ten years." Ten years in which Damien had done nothing but search the Ancient Seas. Ten long miserable years waiting to avenge his father's death. And ten years before that. During that time, he'd paid handsomely for eyes and ears in every major port. The mermaid would choose a place heavily populated with vulnerable men, and when she surfaced, Damien would hear about it. Just as he did three nights ago. It had taken him another two nights to arrive at Hoffnung. Apparently it was worth the trip.

This was the best lead he'd had in years. He fingered the rare Caestrian lace on his sleeves.

One of his colleagues ordered a drink and rubbed his hands together. "I can almost hear the chink of coins!"

The other man's eyes flashed. "Is it true her tears turn to pearls?"

Damien nodded. "We'll make a fortune off her. She'll also fetch a pretty price from people wanting to see a real mermaid. And another thing." He leaned toward them. "They say she has healing powers too."

His men were near salivating.

"What d'ye need more money for?" one of them asked, wiping his mouth on his sleeve. "You already own two islands filled with sugar and coffee plantations an' enough slaves to mine for yer silver. Plus you have the ear of Natas."

Damien smiled. He'd worked hard to ally himself with the most powerful man in Erden. He twisted the oversized ruby on his finger, drawing the attention of one of the trollops, along with several men. He could feel the envy of these commoners, could feel their admiration. "One can never have enough riches. Or power," he finally said. And he intended to get more of both.

"D'ye know who commands this *Scepter*?" his man asked with a sinister grin.

"Yes, and we shouldn't have any trouble finding him. And the mermaid with him."

When Damien captured her, she'd pay for his father's death by a life of imprisonment, making Damien the wealthiest and most powerful man in Erden. Even more powerful than Natas.

Ignoring Savion's command to stay below, Perdita made her way through the companionway, wincing and groaning as the bucking ship slammed her into the bulkhead on one side of the narrow hallway and then into the other. Once she made it above deck, she fared no better. A fist of wind nearly scooped her up and tossed her overboard. Thankfully, she managed to brace herself against the mainmast. Rain stabbed her like liquid arrows. The ship vaulted, lifting her from the deck and slamming her down as if she were but a doll and the ship naught but a toy. Thunder roared in laughter.

Savion's voice passed over her in broken clips of commands and encouragements. She found him above on the quarterdeck assisting his helmsman with the wheel and shouting orders to those within earshot. Sodden hair whipped around his face, and his shirt lashed his chest and arms. Yet, despite it all, an odd peace surrounded him. A confidence. What a remarkable man. His eyes met hers, and she could sense his displeasure at seeing her above.

The ship canted. Losing her grip, she toppled over the deck and finally grabbed onto a latch grating. Terrified shouts assailed her from above where men clung to yards and lines, adjusting sail.

The ship righted and Petrok, hair plastered to his bearded face, charged toward her and shouted over the storm. "Captain says to go below. It's not safe!"

"Are we going to die?" She pretended to be alarmed.

Hona appeared beside her. Taking her arm, he helped her to stand. "No, miss. We've survived far worse than this." He led her down companionway and halfway to the cabin, then released her and turned to leave.

"Can the captain swim?" Her shout spun him to face her.

Rain plastered blond hair to his head, the ends dripping onto his shirt. "Aye, miss, not to worry. He's the best swimmer of all of us. But never fear, there'll be no need for that."

The sweet lad gave her a sincere smile, and she suddenly regretted what she must do. But there was naught to be done for it. Creeping back to the ladder, she glanced above at the raging torrent. Water gushed down on her, slapping her face. She probably deserved it.

She hesitated there, clinging to the ladder as the ship tossed her back and forth, debating what she was about to do. Savion's commanding voice sounded from above, sparking something within her she dared not admit. She'd come to know him these past days: wise, understanding, brave—not to mention the kindest, most unselfish man she'd ever known. The chances of him risking his life for her were beyond good. But what if he died? How could she bear it?

The ship bucked and shoved her backward. Her behind hit the hard wood at the bottom of the ladder. Pain shot up her spine as water sloshed over the deck and seeped through her already-wet gown. Gripping the bottom rung, she dragged herself up and fought her way to the main deck.

She could do this. She *had* to do this. They'd be in Kadon tomorrow, and Savion would deposit her on shore as promised. Even if he had grown fond of her—which she wasn't altogether sure of—he was too honorable a man to keep her on the ship. She would never see him again.

Lunging onto the slippery deck, she covered her face with her arms against the wind, and headed toward the railing. Rain stung. Wind shoved. And more than once she nearly slipped. But she finally made it, gripped the saturated wood, and glanced at the seething, dark water flinging the ship up and down like a teeter-totter.

She could do this. Gulping down her fear, she glanced over her shoulder at Savion still on the quarterdeck. Good. He saw her. His jaw stiffened, and he started across the deck. A flash of light appeared beside him. The outline of a man. There one second, and then gone.

She faced forward again. She was seeing things. If her plan failed … if it failed, she'd drift at sea for twenty more days at the mercy of tide and water. She didn't relish the pain. Or the loneliness and despair.

How could she be sure Savion would rescue her? Or that he wouldn't simply send one of his crew? Nay, he was not the type of man to allow a woman to drown *or* send others to risk their lives in his place.

One more glance told her Savion was nearly upon her. So she did what she must. She climbed atop the bulwarks and jumped into the raging sea.

Savion's chest constricted. He swiped water from his eyes, hoping he was seeing things. But no. Perdita had been standing there. And now she was gone. He dashed to the railing and nearly slipped overboard himself. Rain pelted him as he tried to focus on the churning water. There. He spotted her, arms flailing, head bobbing.

"A rope!" he shouted to Petrok, who appeared beside him, his expression equally shocked.

"But Captain—"

"A rope! Tie it to the mast!"

Petrok did as he was told and handed the end to Savion. He looped it around his waist, secured it, and made for the railing.

"Captain!" Petrok shouted above the storm. "She's gone! It's too late!"

But Savion couldn't think of that now. All he knew was that if he didn't at least try, Perdita would drown. He scanned the sea one last time, seeking the peace within. The ship lurched. He tightened his grip on the railing and hunched against a wave crashing over them. Movement caught his eye, and he turned to see the bright outline of a man standing on the foredeck, wearing the full armor of Nevaeh, unhindered by either the leap of the ship or crash of waves. A blast of wind and he was gone.

Reassured, Savion leapt on the railing and dove into the water.

The force of the storm slapped him like an old enemy—an enemy that was soon muted as water caved in on Savion and shoved him deeper and deeper. The peace beneath the storm was a false peace—a peace that would lead to death. True peace came from within. That peace rose within him now, warmed the medallion on his chest, and forced him to surface. Thunder met him with a growl, but lightning revealed someone in the distance rising on the crest of a wave. A scream sped past his ears, and he started in that direction, fighting off every punch of water and thrust of wind—his one thought to save Perdita. Foolish, stubborn woman!

One glance at his ship told him Petrok was raising storm sails in an effort to gain some maneuverability while most of his crew lined the railing staring at the scene in horror. A wave flung Savion into the air, then abandoned him. He dropped several feet back into the water. The sea struck him like a brick. Pain scraped his back and pierced the wound in his side.

But he'd seen the Guardian, and the peace remained. Still, waves beat him down, water flooded his nose and lungs. He pressed on, unsure of where the woman was but sensing the direction … following the inward guidance he'd grown to trust.

Lightning scored the sky. The rope grew taut and yanked him back. A massive swell rose above him, and he dove into its base. He punched through the surface, coughing and spitting out water. And there she was, right before him! He grabbed her and turned to signal his crew.

Perdita wore a long gown of white satin with gold embroidery at the hem and cuffs, a stomacher embedded with pearls, and a crown of gold from which a silvery net of gems fell upon her hair. She was in Savion's arms, dancing across a floor that looked like glass in a majestic hall with thick columns and a gilded ceiling. Surrounding them, a crowd of onlookers admired the couple with smiles and sighs and approving nods.

Savion was dressed in an exquisite black suit with silver-buckled boots and a high-collared purple cloak only worn by royals. His movements were all grace and poise and confidence as he swept her across the floor to the sound of the most beautiful orchestra she'd ever heard.

With one hand pressed possessively on her back and the other interlaced with her fingers, he looked at her as no man ever had—a gaze that penetrated her soul, where together they seemed to connect in a union far exceeding the physical.

She had succeeded! She was human again. And loved. Finally, she was worthy of someone's sacrifice.

Pain skewered down her legs. The glass floor became mud, the columns palm trees, the gilded ceiling a stormy sky, and the crowd withered to but three men. Former Ivans all, save for Savion, who joined them. Her dress shriveled, her bare breasts exposed. She covered them with her hands as her legs gave out and melded together into a tail. Collapsing to the ground, she flopped like a fish.

The Ivans pointed at her and bent over laughing, slapping one another and saying, "And she thought we would love her. Look at her! She's just an ugly fish."

Perdita lurched and struck her head. "Ouch!" She touched her forehead and pried her eyes open to see the stained wood of the bulkhead beside Savion's bed. Rolling over, she spotted her feet sticking from beneath her damp chemise and wiggled her toes, heaving a sigh of relief. Just a dream. But the pain wasn't a dream. She remembered that. Waves of agony shearing over her. Her lungs filling with water, her chest constricting, her body pummeled by wind and wave with no control. Yet death remained elusive. As always.

Savion had jumped in after her as she knew he would.

Savion? Terror buzzed through her. If her plan worked, he might be dead. But had her plan worked? Heart in her throat, she slowly lifted her chemise. Three tiny slits remained on her right side just above her hip. She hung her head, longing to cry, but knowing she could not.

The door creaked open, and Savion peeked in, smiling when he saw her. The sight of him swept away her despair. Shoving down her chemise, she lifted the quilt to cover herself, then wondered why she was being modest when all she wanted to do was seduce this man. Yet for the look of approval in his eyes at her action, she'd gladly don a nun's habit.

"How are you feeling?" He yanked a chair forward and straddled it, leaning his arms across the back.

"Well enough, I suppose, for nearly drowning." She moved her legs over the edge of the bed and suddenly felt like a child in his presence—an unruly child. "I can't believe you jumped in after me." He studied her with a look she could not identify. It made her squirm. It made tears burn behind her eyes. She forced them back.

He rubbed the back of his neck. "I can't believe you jumped in in the first place."

"I slipped," she returned quickly.

He rose and shoved the chair aside. A ray of sun teetered over him from the window, accentuating the tightness in his jaw. "You leapt on the bulwarks during a squall. What did you expect? What were you doing above deck anyway?" He strode to the windows and crossed arms over his chest. "Have you ballast for brains, woman?"

"Have a care, Savion. A lady might think you have affections for her with such anger."

He swung about. "I'm angry because you put me and my entire crew in jeopardy."

His voice was harsh, and she regretted her teasing. "You didn't have to come after me." She fought back those tears again.

Seconds passed with naught but the creak of wood and whistle of wind to answer her. Savion sighed once, then twice, and finally came and knelt before her, taking her hands. "Of course I did." Golden eyes examined her with relief.

She sighed. He *did* care for her. But why hadn't his sacrifice broken the curse? "I am truly sorry, Savion." Not a lie, for she felt unusual regret in the pit of her stomach. "You could have died."

"I'm a good swimmer." He pressed his side and winced.

"Your wound. Did it reopen? Is it bleeding?" She attempted to rise, but his upraised hand kept her in place.

"It's all right. Haddeus took care of it."

"You shouldn't have come after me with such a fresh wound." Oddly, she meant it, as ludicrous as it sounded.

He cocked a brow. "Do you really think I wouldn't do everything in my power to save you? To save anyone?"

"Even risking death?"

"Of course." He shrugged. "But there was little chance of that. There are those watching out for me."

Did he mean his crew? "So you never believed you would die?"

"No."

So, that is why the curse remained. Whether it could be broken by intent and risk alone, she had no idea. But that it could not be broken without either, 'twas obvious.

His dark brows drew together as he studied her, and she had the odd sense he could see into her soul. "Did you wish me to risk my life? Is that what this is about? Some cruel pursuit of sacrifice to appease your vanity."

"Nay, of course not." She stared at the floor.

He tried to tug his hand away, but she squeezed it with both of hers. In the process, the quilt slipped, dragging her chemise off one shoulder.

"I would never wish you to die, Savion." That much was true. Truer every moment she spent with him.

He saw her bare shoulder and looked away. "I grow tired of your seduction." He jerked his hand back and rose.

"I was not …" At least not this time. But what was the use? She was beginning to feel rather small and dirty in the presence of this great man.

She covered her shoulder and felt his eyes upon her, boring into her soul.

"We will make port in Kadon tomorrow evening." Turning, he marched out the door.

And then he would leave her. Just like all the rest.

CHAPTER 12

Frustrated and confused, Savion stormed from his cabin. Not only could he make no sense of the woman's ramblings, but when he sought the wisdom within, he found nothing but a jumble of emotions. He'd seen her jump overboard, yet she denied it. Her behavior made him believe she'd wanted him to dive in after her. But why? And why risk her life? To appease her vanity? That made no sense either. There was so much more to this woman than she revealed. And that alone should force him far away. Yet he sensed a deep sorrow clouding her soul that made his own ache to help her.

Popping above deck, he made his way to the railing. The edge of the sun dipped below the horizon, transforming the sea into shimmering turquoise. He would never get over the beauty of Erden and the Ancient Seas—the wonder of creation. Yet his longing to return home left a gaping hole in his heart. Would he ever see the shores of Nevaeh again?

Petrok's commands to adjust sail echoed over the ship while Hona slid behind Savion, his light hair flapping in the stiff breeze.

"How fares our passenger?" he asked with a grin.

"Well enough, considering her ordeal."

Savion could feel the man studying him. While part of him longed to be left alone with his thoughts, part of him longed to share his mind with the young quartermaster—the man Savion considered his best friend.

"Something troubles you, Captain …" was all it took for Savion to turn toward Hona and relay his confusion over the beauty below.

While water purled against the hull, wind roared in the sails, men shouted and wood creaked, Hona listened intently.

"I've never seen a woman distress you so, Captain."

"Indeed." Savion released a heavy sigh.

"It's odd, really." Hona scratched his head. "You can sense evil miles away, feel needs and injustice in other lands. Yet this woman, who is but a few feet away, baffles you."

"Ah, you see my struggle, then." Savion said, wondering too, why Perdita's soul was closed to him when he could read all others. He gripped the railing as an idea sparked in his mind. "She is a test. That has to be it. A test." Perhaps sent by his father in order to determine whether he could be trusted to choose a mate wisely—not fall for beauty and deceit as he had done before.

One final test before he was called home. Excitement prickled his skin.

"A test?" Hona asked. "For what purpose?"

Savion smiled. The time was not right to tell his friend the entire truth. "A test of my willpower, my strength. The king tests each of us from time to time, does he not?"

"I suppose." Hona gazed at the sunset, a collage of amber and coral and vermilion splattered across the sky. "Whatever the test is, I hope you pass it, Captain."

"I will." He slapped his friend on the back. "Now tell me, what damage did the storm cause our fair ship?"

"A few torn sails, split booms, and one of the guns that wasn't lashed down punched a hole in the hull. Should take no more than a couple days at most to fix if we can find the materials."

Good, the sooner he settled Perdita in Kadon, the better. Once he left her there, the test would conclude, Savion would be victorious.

And his father would call him home.

Savion had said no more than two words to Perdita since retrieving her from his cabin and rowing her ashore. Even in the jolly boat, he sat stiffly at the stern, his light hair blowing in the breeze, his jaw tight, and his focus on the port town of Kadon. Shielding her eyes, she glanced past him to the majestic *Scepter,* a graceful outline against the setting sun, and wondered if she'd ever board her again. With each dip of the oar into the water, she felt her heart dip a little deeper into despair.

What did it matter? She still had twenty days to find someone else who would be willing to die for her. Yet, even as the thought crossed her mind, she knew she would never find such a man—or at least another man like Savion. Even if she had a lifetime of days. She stole another peek at him, longing for him to look her way. He was a rare find indeed. A good, honorable man with a heart that surpassed all others. Leave it to her to find the one man in Erden who was unmoved by her seductive charms. Even worse, he had no fear of death! How could she get someone to die for her if he never thought he would actually die?

When he refused to look her way, she faced Kadon, a city like any other port town in the Ancient Seas with its wharves and ships and workmen, warehouses and taverns and shops rising from the sand and climbing the hills beyond. Bells rang, birds squawked, wagons creaked, and shouts and chatter permeated the air.

Once at the dock, Savion helped her from the wobbly boat, and with two of his men, walked her ashore. When he inquired of the friends she mentioned who lived here, she stated she'd find them on her own, and against everything within her, turned to leave. But he followed her nonetheless and led her to a boardinghouse, where he paid for a room for a week.

Worse than being abandoned was the sense that all the camaraderie, the friendship, the bond they'd developed over the past ten days had somehow dissipated in the tropical heat. She could not imagine what she had done to cause his disdain except perchance that Savion had discovered her duplicity through his powers of discernment.

With a tip of his cocked hat, he turned to leave. Just like that. And just like that her heart turned to wax. She sped after him, and after much urging, pulled him aside to a quiet corner of the boardinghouse parlor.

"Savion, please let me stay with you and your crew," she said with pouty lips and desperate eyes.

He shook his head and stared out the window as if she weren't worthy of his gaze. "That would hardly be proper."

"I could join your crew. Cook or mend sails." Though she knew how to do neither. But how could she let the only man in the Ancient Seas who could break the curse walk out of her life?

"I'm sorry, Perdita, it is not meant to be." But the battle brewing in his golden eyes said otherwise. "I would never tempt my crew so."

"Is that all I am to you? A temptation?" She glanced down. "Or mayhap just a bother."

At this he seemed to soften, and a shake of his head gave her hope. "You were never a bother. But I have a mission, things I must do. Things that aren't safe for a lady."

"In case you hadn't noticed, I don't give a care about being safe."

"Precisely the problem." He shifted his stance and finally faced her. "I wish you well, Perdita." He placed a kiss upon her hand, then put on his hat and strolled out the door.

And her heart strolled out with him.

Clutching her skirts, she dashed up the stairs to her room, fell onto her bed, and sobbed. An hour later, she collected two handfuls of pearls from the quilt where her tears had fallen. She thought to toss them from the window, but she could use a new gown. And some food, of course. Something sinfully delicious. At least she had that to look forward to.

Rising, she examined herself in the full-length mirror. Even with her hair a mess and an ill-fitting gown, she could not deny her beauty far surpassed most human females. Why, then did Savion not grovel at her feet like every other man?

Had she lost her touch? Her appeal? She turned and glanced at her side view and then spun to see her backside. Nay. Everything was in perfect proportion. As she'd been told by every man she'd ever known.

Every man but Savion.

Shoulders slumping as much as her spirits, she made her way to the window and looked over the city and docks beyond. Several ships rocked in the bay, and she searched for one in particular before the sun stole all the remaining light. There it was, the *Scepter.*

An ache formed in her heart, and she blew out a ragged sigh. She was cursed, indeed. Not just cursed to be a mermaid, but cursed to be unloved forever. Did anyone really love anyone else? Below her on the street, people darted to and fro: women with small children, slaves, dockworkers, merchants, the upper crust traveling in their carriages with primly-dressed coachmen, fancy ladies twirling lace parasols above their pearl-embedded coiffures.

Mayhap no one *was* truly loved. But at least these people would die someday and their pain would cease.

She must endure it forever.

Could a heart be broken so many times that even an eternal one would finally stop beating? That was her only hope. That and the hope that Savion would risk his life for her yet again. And that the next time, he would mean it.

Nay! She would not give up. She would fight hard during her last days on land. And she would do everything in her power to win the heart of Savion Ryne.

He sensed when evil was afoot, did he? Well mayhap that's just what she would give him.

With every step Savion took away from the mysterious Perdita, his feet grew heavier until it felt as if he slogged through mud. When he sought the reason within, all was silent. So he continued down the main street, flanked by his men, returning greetings from those who knew him and trying to focus on the task at hand: repair his ship as soon as possible and discern where he was to go next, what attack he was to thwart, what disaster he could deter, whom he needed to rescue.

And wait for his father to call him home.

Turning a corner, he wiped sweat from his brow, stepped over a pile of horse droppings, and then leapt aside to avoid an oncoming wagon. He stopped and gripped his medallion, searching for that sense of evil normally so strong in Kadon, as in most port towns, but found it conspicuously absent.

"Notice anything different?" he asked Petrok who stood beside him.

"You sense something?" Petrok's eyes flashed as if anxious for a fight.

"No." Savion flattened his lips. "That's just it. Where are the Malum who usually patrol these streets?"

His men glanced up and down the busy avenue.

"Odd, yes," Nuto finally said. "Perhaps they were called elsewhere."

"Perhaps they heard you were coming and ran for fear of your power," Petrok added with a wink.

Except … when had the Malum ever done that?

Back at the ship, Savion found the remainder of his crew hard at work making repairs. During the short time he'd been gone, they'd been able to procure all the necessary materials to fix the torn sails, broken lines, cracked booms, and the hole in the hull. Another oddity, for normally it took more than a week to acquire such materials, especially in a port where so many ships were in need.

During the next few days, Savion worked side by side with his men. Stripped of his shirt in the blazing sun, he used the remedy of hard labor and sore muscles to help him forget about the strange lady he'd abandoned in town. Nighttime was another matter. She invaded his dreams in a way no woman had. Not even Lorelei. And that bothered him the most. Perdita came to him in glowing mists, leaning over him, tending to his wounds, singing … always singing, sometimes sweet, sometimes off-key. Always songs he'd never heard before—sweet melodies filled with such sorrow they lured him deeper into a world where peace reigned. Tears fell from her eyes as she caressed his cheek, drops that glistened like pearls as they fell to her lap. Then he would always wake, sweat-laden and breathing hard as if he'd just fought a battle.

Though he ventured into town a few times with his men seeking refreshments, he never saw her. He hoped she had found her friends, along with some honorable employment, but he was careful to direct his thoughts elsewhere. The last thing he wanted was to be drawn into her trap again. No, he must pass this final test. He must.

On the third day, a pervading sense of trouble invaded his soul. A sense of suffering and pain in a distant port named Brayton. With the ship repaired, he normally would have set sail immediately, but this particular sense was different from the others. It didn't originate in the same peaceful place within his soul, but instead came from outside himself, from a dark place fraught with anxiety and desperation.

Swallowing the sour taste in her mouth, Perdita wove through the tables and chairs in the punch house and approached the man she had spotted in the back. Smelly Sal Burns—aptly named due to his aversion to bathing and his delight in setting his enemies on fire. She'd crossed paths with the bloater ten years ago in this same town and was pleased to discover he was still in charge—at least over most of the dock area, where he extorted money from patrons in exchange for protection from roving bandits, pirates, and other disreputable sorts.

Ignoring the catcalls and whistles flung her way as she passed, she stopped before his table, circled by several of his worshiping toadies. Delight twinkled in the eyes of the two burly guards flanking the corpulent man. One of them cleared his throat, and ole Smelly Sal looked up from his drink, his brows rising and his ever-present bawdy sneer growing wider.

"Perdita! My sweet Perdita. Do me bloomin' eyes deceive me?" He struggled to lift his wide frame from the chair and then attempted to squeeze through the crowd. Cursing, he shoved his men aside and gripped Perdita's shoulders, wafting her with a stench that stung her nose. "Why, look at ye!" He took a step back. "Ye haven't aged a bit."

But Smelly Sal had. Amazing what ten years of dissipated living could do to a man. Which made her thankful more than ever that she had not given herself to this stinky oaf. Nay, 'twas one of his men who'd caught her eye instead. A swarthy man with exotic looks, a keen mind, and the heart of a saint. Or so she'd thought.

"We all age." She gave Sal a coy look. "Some more than others, apparently." She tugged on his gray beard while studying his prominent belly. His men laughed. Thankfully so did Sal. Though he was the most feared and ruthless man in town, his infatuation with her had always given her a speck of freedom. Within reason, of course. She knew there was a line she could never cross with this dangerous man.

Which was precisely why she'd sought him out.

"Have a seat, my fair one." He hoisted one of his men by the collar and shoved him away, gesturing toward the seat. "Tell old Sal what a beauty like you has been up to since I seen you last." Perdita sat, and Sal pushed one of his men's untouched mugs of ale her way. Grumbling, the man rose and left.

"We ain't seen ye since Waden died." Sal's right-hand man said with a hint of suspicion.

Perdita studied the foam atop her ale, trying to hide the fact that her heart sank into her stomach. Waden, Ivan number twenty-nine, had died because of her. Not directly, but on his way to help her, his ship went down in a storm. Of course, if he'd made it to the island she'd directed him to, he would have faced fifty savages who would have accused him of stealing their golden idol. But that was another story.

Sal leaned toward her, a twinkle in his hooded eyes. "Come back to grovel at me feet? Regret not takin' me up on me offer?"

Her sumptuous dinner of roast beef with mushroom cream sauce curdled in her stomach. "Tempting." She smiled. "However, I have a different sort of offer in mind."

She sipped the ale, and her lips puckered. She never did like the taste of it.

"From this angle, I see only one offer which'll please me." He scooted his chair back and slapped his knee. "Come sit on ole Sal's lap."

She'd rather boil in oil.

A breeze swept in, flickering the lantern on the table as Sal's men eyed her expectantly, knowing that no one defied one of Sal's orders and lived.

A strident tune blared from a piano in the corner, grating over her already tight nerves. Trying to gather herself, she leaned back in her chair and fingered the embroidered ruffle at the end of her sleeve.

"I have a better proposition—that I come work for you," she said with a confident tone.

"Just the thing I had in mind." Sal licked his lips, and his men chuckled and grunted like pigs in heat.

Ignoring them, Perdita feigned a look of nonchalance. "Word about town is that Major Tombay sits on a fortune in gold coin at that well-guarded estate of his. I also hear he still owns half the town just like he did ten years ago, taking money from citizens to protect them from you." Corrupt politicians disgusted her more than thieves and thugs. At least the latter were honest about their sins. "Pray, do tell me what it is like playing second fiddle to the likes of him all these years?"

Tension strung over Sal's men like rope in a tight wind. Some backed their chairs away from the table, out of the path of retribution, she suspected. The guards framing the chubby sod drew close, glaring at Perdita as if they would run her through. She dared them with her eyes to do just that. If only it were that easy.

Sal's face bloated like a puffer fish, his eyes narrowing to pointy spears, and for a moment she thought he'd do to her what he'd done to so many who dared defy or insult him—torture them for days and then set them on fire. A rather gruesome prospect for one who wouldn't die.

But then his half-smiled revealed yellowed teeth, and his belch preceded laughter that was immediately mimicked by his dutiful parrots.

"An' just what type of work are ye proposin', fair one?"

"What you asked me to do before. What you know I'm fully capable of doing." She smiled sensuously.

"Aye, I'll not deny that. But why the change o' heart after ten years?"

"Let's just say I'm in need of some money."

He glanced at the new gown she'd purchased today and disbelief traveled across his lined features, but then he took a swig of ale. "An' what's in it fer me?"

"Need you ask? His fortune—minus my share—and his humiliation. And a way into his estate to rid him of the army he's hired to protect his interests."

"An' what of you? You could no doubt work your way into his graces and get his money without my help."

"I detest the man," she returned with spite. Though, in truth, she'd never met him. When Sal eyed her with suspicion, she added, "He banished a lover of mine from town."

This seemed to appease him as he nodded with a snort.

Perdita grinned. "Just think, you'll be king of Kadon within days."

The resulting pride and greed swept away any misgivings Sal might have had as he raised his mug to her in a toast.

She tapped her fingers on the table. Good. The trap was set. She had only to do what she did best and then hope Savion would come to her rescue.

CHAPTER 13

The uneasiness that had begun in Savion two days ago grew stronger with each passing minute. Unsure whether to leave for Brayton or stay in Kadon stirred his normal confidence into a cauldron of uncertainty.

"You don't seem yourself, Captain." Nuto's loud remark drew Savion's gaze to the lithe man sitting across from him.

"Aye, something bothering you?" Petrok said between mouthfuls of roasted boar, yams, and biscuits—fresh food they normally didn't get while out at sea. Orange slices peeked above a bowl at the center of the table like myriad rising suns. Plucking one, Hona slid it into his mouth.

"Nothing. Just determining our next course." The ship creaked and groaned over a wavelet while a breeze entered through the open stern windows and fluttered the candles atop the table.

"The ship's been ready for days," Verrad pointed out. "I found a merchant in need of transport for his goods: foodstuffs and tools. Why not just head out? I grow tired of this town."

"Gone through all the women and wine already?" Petrok snickered, causing Verrad to grin mischievously.

Shaking his head, the first mate turned to Savion. "You sensed trouble in Brayton, did you not? I say we go there and teach those Malum another lesson."

"Always anxious for a fight, Petrok." Savion smiled. "Sometimes it's best to wait and make sure your move is the right one."

"With that I will agree." Verrad set down his fork and poured more wine into his cup. "It's foolish to continue with these minor skirmishes—saving one person here and one there, a small village and then a fishing boat or merchantman. How is that going to help our cause in the long run?"

Hona frowned. "It's not about a cause, Verrad. It's about people."

Verrad's dark eyes shifted to Savion. "Yet our cause is to save as many people as possible from Natas's clutches, isn't that right, Captain? Why help one or two when we can help thousands?" He sipped his wine, then lowered the mug with an ominous clank. "When we defeat Natas and we—I mean you—finally rule over the Ancient Seas, think of the good we could do."

Yet the sparkle in his eyes was not of benevolence but of power and greed.

Nuto slumped in his chair. "We can never defeat Natas. He has too many warriors. He's crushed every force that has come against him. Who are we but a ship full of do-gooders?"

"Ah, but that is where you are wrong." Petrok pointed his knife at the man. "We have Savion Ryne as captain." He faced Savion. "And the power that rests on you is not of Erden. We have all seen it"—he glanced over the others—"and we cannot deny that it is Savion's destiny to rule the people in goodness and truth."

Though touched by the man's confidence in him, a piece of Savion's heart began to chip away as he listened to his men. "So you all wish to rule? Is that why you joined my crew?"

"No, Captain." Hona spoke up with urgency. "I follow you because I cannot do otherwise. You are good and strong and kind, and those few we save from Natas are enough."

Savion gripped Hona's arm, warmed by his friend's affection.

Verrad tossed his drink to the back of his mouth and poured another cup.

Nuto helped himself to more rice. "You are our friend and our captain, Savion. Being with you and serving on the *Scepter* is an honor."

Petrok looked up, his eyes flashing. "But should you desire to rule, Captain, we would be honored to serve you. I have grown quite fond of saving the world. I will always stand with you. No matter what."

"Even should we face certain death?" Savion raised a brow.

"Of course!" Petrok gave an indignant huff, and the others added their agreement.

Later that night, after most of his crew had retired, Savion stood at the stern of the ship gazing over the flickering lights of Kadon, fingering his medallion and searching for wisdom, strength, and direction. The pull to go fight in Brayton was strong, but a stronger sense had emerged from within him, deep in his spirit. It called to him from Kadon, hailing him from the streets, whispering to him in a siren's song.

Something or someone was trying to get him to leave this city. The absence of Malum, the miraculous ease and rapidity of his ship repairs, this lure from Brayton that came not from within but from without. Something was amiss. His spirit could not find peace. And until it did and he received clear direction, he intended to stay where he was.

It hadn't been easy to track the *Scepter,* especially through a summer squall, but Damien's life had never been easy, and he'd grown accustomed to the disfavor of the gods. Regardless, he always won in the end. Not with luck—with hard work, wits, and drive. That's all a man needed. If the gods hadn't wanted him to succeed, they shouldn't have given him all three of those qualities. During his forty years in Erden, he'd battled his way up from being a poor orphaned son to a man who owned two islands and ran three of the most successful businesses in the Ancient Seas. Not only that, he was allied with the most powerful general of all time. Every citizen in every port on every street parted the way for Damien when he passed. Men bowed before his wealth and power. The strong conquered the weak. It was the way of the world.

And because he was strong, he *would* have revenge for his father's death.

Though Damien detested politics, he rather liked Natas's way of governing—by fear and force—as long as Damien was the one invoking both. After all, he was doing the people of Erden a favor. Most were so ignorant and inept they couldn't care for themselves. They needed someone to tell them what to do, how to live, what to eat, even what to believe. Yes indeed, Damien was just the man for the job. He didn't even mind sharing the power with Natas, as long as the general accomplished what he promised he'd do—take the kingdom from King Abbas. Then Damien's final dream would come true. Traveling to Nevaeh where he'd heard the streets were paved in gold and the walls and gates were made of gemstones! Ah, the riches King Abbas hoarded for himself. But soon they would be Damien's.

The only thing standing in his way was one silly mermaid.

Now, as his men rowed him to Kadon's shore, he could almost smell her fishy scent, could almost see the pearls streaming down her cheeks. Once he captured her, not only his revenge but his wealth and power would be complete.

All it took was two days—two days of Perdita's feminine charms—and she had Mayor Tombay following her around, begging her favors like a starving puppy. She was quite pleased with herself, actually. After Savion's constant dismissal, she'd started to believe she'd lost her touch. Not true. Even the stodgy, distrusting recluse of a mayor had been bewitched the minute she'd turned her charm on him.

She distracted the guard on the east gate of the mayor's estate, knocked him out, tied him up, and then left the gate open. Now, all there was to do was get the mayor drunk and find the gold. Soon, Sal and his men would arrive. During their fight with the guards, Perdita would escape with a good portion of the pompous man's fortune.

When Sal discovered her betrayal, it would infuriate him to the point of boiling.

She hoped he'd follow his normal punishment of first flogging her in public. That should give Savion enough time to rescue her before Sal burned her at the stake. She shivered at the thought of enduring that kind of pain without the release death would bring. But surely Savion would come. The *Scepter* was still in the harbor, and she had seen his men around town. If he could sense distress and injustice miles away, he would certainly sense the danger surrounding her.

Two hours later, with the mayor passed out on his bed and most of his gold in two pouches hidden behind a Cassia tree near the back entrance, Perdita opened the gate for Smelly Sal and his men. He placed a wet kiss on her cheek as he passed, leading his band of ruffians into the courtyard and house. She swiped his saliva away with the sleeve of her gown as the clank of blade and the crack of pistol soon saturated the air, joined by shouts and shrieks.

Grabbing the bags of gold, Perdita slipped out the gate and sped into the night. Sal was no fool. She must hide herself as if she were *truly* trying to evade capture, or the man would smell a trap. Though to what end, he would never imagine. First, she would enjoy doing something that would only increase Sal's fury when he found out.

Give all the money to the poor.

'Twas one of her favorite pastimes during the ephemeral redemption, which she always tried to squeeze in between seducing her latest would-be-lover. Now, carrying two bags bulging with coin, she combed the dark streets, seeking those in need. Kadon harbored many such unfortunates: a woman and her two children curled up in an alleyway; a lame man, skin leathered by the sun, hand outstretched to passersby; a band of orphans scouring through refuse for scraps to eat.

She spread her gold among them all until there was no more, her heart lighter than it had been in weeks. Then after paying the rest to a drunken sailor for a spot in the hold of a ship departing the next day, she settled down with the bilge and the rats and waited to be found.

By first light, as expected, the sailor's loose tongue had spread tales of a beautiful woman aboard his ship, and ole Smelly Sal Burns descended into the hold, eyes crazed with hatred and death stalking in his wake.

Clutching her arm, he dragged her back to port, cursing and spitting and foaming like some mad monster from a mythical tale. "Ye know what I do with those who betray me? I make them wish for death!"

Too late, she already did.

"Captain, the odds are not good … even for you." Hona yanked Savion's arm back, forcefully stopping the captain's determined march into the center of the mob.

Wrenching his arm away, Savion growled, focusing on the disturbing scene before him. Why did the daft woman always cause trouble? Why could she not behave? But more importantly, why could he not leave her be? His heart rattled with every jangle of the chains pinning her to the whipping post. His anger grew at the blood streaming from her bound wrists, the scratches covering the bare skin of her back, exposed through her shredded gown, and her defeated silence.

He wiped the sweat from his brow and scanned the crowd shouting with raised fists for her to be flogged—the wealthiest of the townsfolk in their plumed hats, lace cravats, and silk flounces shimmering in the noonday sun. His eyes landed on Smelly Sal Burns. Savion had no quarrel with him, though he was sure the man was not without fault. His reputation as a bully and a crook were well known throughout Kadon. In fact, Savion had rescued more than one person from his clutches over the years.

As he would have to do now. Even though Perdita had obviously stolen from him. Or from someone. And then given it all to the poor! Savion squeezed the bridge of his nose, still trying to make sense of it. Word of her actions spread rapidly throughout the sleepy city until in the wee hours of the morning one of Savion's powder boys, who'd spent the night in town, came rowing out to the ship with news of a strange woman's charity—a rare occurrence in this town.

Rarer still for a woman as self-serving as Perdita. Perhaps he had misjudged her.

A commotion pulled Savion's attention to a band of armed men pressing in at the back of the crowd. A tall, regal-looking man in a satin jerkin braided in gold with a fountain of Caestrian lace at his throat marched through the mob that parted for him as if he were royalty. He stopped in the center of the square as if he owned it and stared at Perdita with intense interest before sweeping a look of dismissal at Savion. Verrad jolted beside him.

Ignoring the newcomer, Savion pushed forward and raised his voice over the crowd. "Let her go, Sal. She's but a foolish woman."

"I agree with the foolish part." Sal motioned for his henchman to grab the whip. "As to the lettin' go, she deserves her punishment."

"I'll take her away from here and promise you she'll never return."

"She'll ne'er return, all right. I'll make sure o' that." He chuckled. "But she'll get a fittin' punishment fer stealing from ole Sal." He glared at the mob. "A warnin' to ye all."

"From what I understand, the money was not even yours but the mayor's," Savion returned.

Ole Sal spit to the side. "Unfortunately, the mayor has met an early grave, bequeathin' his fortune to me."

Savion gripped the hilt of the sword hanging at his hip, his men following his lead. "Release her at once, or answer to me and my men."

The tall, well-dressed man tilted his head toward Savion. "This is none of your affair, sailor! Begone! You would risk your life and your men's lives for this wench, this whore? Besides, she is a thief and deserves her punishment."

Verrad leaned toward Savion. "He has a point, Captain. The *Scepter* is loaded with goods and ready to sail. We've done enough for this woman. Do we dare defy the law?"

Savion flattened his lips. The law. The law demanded punishment. He thought of his father: pure goodness, wisdom, love, justice … mercy. Yes, what of mercy? What of second chances? What would his father do? Savion faced the angry mob. "Perhaps she does deserve to be punished, but don't we *all* deserve the same for our stupid actions? Haven't we *all* stolen or lied or hurt others?"

Silence descended on the crowd. Some gaped at him as if he'd told them they were naked.

A few of Sal's men scratched their heads and lowered their blades. But Sal pushed his beefy body in front of Savion's and yelled, "Thieves must be punished or chaos will reign." He sneered at Savion. "What are you going to do? Fight my forty men with your twenty?"

Not just forty. From the looks of things, the well-dressed man had an additional fifty with him.

"No." Savion had no interest in bloodshed. Especially not his crew's. "But if punishment is what you want, punishment is what you'll get. I will take the flogging in her stead."

CHAPTER 14

Perdita could not believe her ears. Even as the words sifted through her mind, they stabbed her heart with both shock *and grief*. Nay! This is not how it was supposed to happen. Savion was supposed to dash to her rescue, risk his life in a battle against overwhelming odds—as he had done in Skivia when he'd singlehandedly fought three Malum. Why else would Perdita risk being burned at the stake?

"Nay, Savion!" She started to sob but forced back tears that would betray her. She'd rather see him leave than suffer the punishment that was her due. "Go away! I don't want you here!" She twisted for a glimpse of him, the irons biting her wrists.

His golden eyes met hers—the look he gave her powerful yet tender, holding more compassion than the anger she deserved.

"Go!" She turned away.

Chuckling sounded from Sal's direction, followed by laughter from the crowd. "You would suffer agony and humiliation for this wanton maid? I heard you were a mighty warrior, a defender of the weak, not some nimby-hearted cod."

"Do you accept my offer or not?" Savion's tone bore annoyance.

"I do not. Bring the whip!"

Relief loosened Perdita's tight chest, even as she braced her back for the flogging. Shuffling sounded. Part of her hoped 'twas the sound of Savion and his men leaving. If they weren't going to rescue her, she preferred they not watch her humiliation.

One glance told her she was correct. She was not worthy of the kind of love that would sacrifice all.

Stupid, stupid girl! Now she would suffer the flames as well.

"I will pay money for her!"

'Twas Damien Gund's voice. She'd heard him strut into the clearing like a bloated goose and announce her as naught but a whore. And the sweat trickling down her back had turned to ice. Now as she strained to see him, his eyes locked upon her like cannons on a target, and a victorious grin masked his normal vicious scowl.

She hung her head. Two fates awaited her: tortured for life or burned at the stake. She didn't know which she preferred.

Ole Smelly Sal eyed the man with suspicion. "Didn't you just say she deserved her punishment?"

"Aye, and it'll be my pleasure meting it out to her."

"She stole from me, not you," Sal returned.

Damien gave an incredulous huff. "Do you know who I am?"

"Everyone knows who you are, Mr. Gund."

"Then you know how miserable I can make your life, Smelly."

Sal's face grew tight. "That's Sal to ye."

"Sal, Smelly, who cares?" Damien snapped his fingers, and several well-armed men emerged from the crowd. "I will give you one last chance to accept my offer."

Perdita's stomach soured. Damien hadn't changed a bit. He was still as vile and greedy and determined as ever. Sunlight caught the silver streaking his dark hair and manicured beard as he stood in the center of the square as if he were king. He was imposing enough without all the black satin, silver embroidery, lace, and brass-buckled boots—attire that made him look like royalty. No doubt he thought he *was* royalty with all the power he wielded. And now that he had found her, she knew he'd never let her go.

She would spend the rest of eternity adding to the fiend's fortune as the lead exhibition in a traveling show, while he tortured her for pearls each night.

"What sort of price are we talking about?" Sal scratched his scraggly beard.

"How about the price of your life." Damien and his men whipped out countless knives and pistols, shocking the throng into silence. Several began slinking away.

Sal gave a nervous chuckle as he took in the growing number of men emerging from the mob to stand beside Damien.

Perdita faced the wooden post again, her heart thrashing in her chest. Damien would win. He always won. Zost! She should have spent this ethereal redemption in her cave as she'd planned. Not embarked on some fool's quest after a man who'd never done a vile thing in his life.

The battle began. Grunts and groans and the chime of blade and roar of pistols burst into the air like fireworks in some maniacal carnival. She dared not peek. What did it matter anyway? To either victor she would be a prisoner. In either of their hands, she would be tortured. And with Savion gone, her only hope of becoming mortal had vanished.

She leaned her head against the rough wood, and thought to appeal again to King Abbas. He was supposed to be a benevolent king, merciful and kind. Yet, he had not answered her last prayer for peace. Instead, Savion had appeared, and now she found her situation far worse. Regardless, she whispered a prayer anyway and then gripped the post, awaiting her fate.

Hands grabbed her shoulders. Damien's men or Sal's, she didn't know. Sunlight glinted off the blade of a large ax, blinding her. Leaning away, she trembled. Zost! *This was going to hurt!* Someone shoved her against a hard chest as arms surrounded her from behind. Still, the battle raged in the background. Gun smoke and the metallic smell of blood clogged her nose. Along with the sweat of the man behind her.

"Stay still!" he ordered. Heart leaping, she turned her head to see Savion's stubbled jaw rubbing her cheek, his eyes on Petrok standing above Perdita with the ax.

Thwack!

Metal on metal clanked, jerking against her wrists.

Thwack!

The chains slipped from her hands. Savion pulled her to her feet and swung an arm around her waist to help her walk. Then, with his crew forming a barricade around them—fighting off the few men who noticed what they were doing—they dashed down the street. Mud oozed between her bare toes as they wove around wagons, coaches, horses, and curious stares to the docks and into a small boat. Rapid rowing by six of Savion's crew brought them to the *Scepter* within minutes, while a string of commands from his mouth sent his men hoisting the boat into its cradle and unfurling sail. The anchor was raised, canvas thundered above in a hearty boom as it caught the wind, and the *Scepter* veered to port and sailed from the harbor.

Perdita gripped the railing and gazed at Kadon, where pistol shots still split the air. She smiled. How long would it take before they realized the object of their battle had disappeared?

Inside, her own battle raged between being thrilled to not be facing torture, ecstatic that Savion had come back for her, and disappointed that her plan had not worked and she was still under the curse.

Immortal and trapped instead of mortal and free.

Wind blasted over her, and strands of her hair tickled her back—her nearly-bare back. Oh my, she'd forgotten. She spun around to find some of the crew gaping at her with the expected desire, and one of them—Verrad, if she remembered his name—eyeing her as if he'd just won a race and she was the trophy. Before she could make her escape below, Savion leapt down from the quarterdeck, shouted a few orders to Petrok at the helm, and took her arm. Halfway down the companionway, the ship canted, and he laid a hand on her back to steady her. Heat spiraled through her at his touch to her bare skin. He must have felt it too, for he jerked away so fast, she felt a breeze. An angry breeze, no doubt, as he all but shoved her into his cabin, entered behind her, and slammed the door.

Savion eyed the woman as she inched toward a chair. A ray of sunlight shimmered over the silky skin of her back as raven locks caressed her waist with each rock of the ship. He swallowed and looked way, trying to regain his fury. Ah, there it was.

He grabbed a waistcoat from his trunk. "Woman."

She turned. He tossed it at her. "Cover yourself." Frowning, she slipped on the garment, then sank into a chair. "Why are you—"

"Angry?" He rubbed the back of his neck. "Because I find you once again *on my ship*! You're like a fungus, an insidious fungus that returns again and again after I think it's gone for good."

The hurt in her eyes made him instantly regret his words. He stormed toward the stern windows. "I gave you money and a room for a week. Plenty of time to locate your friends or find gainful employment." Balancing on the heaving deck, he crossed arms over his chest and gazed at Kadon growing fainter in the distance. Could the woman have been the reason he sensed he must stay in Kadon?

That urgency, that sense of danger, had vanished now that she was on board. But why?

He swung about, trying to restrain his frustration. "Instead of doing the *good* thing, the *right* thing, you decide it would be a better idea to steal the mayor's fortune!"

"You didn't have to save me." She fingered a lock of hair and stared at the floor.

"Next time I won't." And he meant it. It was not good for someone to be rescued from their own consequences. How would they ever learn?

She looked up at him, her nose and cheeks pink from the sun, her lashes a silken forest, her green eyes moist with wonder. "You offered to be flogged in my stead? Why? When you obviously loathe me."

Savion looked away from the pain in her eyes, the longing that did disturbing things to his insides. The ship tilted. Water roared against the hull like the blood through his veins. "I don't loathe you," he finally said. He wove around his desk and leaned back on the top, staring at the floorboards. "I couldn't bear to see you … any woman suffer like that."

"You are unlike any man I have known, Savion."

"You sound disappointed."

She gave no reply, save a sad smile. "I am sorry for the trouble I've caused you. I didn't ask you to come, though I'm glad you did." Lush black hair tumbled to her lap, tender strands dancing over her face in the breeze from the hatch above. She was *so* beautiful, he could look at her for hours. But she was vain and self-centered, a thief, a liar, a seductress. *A charitable seductress, apparently.*

Indeed, there was good in her. She was educated and intelligent. And kind. He'd seen it when she'd tended his wounds. And now in her charity.

"Why would you steal all that gold only to give it to the poor? Why would you steal at all? Especially from the most powerful man in town?"

"Because he's also the richest. And the money was put to better use."

"That is not for you to decide."

Her eyes sharpened. "Contrary to what you believe, I do actually care about those in need. I hate watching others suffer."

"There are better ways to help. *Legal* ways."

"None within my grasp."

"So you sacrifice your freedom, your very life, to feed the poor? I find that hard to believe." He rose and walked to the bookcase. "Just another one of your half-witted impulses, I'd wager. Or perhaps you had a score to settle with the mayor? I suppose I'll never know since I can't trust a word out of your mouth."

"Alas, you use me monstrously, Savion." Her voice broke in sorrow. "I grieve that you find me so lacking in character."

He turned to face her, looking for tears, anything to prove the remorse in her voice, but found none. "Then prove me wrong. Tell me the truth for once. Why did you take the money?"

The deck tilted, and she clung to the chair arms. "In truth, I was helping a friend. Not by getting him the money but by taking it. I cannot explain further or I will break his confidence."

"Ah, you have no qualms about lying, but divulging secrets, now there's a line you won't cross?"

She cast him a seething glance and frowned. "After I took the gold, I was running through town and noticed those in need. It was nice to be able to help them."

He studied her, seeking the truth of her words. "Odd. But for once, I believe you."

A hint of a smile lit up her face.

"Was that so hard?" He approached and sat beside her. "Let us have another test since you are in the mood for truth. Why did Damien Gund want to buy your freedom?"

She glanced out the window, fidgeting in her seat. "How should I know? I've never seen him before."

Back to lying again. Disappointed, Savion rose. "And we were doing so well."

"Perhaps he was overcome by my beauty." Her tone was desperate. "What else could it be? I have no money or possessions."

"Not every man grovels at your feet, woman."

"So I have discovered." She slumped back in her seat.

Shouts sounded above as the mad rush of the sea heightened against the hull. "Nevertheless, here you are once again aboard my ship and at sea."

"In good sooth, I am sorry to burden you, Captain. Pray, leave me at the next port. In the interim, I shan't be any trouble, I promise."

"Now that I definitely *don't* believe."

CHAPTER 15

After Savion left to attend his duties, Perdita found herself alone once again. She paced the cabin, stared at the glistening sea through the stern windows, and wavered between lying on the bed trying to sleep or flipping through the many books lining Savion's shelves. One would think she'd have grown accustomed to being alone, but it never failed to bring her spirits low. Especially during the only month she had to enjoy the company of others. So, when Bart brought a clean gown and some boiled pork, biscuits, and papaya, she begged the grouchy old sailor to stay. He stared at her curiously, scratched his thick beard, and darted from the room as if she had the plague.

Mayhap she *was* a fungus, just as Savion had said.

As night fell, her thoughts drifted to Damien. And the pork she'd eaten for supper—as delicious as it was—soured in her stomach. The vile man had finally found her! A shiver overtook her. Striking flint to steel, she lit two lanterns, hoping to chase away the shadows along with the chill. Surely, it wouldn't take him long to find out who Savion was and what ship he commanded.

Although, if Damien followed them and attacked, it *would* provide another opportunity for Savion to break the curse. It would also put Perdita at great risk. Hugging herself, she lowered to the cushioned window ledge and watched the moon sprinkle silvery dust atop waves. The rhythmic creak and groan of the ship should have lulled her exhausted body to sleep, but her nerves were too tight, her despair too overwhelming. She had only twelve days left before she faced another ten years of torturous loneliness.

This time she didn't think she could bear it.

Hours later, the door latch clicked and Savion entered the cabin. Thankfully, his anger seemed to have evaporated. He stepped into the lantern light, and she wondered once again how she could have ever thought him plain. There was so much more to this man than his appearance—his spirit and soul so strong, so noble, they made his looks more than appealing.

Was that the reason he found her so hideous? Did her ugly soul overpower her beauty?

Setting his sword on the desk, he approached. "You look frightened."

"I am." She hugged herself.

One brow rose. "You? The woman who singlehandedly fights villains off on a beach, braves battles against Malum warriors, and steals a ruthless mayor's fortune? *That* woman is frightened?"

She smiled. "Mayhap I have reached my limit of adventures."

"Ah, let it be so!" He chuckled.

If he only knew how many preposterous adventures she'd embarked on in her long life, how many times she'd tried to lure men to their deaths—and in how many different ways. In truth, she'd run out of ideas. Now, here stood this enigma before her. This man who, by all accounts, would leap to his death to save her—or anyone, for that matter—but who was somehow protected by a force she dared not acknowledge.

By now she should have had him seduced to the point of declaring his love for her on bended knee. The next step would be to give her body to him, receiving his admiration and love, hearing his words of devotion whispered in her ears through the long, passionate night.

Of course every man who had done that had ended up abandoning her.

Alas, this man placed no value on sexuality or beauty. She'd not missed the admiration in his eyes when he mentioned her gifts to the poor, when he'd caught her telling the truth. Nay, this man valued honor, truth, and charity.

But how could she give him things she didn't possess?

"You don't have to be frightened," he finally said, raising his hand to touch her but then dropping it to his side. "You are safe here."

There it was, the longing again in his eyes. So, he *did* find her appealing. He *did* long to touch her. "Thank you, Savion." She rose and threw herself into his arms, releasing a shuddering sob she wished she could give in to, for tears truly did fill her eyes. Especially when his strength surrounding her felt so good, so right, and made her feel so safe. Drawing her close, he embraced her tighter, and rested his chin atop her head.

"It's all right, Perdita. You must learn to stay out of trouble." He chuckled then grew silent as he stroked the hair falling down her back.

A cyclone rose in her belly—a pleasurable one that radiated through her body. 'Twas the usual desire, but yet so much more—'twas peace and safety and hope like she'd never known before. There, in his arms, she felt as though she'd come home, and the past three hundred years were but a bad dream. She breathed deeply of him and relaxed in his embrace—wanting to remember everything about this moment.

His body stiffened, and he pushed her away. Flustered and breathing hard, he retreated around the desk, grabbed his sword, and sheathed it.

"What did I do? Forgive me if I offended you." She squeezed back tears. "Oh, Savion, why don't you love me?"

"Love? I hardly know you, Perdita. Love must grow out of mutual respect and admiration."

Perdita couldn't help but huff. "That sounds more like fealty between servant and master than love. Love between a man and a woman starts with attraction, chemistry." She searched his eyes for the attraction she'd seen there so often.

But instead, they were cold and filled with pity. "If you believe that, you know nothing of love."

"And what do you know of it? Have you ever loved a woman?"

She regretted her harsh tone when pain etched across his face. "I have. Much to my regret." He swallowed. "And I can tell you that what is between you and me is not love, Perdita. Love doesn't badger. It doesn't lie. It doesn't cause the object of its affections pain. It doesn't get angry, isn't jealous. It does not seek its own pleasure but the pleasure of the one it loves."

Anger, lying, seeking her own pleasure, causing pain—all the things she had done to him and so many others. Suddenly she felt as small and worthless as a ship mouse.

"Besides," he added. "You are but a test I must pass. That is all."

A sharp pain twisted her insides. Backing away, she averted her eyes from his piercing stare and almost wished he would leave before he wounded her further.

He did.

The slam of the door struck her heart with the finality.

Still tingling from his embrace, Perdita staggered to sit on the bed and fought back tears. She had thought she could no longer feel the pain of rejection, but this man, this Savion, touched her heart in places she didn't know existed.

And he thought *she* was difficult to understand.

In his absence, a chill swept through the cabin, trying to steal the sensation, the smell of him away. She didn't want it to leave. She wanted to remember him forever. Even if, in his naivety, he referred to love as if it were some sort of contract or friendship, cold and without passion, when in truth, it was magical and mysterious and made one feel alive and special. He'd probably never even been with a woman. What did he know?

She drifted in and out of a restless sleep in which Ivan number fifteen made an appearance—McKale Wolf. Hair the color of bronze with muscles equal to the metal's strength, he was a colonel in King Abbas's army. Courageous, passionate, mighty—what better choice of a man to risk his life for her? Though he could have his pick of women, he'd been easy enough to charm, and within days she'd had him falling at her feet like a limp noodle. In the weeks that followed, she found herself caring for the man despite his bumbling attempts to woo her. For a warrior, he was kind and thoughtful, albeit a bit vain, and he didn't hide the fact that he adored her. In truth, he made her feel like a princess, as if she truly had value and worth. She never wanted their time together to end.

The skirmish between Abbas's 5th Calvary and Natas's horde of Malum had lasted for hours. Hiding amongst the shrubs on the edge of the battlefield, Perdita waited, watching, admiring McKale's skill at fighting, but seeking that one moment when she could enter the fray and cause him to risk himself to save her. He'd more than proven both his courage and his love for her. This was the moment! Soon she would be free.

The battle turned in favor of the Malum, and soon Abbas's forces issued a retreat. The Malum gave chase. Now! Perdita ran into the center of the field between the two forces and called out McKale's name. He spun on his horse and gaped at her, at first with shock, then with fear as he eyed the advancing Malum. Seconds passed as Perdita's heart vaulted in her chest like one of the horses galloping toward her.

He mouthed the word *sorry,* then jerked the reins and sped away. Unable to breathe for her severed heart, she started to run, but her legs wouldn't move. The Malum horde struck her, the hooves of their horses trampling her over and over.

Thinking her dead, they left her lying face down in the mud. She'd spent days in excruciating pain, gnawed on by bugs and other vermin and breathing in dirt and horse manure until some of her strength returned, and she crawled to shore and slipped into the sea.

Rejected again. And from a man to whom she had given her all and would have loved forever.

Something slid down her cheek, tickling. She reached up and felt a pearl. Jarring awake, she sat, heart pounding, and blinked to dry her eyes lest any more tears escape. She must be more careful. She must have no more dreams that would cause her to cry. Swinging her feet over the edge of the bed, she rose, pressed down her gown, and headed out the door. She needed fresh air. She needed to clear her head of her haunting past—of the wounds she would forever carry in her heart.

With most of the sails furled for the night, only a few sailors roamed about the ship. Standing at the railing, she allowed the wind to ease fingers through her hair, a sensation she missed sorely when she lived in the water. With twelve days left, she was out of ideas to make Savion fall in love with her. If his idea of love was truly all the qualities he mentioned, not only did she possess none of them, they were all things freely given to the one loved. She could not force them or lure them or seduce them from him. She could not even use her beauty and her body to draw them out.

Who loved so unselfishly anyway? No one she'd ever met.

Yet … she *did* see desire in his eyes. Alas, whenever it appeared, he retreated quicker than a startled sea anemone. Mayhap 'twas hopeless. Mayhap she should allow him to leave her in some town where she could at least enjoy good food and the camaraderie of others during her last days on land.

"Good evening, Miss Mulier." The sultry voice caused her to jump.

Verrad slipped beside her and gave her a disingenuous smile.

"Good evening, Mr. …"

"Verrad Jud. But please call me Verrad. Can't sleep?" He cocked his head at her, and the malicious look in his eyes made her skin crawl.

"Or do mermaids not need to sleep?"

Chapter 16

There wasn't a spot on Perdita's body that didn't scream in pain. From the raw skin beneath the ropes that bound her legs and hands, to the roots of her hair that had been yanked repeatedly, to the bruises where she'd been punched and slapped, down to the burns on the bottom of her feet—each torture inflicted by the madman now pacing before her in a small storeroom in the bowels of the *Scepter.*

He rubbed the dark stubble on his chin and glared at her with eyes like a sea serpent. "What does it take to make you cry, *mermaid*?"

Perdita struggled against the twine that bound her to the chair and fought back the tears this man so diligently and desperately had tried to extract from her for hours. "I told you I am not a mermaid."

"Then shed a tear and prove it!"

Monstrous shadows, cast by the light of a single lantern, stalked across the bulkhead, witnesses of her judgment. "I don't know what I have done to make you torture me, Mr. Verrad, but I beg you, please let me go." She tasted blood on her lips and prayed his strikes to her face had not marred her beauty overmuch.

He snorted. "If you would only cry—just one tear—I would release you. It is a simple request." He leaned to study her as one would a strange fish caught in a net. "Yet for some reason you've not shed a single tear when most women would have been reduced to a sobbing puddle. Why is that?" He brushed a lock of hair from her face.

"I told you I don't cry easily."

"Humph. Apparently." He brought himself up and drew his long knife. "Could you not make an exception for Verrad? Hmm? Most women—if you even are one—are experts at conjuring up tears on a moment's notice."

"I am not most women." Light flashed at her from the blade, and she trembled at how far he would go to prove his theory.

"Precisely." He grinned. "Which is what has brought us here."

The ship creaked and groaned as her insides were doing, and Perdita searched her memories of when she had slipped up, for the mistake that had roused his suspicions.

"What makes you think I'm a mermaid?"

Verrad shoved his disheveled hair back, his eyes dark and sinister. "Damien Gund believes you to be so. That's good enough for me. Ah, yes. I see it in your eyes. I also saw it in your eyes when he sauntered into the clearing. The terror, the knowing. He's been searching for the mermaid who murdered his father. And he won't give up until he finds her." He slapped the blade against his palm. "By his actions yesterday, I'd say he believes you are she."

"He's as mad as you are."

The ship tilted. Balancing on the heaving deck, Verrad came alongside her and leveled the knife at her neck. The tip pierced her skin. Her breath came fast. Stepping back, he raised his hand and slapped her across the face. Pain seared her cheek and down her neck. She thought of happy moments: flowers and butterflies, the feel of land beneath her feet, and delicious food—anything to stop the tears from flowing. For if they did, this man would either sell her to Damien or keep her for himself.

Placing hands on his knees, he leaned over to peer in her eyes. "Still no tears? Hmm. Pain doesn't work. But what will?" He wiped the blood on his knife on his sleeve. "Ah, perhaps a different kind of pain." Pulling up a crate he sat down. "You seem interested in my captain for some reason . . . perhaps in gaining his love? If I recall what Damien Gund told me, that was your tactic with his father as well. *Love.* Something which eludes you, I'm guessing?" His smile turned victorious, biting.

Perdita stared at her lap, ignoring the pang in her heart.

"Aha. So that's it. You've been rejected. Had your heart broken, have you?" He leaned over, elbows on his knees, and studied her. "Has nobody ever loved poor Perdita? Poor unloved, unwanted Perdita. You may be beautiful on the outside, but you are an empty shell on the inside, aren't you? Unable to attract the affections of anyone longer than it takes for them to bed you and toss you aside like the refuse you are."

Perdita's eyes filled with uncontrollable tears.

Petrok snored. Louder than the groan of the ship and the thunder of sails. So loud it rattled Savion's brain. Yet that was not what kept him awake. It was the woman gracing his cabin, his bed, forcing him to share sleeping quarters with his first mate. It was the woman who had his insides all twisted in confusion, who had nothing to recommend her except her beauty. And yet, the one who had a grip on his heart like no other. It was the woman he regretted informing she was just a test he had to pass, a means to an end. The pain in her eyes haunted him. How could he have been so cruel? Everyone had value in the Kingdom of Erden. In his longing to go home, had he forgotten all that his father had taught him?

The eerie whistle of wind through the rigging above sent a chord of unease through him. Something was amiss. A disturbing sensation—aside from his guilt—that forbade sleep. And unlike most of his premonitions, this one came from nearby, not hailing from some distant shore. Tossing off his coverlet, he sat and rubbed his eyes, seeking guidance from within. Yet all he sensed was a strong desire to throw a pillow atop Petrok's snoring face.

Instead, he stood, threw a shirt over his head, and started out the door, following the leading of the medallion and the agitation in his gut. After ensuring all was well on the main deck, he started down the ladder to the gun deck, where most of the men were asleep in their shifting hammocks, snoring even louder than Petrok. He descended another ladder into the hold.

A woman's groan lifted the hairs on his arms. Male laughter sent him storming toward a set of storage cabins at the stern. Lantern light slithered through the bottom of a closed door, and he barreled into it with his shoulder. It flung open to a sight that froze Savion in his tracks: Perdita, lip and cheek red and swollen, hair dangling in her face, tied to a chair with Verrad standing over her like the henchman of an evil king.

"What is the meaning of this? What have you done?" Savion threw him aside, then knelt to untie her bonds, the raw skin beneath the ropes incensing his anger.

Verrad leapt back toward her. "Look at her eyes, Captain. Watch her eyes! She's about to cry!"

Savion freed her arms and feet and glanced at her face. Tear-filled eyes gazed at him with both sorrow and relief. Blood seeped from a gash on her arm. Fuming, he rose, knocked the bloody knife out of Verrad's grip, then grabbed the man by the lapels of his waistcoat, and shoved him against the bulkhead. "Of course she's about to cry. You're torturing her!" he seethed, longing to pummel

Verrad as the man had done to Perdita. Instead, he released him and backed away. "By the stars of Lemox, what possessed you to strike a woman?"

Petrok stormed through the door, but with one look from Savion, held his ground.

The hatred in Verrad's eyes set Savion aback. The purser ran the back of his hand over his mouth, then pointed at Perdita. "She's a mermaid."

Petrok laughed.

Savion blinked at the ridiculous notion. He took a step toward Verrad and sniffed. "Are you drunk, man? Or perhaps all the liquor you consume has finally eaten away your brain."

"It's true. She is here to lure you to your death beneath the seas."

"Don't be absurd! Mermaids are only fables, Verrad. Myths fabricated from sailors exposed to too much sun and rum."

"Her tears turn to pearls," Verrad insisted.

Petrok gave a snort of disgust. "We always wondered about your sanity, Verrad."

"You tortured her to make her cry!" Savion's disbelief rose with his fury.

"To prove to you who … *what* she is! But the wench refuses to cry." Verrad raised his voice. "Have you ever seen her cry? Just once?"

A worm of doubt inched its way through Savion's mind. "Rubbish! She was in the sea and no tail appeared."

"I know. I don't understand that." Verrad shook his head and frowned.

"I'll hear no more of it! Petrok, lock Verrad in his quarters until I decide what to do with him." Then, drawing an arm around her, Savion helped Perdita to her feet. She winced, and he sat her back down to examine her feet. "You burned her feet?" He rose, hands fisted, and glared at Verrad.

But the purser made no response.

"Get him out of here!" Savion shouted as he swept Perdita in his arms.

Petrok yanked the man out the door just as a muffled boom thundered through the hull, shaking the timbers and raining down dust. Footsteps thudded above deck. The ladder creaked as someone descended in a hurry, but Savion knew they'd been fired upon before he heard the man's anxious report.

Charging up the ladder, Perdita in his arms, he exchanged a worried glance with Petrok and bellowed, "Battle Stations!"

CHAPTER 17

After carrying Perdita safely to his cabin and calling Haddeus to tend to her wounds, Savion marched across the main deck and focused his attention on the ship that loomed large against dawn's glow on the horizon. As if her black sails weren't enough proof, focusing his telescope on the flag bearing a dragon's skull with red glowing eyes and pierced by six swords convinced him it was a Malum ship.

"Malum," Petrok confirmed from beside him.

"Yes, but why attack us?" Savion lowered his scope. "They've always set traps or attacked by sabotage, never head-on."

"Indeed. Most curious." Petrok rubbed his hands together. "But we can take them, can't we, Captain?"

Savion gave a confident huff. "Of course."

Nuto approached. "Orders, Captain?"

"Prime and load the guns, Nuto, and run them out. Fire upon my order."

With a nod, the man ran off.

Turning, Savion leapt onto the quarterdeck ladder, grabbed a line to steady himself, then turned and drew his crew's attention. "These Malum intend to take our ship, gentlemen. Most likely to kill us since we have nothing of value on board. But we will not let them, will we?"

"No!" Fists went into the air.

"For King Abbas!" Savion shouted.

"King Abbas!"

"Then, let's to it, men! Clew up the mainsail! Let's give our new friends a proper greeting, shall we? Twenty degrees to starboard, Hona!"

"Twenty degrees, Captain!"

The *Scepter* tacked to starboard, the deck tilting until sea foam bubbled over the railing.

Clinging to a line, Petrok shouted above. "Slack off the headsail sheets!"

The top men went to work while Savion marched to the quarterdeck and stood brazenly by the helm. After giving Hona a reassuring nod, he raised his scope for another look at their enemy. The Malum ship rose and plunged through the seas like a drunken black hornet. Carronades lined her railing while bow-chasers were expertly aimed right at the *Scepter,* ready to sting.

"Brace around forward; set the main!" Savion shouted to Petrok. "Haul to the wind and bring us on her weather quarter!"

Petrok repeated the orders, and the crew scrambled to task. Tension stalked the deck, pricking nerves and silencing the men. Savion's crew were good sailors and better warriors, but most of their battles had been on land with sword and pistol, not at sea with sail and cannon.

The *Scepter* veered once again, creaking and groaning in complaint. Sea spray showered over Savion as he gripped the railing and studied his enemy. Just a few more minutes and they'd be within firing range. But that would bring his ship right in the line of the Malum guns.

A jet of orange smoke spat from the enemy ship.

"Hit the deck!" Savion ordered as an explosion racked the sky.

Perdita could not shake the vision of Savion as he'd charged into the room to rescue her from Verrad—the horror and anger on his face. Nor could she forget the way he'd shoved the scoundrel against the wall in his righteous rage, nor the strength of his arms as he'd swept her off her feet and carried her to his cabin. 'Twas the stuff of fairy tales ... of dreams. And not the way of cursed mermaids. Still, she would savor such moments. They would keep her company during the next decade of lonely years.

After the doctor bandaged up her feet, patched the slash on her arm, and examined her swollen lip, he scurried away, no doubt to join the battle above. Remarkably, in the past three hundred years, Perdita had never found herself in the midst of a ship battle. She'd watched them from afar and from beneath the waves, but never from on board one of the majestic ships. Excited to experience something new, she forsook the safety of the cabin, limped down the companionway and up the ladder, ignoring—or trying to—the pain in her feet. Fear made her halt on deck at the sight of the crew rushing here and there with nervous looks on their faces and weapons in their hands. What if one of them should get hurt or killed? What if something happened to Savion?

The sound of his voice turned her to see him on the quarterdeck, armed with cutlass and a brace of pistols, directing his men to task with courage and confidence. His determined gaze shifted toward the pursuing ship. "Bear off, haul your braces, ease sheets, starboard guns stand by! Fire as you bear!"

A volcano belched from several cannons in rapid succession, filling the air with thunder and smoke and sending a quiver through the ship. Perdita's ears rung like an ancient gong. The sting of gunpowder burned her nose. Grabbing her skirts, she stumbled around rushing men and nearly fell against the starboard railing. A ship with black sails heaved through the sea toward them, a foamy mustache at her bow and a dragon's skull on her ensign. A dark mist hovered around her. Only one of Savion's shots had met its mark—unfortunately above the waterline.

"Hard a port!" Savion shouted, marching back to the helm.

"She's preparing to fire!" Petrok yelled.

Yellow flames jetted from the Malum ship. A muffled shout ordered all hands to the deck. Perdita didn't have to be told twice. Oak and tar filled her nose as she pressed her cheek to the wood. *Boom! Boom! Boom!* The sky trembled. The eerie sound of wood cracking and a wail of pain sliced through the air.

Perdita dared to lift her head. A cannonball had crashed through the bulwarks and struck the mainmast, firing splintered wood at a nearby sailor. He lay on the deck moaning, blood spilling from his leg. Savion's quick commands brought the doctor and more men to his aid. They carried him below within seconds while Savion shouted more orders for the ship to veer and her guns reloaded.

Struggling to rise on the bucking ship, Perdita watched as Savion marched across the deck, issuing orders and checking on his men. He spoke with authority, calm and confident, devoid of fear or even anger. His crew respected and trusted him, obeying his orders without question, even though the Malum ship had the advantage of wind and weapons. Her own admiration for this man increased—if that were possible. He'd already proven that he was good, kind, honorable, and a great warrior, but now she could see he was also a skillful leader of men.

He spotted her then. A look of frustration, then concern, crossed his features before Petrok pointed out their enemy tacking in position for another broadside. Fear like Perdita had never known sent her heart racing. Though Malum had never paid her much mind, she'd seen them fight at sea on more than one occasion. She'd seen them sink many a ship into the deep—but not before they tortured the seamen aboard and set them all aflame. They were highly skilled, barbarously brutal. And she couldn't stand the thought of Savion or any of his crew being at their mercy.

The mad rush of water and thunder of sails pounded the air. The deck tilted, and Perdita clung to the railing as Savion brought the *Scepter* into position nigh twenty yards off the Malum ship's quarter.

"Fire!"

Beneath Perdita, a broadside roared and gun smoke filled her lungs. The ship shook so violently she thought it would break apart at the seams. Coughing, she peered toward their enemy, desperately hoping they'd be damaged enough to leave. White smoke curled from a charred hole in the ship's bow between wind and water, and her fore topsail was rent. Yet still she charged onward, finally sweeping alongside the *Scepter* just yards off their starboard side. The black muzzles of ten guns thrust through their ports like rotten teeth in the Devil's mouth.

This was it. They were all going to die. Everyone but Perdita, of course. Which made it only worse.

The sky exploded with such force, the sea quivered. Perdita dropped to the deck and covered her head as the shrill screech of shot zipped past her ears. Wood snapped, canvas ripped, men screamed, the timbers shook, smoke gorged the air. The crackle of a fire met her ears, and she rose to her feet to see their mainmast ablaze.

Savion's calm voice ordered the men to task, forming a line to haul seawater up over the side. But that wasn't the worst of the damage. One shot ripped the main course in two, another damaged their two stern chasers along with the mizzen mast, and two more struck the hull beneath the waterline.

Savion sent men below to patch the holes as best they could and man the pumps. A hail from the Malum ship rang hollow through the smoke—a demand to surrender. With guns reloaded, the enemy ship veered to come about and rake them from behind.

Thankfully, the fire was doused as Savion leapt down on the main deck, Petrok and Hona on his heels.

"Should we raise the white flag?" Hona asked.

"Never." Savion glared at their enemy.

"Our stern chasers are destroyed, Captain. We can't fire at them from behind."

Savion gripped the railing not a yard from where Perdita stood. His eyes met hers—intense, focused, fierce—but then he lowered his gaze to the sea churning against the hull. Hair hung in his face, but she could spot his lips moving as if he were speaking to someone.

Another shout to "surrender or die" came from the Malum ship.

Savion shoved off the railing and turned about. "Arrows. We use flaming arrows, Petrok. Archers to the stern."

Petrok nodded with a smile.

Archers? Perdita approached Savion. "I can help. I'm quite good at archery."

"Get below, woman. I've no time for this now. Hona." He found his quartermaster at the wheel. "Get your musket and join them."

Hona nodded and sped away.

"They are nearly within firing range, Captain," one man shouted.

A chest full of bows and arrows, along with several linstocks, were brought on deck, and the men grabbed them and hurried to the stern. When most had gotten theirs, Perdita grabbed one for herself and followed them, ignoring the pain in her feet and Savion's shout for her to get below at once.

The woman was destined to drive him completely and utterly mad. Perhaps she was a plant by the Malum, after all, to make Savion surrender just to be rid of her. Now, she dared to ignore him—the only one on board who could get away with that—and hobbled across the deck, bow, arrows, and linstock in hand.

He spun to face the oncoming Malum ship, her carronades taunting him from her larboard railing, her warriors shouting at him from on deck, armed, ready to board and slaughter. But Savion would not let them.

He fought in the name of King Abbas and would not be defeated.

Planting his feet firmly on the heaving deck, he kept a confident stance as the seconds dragged like hours until the ship was in range. Would his archers be able to fire their arrows before the Malum cannons pulverized the *Scepter*? Savion's heart crashed against his ribs. *Guardians of Erden, be with me.* The Malum ship eased closer and closer, her crew thrusting defiant fists in the air, roaring in celebration over their conquest. Another second …

He glanced at the twenty archers crouched behind the stern railing, arrows strung tight in their bows, other men holding lit linstocks, awaiting his order. To his dismay, Perdita had positioned herself on the far right, her bow drawn and ready.

CHAPTER 18

"Fire!" Savion bellowed and Perdita lit her arrow, stood, and along with her fellow archers released her bow. Dozens of arrows arched flames across the sky, most hitting their mark as if they could do naught else. Sails went ablaze in seconds. Malum darted across the ship in a frenzied attempt to put out the fire.

"Hard to starboard!" Savion shouted, and the *Scepter* veered to the right, deck tilting, sails thundering, and water spewing from her larboard quarter.

The roar of carronades followed, pummeling the air. The crew dropped to the deck, clinging to hatch gratings, lines, and masts—anything they could find to keep from tumbling overboard. Perdita braced herself against the stern railing. The whine and zip of cannon shot scorched her ears, followed by the ominous crunch of wood. One of the shots punched through the main deck.

The rest splashed into the sea, impotent.

"Praise be King Abbas!" Savion's crew cheered as they rose to their feet. "Praise be King Abbas!"

"All sail to the wind!" Savion ordered, and soon, with all canvas billowing in a stiff breeze, the crippled *Scepter* sliced a path through the turquoise seas. When Perdita's bandaged feet finally dared to move again, she rose and sought the Malum ship—now naught but a fireball on the horizon.

Amazing. She'd never seen anyone escape such overwhelming odds. Shielding her eyes from the afternoon sun, she found Savion on the quarterdeck, map spread before him, conversing with Petrok and a few of his crew, who held down the edges against the wind.

A thin man emerged from one of the hatches, his ragged clothes dripping on the deck. "Captain, the pumps can't keep up. We're takin' on too much water."

Savion nodded, yet his expression revealed none of the fear now rising within Perdita.

"Do what you can," he replied, then folded up the map as Petrok dispatched orders for the crew to adjust sail and course.

Perdita's aching feet drew her down to Savion's cabin once again. The pain reminded her of how close she'd come to crying in front of Verrad. *Zost* on the scamp! How could one of Savion's crew be acquainted with that fiend Damien? Of all the luck of Neptune! At least Verrad was locked in his cabin for now. In the meantime, they had bigger problems, it would seem. Sinking to the depths for one. Yet, for all their trials, Perdita was beginning to believe there wasn't anything Savion couldn't save them from. Forsooth, he seemed to be in the business of saving everyone who crossed his path.

Everyone but her.

Eleven more days. She had but eleven more days to convince him to do just that.

By twilight, the *Scepter* sailed into the cove of an island Perdita recognized as one she'd almost claimed as her home nearly two hundred years past. Small, uninhabited, with lush jungles, gorgeous shores, and towering cliffs, it had everything she required, all save the safety of an underwater cave. Now as she sat on the stern window ledge and admired the setting sun sprinkling amber and gold over the turquoise bay and waving palms, she remembered why she'd loved it so much.

The ship halted, the anchor splashed home, and Savion marched into the cabin with the authority that was his due.

A breeze followed him in, showering her with his scent of sweat and man. His open white shirt revealed a power chest, glistening with sweat. Breeches hugged muscular thighs and disappeared into knee-high boots. He tore off his brace of pistols and laid them on the desk. And against her will, her heart skipped in her chest.

"I told you to stay below." Though his gaze was pointed, his voice bore no anger.

She swung her legs over the window ledge and frowned. "I'm not some helpless, swooning female that I need to be coddled."

His brows rose. "I'll admit you are a good shot with bow and arrow, woman, but if memory serves, wasn't it just last night I found you bound below helpless *and swooning*?"

"Bound yes. Helpless, mayhap." She raised her chin. "But I *never* swoon."

He narrowed his eyes as a tiny smile appeared on his lips. "No, I suppose not. And you certainly weren't helpless today. Where did you learn archery? It's not a normal skill for a woman."

"Here and there." She twirled a strand of hair that had fallen in her lap. "I can hardly lift a sword, and a pistol has but one shot. Hence, the bow and arrow seemed the logical choice."

"Hmm." He drew a deep sigh and crossed arms over his chest. "Not much need for that beneath the sea, I suppose."

Her heart sped up and she looked away. "I beg your pardon?"

He cocked his head and studied her. "Do be honest with me for once, Perdita. *Are* you a mermaid?"

She sensed teasing in his voice, but still her heart clamped in fear. She faced him with a beguiling smile. "Do you wish me to be?"

Disappointment shadowed his brow as he huffed out a sigh. "Will you never cease your seductions?"

"Of course. When you give in, Captain."

He grunted, but another smile peeked from the corner of his lips. "I came to inform you we will spend the night on the ship and go ashore in the morning."

She glanced out the window. "What drew you to this particular island? Have you sensed some desperate need, some impending tragedy only *you* can divert?" She was toying with him, but he grew serious.

"Much-needed repairs, as you well know." He followed her gaze out the window, where darkness had blanketed the island. "However, I *am* sensing a need here."

At her questioning look, he continued, "It will soon reveal itself. How are your feet?" He glanced at the bandages.

"I'll live." *Unfortunately.*

"And your arm." He knelt before her, examined the bandage, then studied her face, where she knew bruises from Verrad's strikes marred her beauty. Anger and pain fired from his eyes, and she lowered her chin, self-conscious of her appearance. He ran a thumb over her swollen lip, his touch warming every inch of her. She closed her eyes and absorbed the memory of his gentleness, the care, the way he made her feel alive … whole … even worthy.

But then he withdrew and stood, and a sudden chill took his place. "I'll have your supper brought to you soon." He turned to leave.

Her cry of "Savion" brought him around.

"I—I've never seen anyone win against such odds."

He studied her as if assessing her sincerity before nodding and closing the door behind him.

Infuriating man! One minute he rescued her and swept her off her feet like some gallant knight, the next he behaved as if she had horns and scales.

The night was filled with demons from her past. She dreamt of Ivan five, a strapping middle-aged plantation owner on the island of Lenkist, who had broken off his engagement to another woman to marry Perdita instead. She stood on the cliffs overlooking the sea—a special secluded place they frequented for picnics. And *other* activities. Wind tossed her hair behind her like shimmering black feathers and molded her already seductive gown to every curve. Beneath her, the indigo sea reached foamy talons to snatch her back into its depths.

She would be there soon enough, for she had only minutes before she became a mermaid again. She lured her lover to the edge and kissed him with a kiss she'd perfected over the years to drive men mad. Then, backing away, she pretended to trip and flung herself into the sea.

He would jump after her. Surely he would. Despite the fact that he couldn't swim. He loved her! Was betrothed to her. And in the state of passion in which she'd left him, he'd no doubt do anything to rescue her. Of course she wouldn't allow him to drown, even though he couldn't know that. But that was the point, wasn't it?

She struck the water hard, the slap radiating outward like the sting of an urchin. But when she surfaced at a distance, he merely stood on the edge of the cliff, staring down at the frothing sea with a forlorn look on his face.

He had not loved her enough.

Or mayhap he hadn't loved her at all.

She woke at dawn covered in sweat. A single pearl lay on her pillow. Pocketing it, she rose, attended her morning toilet, then joined the shouts and pounding of feet emanating from above. Within minutes, she was placed in a small boat and deposited on shore, while the crew continued to hoist supplies from the ship in order to begin repairs. Her stomach grumbled as she lowered to sit on a rock and watch the proceedings, keeping her eye on Savion as he directed his men to task. She caught his gaze upon her more than once, and it made her smile to think that, despite his attempts otherwise, he found her intriguing in some way. But was it enough?

This was the hardest test Savion's father had ever sent his way. That's why he knew if he could only pass, he'd be called home. He didn't blame his father. Savion had risked his family, the kingdom, and everything his father had worked for when Savion had foolishly chosen to wed Lorelei.

His glance wandered to Perdita as, unfortunately, it was prone to do. She looked so alone, so forlorn sitting on the rock down shore. His father had chosen the subject of the trial well. Perdita was the most fascinating woman Savion had ever met. Was she seductress or saint? Scholar or unschooled? Warrior or weakling? Regardless, she never failed to surprise him with her humorous quips, her fluctuating moods, and her unexpected actions. She had lied to him, tried to seduce him, and put him in dangerous situations.

Yet all he wanted to do was take her in his arms.

He *must* resist her. He would choose his bride well. Not based on beauty but on character: kindness, charity, honor, and morality. He would make his father proud.

The swish of leaves brought his attention to the edge of the jungle. His men plucked their swords from their scabbards as people of all colors—dozens of them, all ragged and thin—emerged from the greenery. When their wide, hopeless eyes saw the blades, they froze. Others piled up behind them.

Savion gestured for his men to lower their swords.

A man with a bald head and gray beard stepped forward, his shirt nothing but tattered strips of cloth. Ribs poked the skin of his bony chest. "We knew you would come."

Savion approached him as more and more people squeezed through the jungle like rice through a sieve. "Who are you?"

"We knew you would come," the man repeated as he gripped Savion's arm, his weathered face bright with relief. "We prayed to King Abbas to send help."

Savion glanced over the mob now filtering onto the beach. Dozens upon dozens squeezed from the tangle of green, their hair shaggy and long, their clothing shredded, their faces drawn. Men, women, and children. Savion swallowed down a pang of sorrow.

His men, equally stunned, stared at the sight, still gripping their swords should the newcomers be a threat.

"What happened to you?" Savion asked.

"We've been stranded here for months," the man replied. "We are all that is left of a merchant fleet transporting goods and people from Mirkesh to Zidron. Lost all our ships in a storm."

A young woman covered in red bites and carrying a baby stepped beside the old man. "We've been eating nothing but fruit and bugs. Please, sir, can you spare some food?"

Savion swung to face his crew. "Put away your swords. Petrok, what food stores do we have on board?"

"I don't know." The first mate sheaved his sword. "Verrad keeps track of that."

Hona scanned the needy crowd. "We brought only enough to feed us for our journey."

"Go get it, then, man. And be quick."

"Our food?" Nuto looked alarmed. "You're giving them our food?"

Hona drew Savion aside. "There won't be enough. Not even for a quarter of them. Then what are we to eat when we set sail? What if another storm rises? We could starve before we make port."

"He's right, Captain," Petrok added. "Send them back into the jungle, and when our ship is repaired, we can sail to the nearest port and send back rescue ships loaded with supplies."

"We have to try," a woman's voice chimed in. Not just any woman. A woman who sent Savion's blood racing. "We cannot leave them like this." Perdita slipped beside Savion, her sweet scent drifting past his nose.

He smiled her way then faced his men. "Bring all our sacks, crates, and barrels of food on shore," he ordered. His crew complied—begrudgingly—and within an hour, the sand was lined with one sack of rice, a sack of grain, a cask of salted beef, two barrels of grog, two crates of corn, oranges, and a sack of hard biscuits.

Savion's men gathered wood for two fires, and Perdita helped cook the rice and make flatbreads from the grain.

Once all the food was spread on top of a table made from planks stretched across barrels, Savion grabbed a hard biscuit, faced the crowd, raised the bread toward the sky, and said in a loud voice for all to hear, "Thank you, King Abbas, for all that you provide."

Murmurs of agreement passed through the mob that numbered over two hundred.

Hours later, Savion knew Perdita hadn't eaten anything all day. Yet there she was, bringing plates of food to the starving people, ensuring everyone received enough to fill their bellies, even the aged and infirmed lingering at the edge of the crowd. He couldn't keep his eyes off her as she sashayed amongst them in her stained green skirts and tight cream-colored bodice, her hair spilling from pins like raven silk. She would be beautiful even in rags. Yet it was the gentleness of her touch, the way she smiled and stopped to talk with those who sat alone, her hurried efforts to deliver the food as quickly as she could, that made her glow.

Did the woman never cease to amaze him?

After bringing food to a group of mothers and their children, Perdita returned to the serving table to see if there was anything left. When she'd gathered the last batch, only scraps had remained, and one of Savion's men was about to scoop those onto a plate. Now, stopping before the table, she froze and rubbed her eyes to make sure she wasn't seeing things. There was still some rice and dried pork! She quickly grabbed it and delivered it to those who hadn't received any. When she returned, there was more—just enough to heap onto a single plate. When it happened a third time, Perdita asked Hona—who had just returned for more platefuls—where the extra food was coming from. He simply shrugged, grabbed his portion, and hurried away.

Finally, as the sun made its way toward the horizon, she returned for more food and found the table empty. But it didn't matter, everyone had been fed. She glanced over the crowd spread across the beach. Children played, women chatted amongst themselves, while men lay on the sand, rubbing their full bellies.

Perdita had no idea what had just happened.

Only Savion seemed unaffected by the strange event as he ordered his men to clean up and then strolled through the crowd, talking with people and making sure all was well.

Perdita retreated to her rock down shore. Her stomach grumbled. She'd forgotten to eat anything, and now the food was gone. No matter. Every appreciative smile she received from each plate she delivered had brought her more joy than the most delicious meal she'd ever consumed. How surprising was that? She shook her head, pondering the revelation. Mayhap she had spent too much of her time during her many ephemeral redemptions serving herself and not others.

An hour later, Savion approached, holding a plateful of food. Her nerves tightened when she saw Verrad following behind him, unshackled and smiling at her with that knowing grin that said he knew she was a mermaid, and he wouldn't rest until he proved it to everyone else.

"You haven't eaten." Savion handed her the plate, along with a pouch of water.

"Thank you. I thought there was none left." Rising to her feet, she eyed Verrad, who had stopped a few yards away. "Why did you release him?"

"I couldn't keep him on the ship like it is." Savion glanced over his shoulder at the *Scepter* tilted halfway on its port side. "Rest assured, however, he is being punished severely. I've demoted him to deckhand, and he'll scrub decks, clean the head, and do whatever is asked of him. That is, if I decide to keep him on board." He stared at Verrad, whose eyes remained on the sand. A breeze tossed Savion's hair in his face. He jerked it aside and planted hands on his waist. "He seems contrite, Perdita, and has asked for the chance to apologize."

Verrad inched forward. "I was mistaken, Miss Mulier. What I did to you was reprehensible. I was drunk and not myself."

They both knew that wasn't true.

"I beg your forgiveness for the injury I caused you." The words did not reach his seething eyes.

Savion studied her, gauging her reaction. Of course she would *not* forgive him, especially since he wasn't sorry at all. But Savion expected her to. He wanted her to.

"I forgive you," she finally managed to grind out with a sweet smile.

"And," Savion assured her. "I am keeping him under guard. He will not come near you again." He nodded with assurance before he leaned toward her, a smile on his lips. "I am pleased at your mercy."

But, apparently, not pleased enough to keep her company. She stared at the men walking away. Verrad winked at her over his shoulder, sending a chill spiraling to her feet. After gobbling down her supper, she gathered palm fronds for a bed and lay down to count the stars poking through the dark canopy. How glorious, how magnificent the heavens were! She could never count all the stars. There were thousands upon ten thousands of them. Some said King Abbas had created the heavens. Others said they were formed by a random accident. Perdita couldn't see how anything so beautiful and grandiose and precisely patterned could be an accident. With these thoughts in mind, she drifted off to sleep.

A thousand needles pierced Perdita's legs. Shrieking, she leapt to her feet and tried to focus in the darkness. The stinging continued. Seawater saturated her skirts, dripped from the hem onto the sand. She rubbed her eyes. A torch waved over her legs and feet, the flames dancing … crackling. A figure lunged for her and lifted one edge of her skirts. She slapped the hand and backed away, wondering if she was dreaming.

But then the figure growled out a curse and slogged away, uttering, "I'll prove it one way or another."

Verrad.

She tried to settle her heart. What happened to him being guarded?

A breeze swept over her, plastering her wet skirts to her legs. Shivering, she hugged herself and glanced down the beach toward the main camp, where Savion's men slept around a dwindling fire. Offshore, the gray of dawn perched on the horizon, revealing the *Scepter,* tipped as if it were resting its head on the warm waters of the bay. She wished she could do the same. Rest and peace—two precious gifts that oft eluded Perdita.

And apparently Verrad as well. She watched him grab a bottle from the sand, lift it to his lips, and march away. The man would not give up. She'd lived long enough to spot insatiable greed in someone's eyes. Sooner or later he'd find a way to expose her.

She was wasting her time here, anyway. She had started to believe Savion might care for her—dare she hope—mayhap even love her. But Verrad running loose on the beach proved otherwise. A man in love would do anything to keep his lady safe.

She was wet, cold, and hungry. And worse—alone. Not exactly how she wanted to spend her time on land. Yet staying with Savion was proving to be even *more* tortuous. This island was as good a place as any to spend her remaining ten days. Then she would simply slip into the sea and be forgotten.

Like all the other times.

She scanned the sleeping forms down shore, her eyes latching upon one in particular. Savion. She could tell because his light hair looked like silver in dawn's pre-glow. Even in slumber, he lay with the assurance of authority. She crept toward him, being ever so quiet, keeping an eye out for Verrad, who had no doubt gone off to plot a new scheme to destroy her.

Not daring to come too close, Perdita halted two yards from Savion and watched him as he slept—studying the firm line of his stubbled jaw, the rise and fall of the medallion lying on his powerful chest, the expression of peace and control that always rested upon his face.

Tears clouded her vision and she backed away, needing to leave, but not wanting to, not able to. Not yet. Who *was* this man? This wonderful, incredible man who spent his life helping others, who sensed things no man could sense, who multiplied food and defeated foes, a man who held to a standard of decency and honor she didn't think possible. 'Twas as if he didn't belong in this evil world at all. As if he'd come from another place where men didn't lie and cheat and kill. And abandon. Even now as he lay in slumber, his presence called to every hope within her, luring her into a world she could never enter. A place she could never be.

Because she was cursed.

And cursed she would remain. For she knew now that though this man would risk his life for her, *had* risked his life for her, to allow him to trade his life for hers would be a travesty of epic proportions. What was she worth, anyway? What was her life compared to such a man?

Though it meant another ten years of agonizing isolation, she could never put him in danger again. Kneeling beside him, she kissed her finger and laid it upon his cheek.

"Good-bye, Savion, I wish you well." Tears filled her eyes, and she rose and dove into the jungle before she changed her mind.

Chapter 19

Footsteps faded, leaves shuffled, and Savion looked up to see a flash of black hair and green skirts disappear into the jungle. He'd heard the woman approach, felt her staring at him, and was surprised by the gentle touch of her finger on his face. Even more surprising was her farewell. Where did she think she could run to on an island? And why leave now when it seemed all she ever wanted was to stay with him?

Once again, the woman baffled him. She more than baffled him as a sinking feeling landed hard in his gut at the thought he'd never see her again. But wasn't that the point of passing the test? Never to see her again? Savion stood and rubbed his eyes. Ripples of saffron and rose spread across the horizon and dabbed the sea with color. Another day dawned—another day, and he was still here on the Ancient Seas.

Perhaps he shouldn't have brought Verrad to see Perdita. But the man had been so repentant and had taken his punishment well. Savion's father had told him that mercy was one of Savion's best qualities. Best, and in this case perhaps the most foolish as Savion spotted the two men assigned to guard Verrad slumped against a palm, fast asleep. Great. Surely the man wasn't stupid enough to go after Perdita again.

Regardless, he couldn't very well leave her wandering the jungle alone, where dangerous terrain, poisonous insects, wild animals, and who knew what else awaited her.

Minutes later, Savion slid his sword into his scabbard and checked and stuffed his pistols into his baldric. "I'm going to find her."

Beside him, a sleepy-eyed Petrok scowled. "She obviously doesn't wish to be found."

Gathering his water pouch, Savion flung it over his shoulders then faced his men. Petrok stared at him defiantly, Hona peered into the jungle, and Nuto shifted his foot through the sand.

"I can't very well leave her here all alone on this island."

"She seems like a woman who can take care of herself," Petrok said.

"The captain's right." Hona sighed and ran a hand through his hair. "It wouldn't be right to leave her."

"Even if she wants to be left?" Nuto chimed in.

Verrad stood in the distance, arms crossed over his chest, and Savion wondered if he'd been the reason she'd left so suddenly.

Nuto rubbed his chin. "She's been nothing but trouble. Have you considered that Natas might have sent her to stop your mission … or worse? The Malum never attacked us directly until she was on board."

The man did have a point.

"Nothing but trouble." Nuto shook his head. "Nothing but trouble, I'm telling you."

Petrok grabbed Savion's arm. "Don't go, Captain. I have a bad feeling about this."

"I'm going with you," Hona announced.

"No. I need you here. I won't be gone long. Repair the ship as quickly as you can." He turned and headed toward the jungle, lifting a hand in the air to silence their ensuing protests, even as he wondered if he should heed them. His father had always said that a wise man considered the advice of counselors.

Shoving aside leaves, he entered the green web and sought the peace within—not a web of confusion like the one spanning the canopy above, but a soothing river of peace, an inward knowing that he was on the right path. And there it was, in the warming of his medallion and in the gentle voice deep within. He must go for the woman. Whether she was his mission or not, whether she had anything to recommend her besides her appearance, he knew he must not leave her.

Perdita made her way up a hill to the top of a cliff she remembered from her time on the island before and stood admiring the lush canopy below that stretched beyond the mountains to the azure sea. Birds, so colorful it seemed their wings were dipped in jars of paint, swooped across the green carpet as the chatter of monkeys and buzz of insects filled the air. Despite her burning feet and aching muscles from the climb, she drew in a deep breath of soil and life and sweet nectar and tried her best to appreciate the view she could never see from beneath the waves.

A twig snapped, and she knew without turning around that Savion had followed her. She knew because her heart swelled and her skin began to tingle. *Zost!*

"What are you doing out here?" he asked.

She continued staring over the valley. "Thinking."

He slipped beside her and took in the view. His breathing came hard, and sweat molded his shirt to his muscled chest as if he'd run to catch her. But why? Wind blew his hair behind him as his golden eyes met hers, piercing and so full of life.

"It's not safe out here for you alone. Come back with me."

"Why did you follow me, Savion? I would think you'd be glad to be rid of me."

He heaved a sigh. "Not glad, Perdita. Just a necessity."

"Ah yes, how could I forget? I am merely a test."

Naught but the warble of birds and stir of wind could be heard as he uncomfortably shifted. "I shouldn't have said that. Forgive me."

She said nothing, for there was nothing to forgive. Though her heart still stung.

"You surprised me yesterday, Perdita," he finally said. "Your generosity and kindness to those strangers. It was admirable."

"How could I do otherwise in the face of such misery?"

His smile of approval warmed her to her toes.

"I still have no idea where all that food came from." She suspected he had some powers he hid from others, or mayhap even some he was completely unaware of himself.

"Abbas provides."

Flashes of starving people inhabiting every port she'd ever visited filtered through her mind. "Not always."

"Let's go back, Perdita. I've work to do."

She gave a ladylike snort. "You came to get me because you saw some kindness in me yesterday? I'll save you the trouble. I am *not* kind. Leave me be. I wish to stay."

"But you'll die out here alone."

"If only that were true."

His brows tightened. "Why would you say such a thing?"

"You wouldn't understand." She studied him. "I haven't much hope, I'm afraid."

"There's always hope. Look around you"—he waved a hand over the stunning scenery and the jungle teaming with life—"the beauty of Abbas's creation, the life bursting from within it, the rising and setting of the sun—all this should give you hope. You are young, you have breath in your lungs, you are free."

Young? Free? Breath? The first two she'd not been since the curse. The third she rarely had. But she couldn't tell him that.

Nor, from the look in his eyes, would he go back to camp without her.

She inched closer to the edge of the cliff. "Leave me here or I swear I'll jump!" 'Twas the only thing she could think to do.

Anger and confusion raged on his face. He grabbed her arm and yanked her toward him. "Are you mad, woman?"

"Possibly. But I still mean what I say."

She pushed from him, her feet precariously close to the edge. Wind whipped her skirt. Pebbles flew off the edge and click-clacked as they tumbled below. She didn't relish the thought of the pain she'd endure if she fell, but she couldn't tolerate another day loving a man who would never love her in return.

"Stop behaving like a crazy woman, and come with me this minute!" He pulled her again, his eyes wide as they glanced over the edge. "You're going to get us both killed."

She fought him, tugging against his grip. "Leave me be!" She took a step back. Rock cracked, pebbles fell, her foot landed on air. She lost her balance and started tumbling over the edge.

A flash of green cloth and dark hair skirted the bottom of Savion's vision. He reached blindly to grab ahold, all the while his heart exploded in his chest. Fingers met fabric. It tore. He lunged after her, groping for her arm, her leg, anything! She screamed.

His feet left the ground. Wind blasted his face. His hand clutched warm flesh. *Thud! Crunch!* The woman fell to the dirt. He spun and rolled over her soft flesh. His feet left him again and swung over empty space.

Perdita shrieked.

Savion was falling. Wind roared in his ears. His clothes flapped like wings.

So, this is how he would die. This was his punishment for failing his mission.

He landed on something soft, like sailcloth filled with wind. It cushioned him and slowly began to rise. Glancing to his right and left, he saw the Guardians, faint outlines of light defining their positions. They neither looked at him nor smiled, just carried him up … up to where Perdita's frightened face gaped at him over the lip of a rocky ledge.

He reached for her, grabbed her hand, and hoisted himself up until he sat beside her. She said nothing as he caught his breath. And his thoughts. Had she seen the Guardians? They rarely appeared in front of anyone but Savion. In truth, he hadn't been sure they would come for him this time.

Finally he faced her, searching her for wounds, and upon finding none, felt his anger return. "By the stars of Lemox, what were you thinking?"

Still she gaped at him, a mixture of confusion and astonishment on her face. "You went over the edge … I saw you … over the edge …." she stuttered.

She sat stunned for several minutes before she rose, brushed off her skirts, and started to walk away. Savion dashed after her and spun her around. "What ails you, woman? Why do you wish to die?"

"Why do you wish not to?" she snapped. "And what were those … those lights … those beings who saved you?"

Savion rubbed the back of his neck. So, she *had* seen them. "Let's head back. My crew will be worried."

Patches of sun streaming through the trees dappled her in light, but she held her place. "What are they, Savion? I've seen them before near you."

"Tell you what. You tell me why you wish to die, and I'll tell you what they are." Uneasiness mounted within him as he stared at the fickle madcap woman. He truly did believe her when she'd said she wanted to die. He'd come to know her well enough these past days to tell when she lied, when she flirted, when she was afraid, and when she was serious.

"I wouldn't have jumped, if that is what you mean. 'Twas your fault you fell trying to drag me away!"

"If you hadn't been resisting me!" He fisted his hands, frustration rising.

Her skirts were torn, and one shapely leg appeared. He looked away.

"I'm sorry, Savion."

The sincerity of her tone brought his gaze back to her. "For what?"

"For risking your life." Perspiration beaded on her forehead, reminding him of the pearls Verrad claimed her tears became. "You tried to save me. Why?"

Because for some unfathomable reason, I love you. "It's what I do."

"So, I'm just another one of your missions, another righteous deed you can engrave on a badge and pin to your chest." She took a step back and glanced over her shoulder.

Hopelessness numbed her sea-green eyes. He must discover what wound she bore on her heart that made her so desperate for death. He'd spent so much time saving people from physical harm, he knew nothing about healing broken hearts.

He moved toward her, intending to ask her why she had no hope, when the vixen spun and disappeared into the green web.

Batting aside branches and leaves, Perdita ran as fast as she could, despite the pain in her feet and the perspiration streaming down her back. She ran because the affection and concern in Savion's eyes caused hope to rise.

She ran because she needed to run—away from everything—her fears, her dreams, the curse, her life. But if she were honest, she ran because she longed for Savion to follow her. If he did—if he came after her yet again—then surely it meant he loved her. No man was that good or that noble to endure all the trouble she had caused him. Nay, most would have abandoned her long ago.

She tripped on a root and stumbled. A vine reached out to strangle her. She shoved it aside. Insects buzzed past her ears. A frog croaked, and a growl sounded in the distance. She rushed forward.

Mayhap she *did* have a chance with Savion. If only she could seduce him, then she could show him how much she loved him—unite with him in that physical union that drove men to distraction and made them grovel at her feet. Then he would be hers.

Clutching her skirts with one hand, she batted leaves aside with the other as memories of all the men who had abandoned her after she'd bedded them began to pummel her hope. But Savion was different. His honor would not allow him to leave her after they'd become one.

Though she would have to leave him in ten days.

Still, 'twas better to be in his arms, to enjoy his love, then to spend the rest of her time on land all alone. At least when she slipped back into the sea for another decade, the memory of finally being loved would see her through the long, lonely years.

Halting, her breath heaving, she studied the trees surrounding her, looking for familiar landmarks. The sound of rushing water rode upon the jungle chorus. Yes, she knew exactly how she would finally win Savion's love.

Exasperating woman! Savion charged after Perdita, but she had slipped away too fast. A broken twig, a torn leaf, and scattered footprints led him onward. Several minutes later, his breath came heavy and sweat coated his skin.

Above him, the canopy chirped and buzzed as myriad birds flitted from branch to branch and insects the size of guavas hummed a soothing cadence. Somewhere in the middle of the exotic symphony came the harmony of gurgling water. Savion headed toward it.

The gurgle turned into a trickle, which turned into a gush and finally a roar as Savion shoved aside final branches and emerged into a small clearing. A waterfall tumbled over a rock cliff, sparkling and bubbling into a turquoise pool surrounded by white sand and lush greenery. Ivy speckled in purple and pink flowers draped over the cliff and festooned the low branches of trees, making the scene look surreal in its beauty.

After lifting his baldric over his head and removing his pouch and sword, He peeled off his shirt, kicked off his boots, and dove head first into the glistening pool. Cool water swept over him, washing off the sweat, heat, and grime of the jungle. Nothing had ever felt so good. He swam to the deepest part of the pool, touched the silt, then shot off the bottom straight to the surface. Sunlight warmed his face, and he gulped in a lungful of air before opening his eyes.

A boulder rose from the water not four feet from where he'd surfaced. He started toward it but movement halted him. Someone sat upon it. A woman. Silken strands of ebony hair waved across her back. With a start, she spun to face him.

It was Perdita. And she was completely naked.

CHAPTER 20

Perdita! Shock kept Savion staring at her, his eyes unwillingly roving to places they shouldn't, curves that caused heat to storm through him. She flung her arms up to cover herself. He spun around in the water, a thousand emotions and sensations raging within him.

"What are you doing here?" he demanded.

"I should ask you the same thing," she gasped out, indignant.

"Where are your clothes?"

"Same place I imagine yours are."

He scanned the beach in the distance, spotted his own discarded attire, and then found her skirts and underthings hanging on a tree limb to the side. Why had he not seen them?

"I insist you get dressed at once," he commanded.

"Very well." Her tone no longer bore fear or shock. He heard her splash into the water and swim his way and pictured her beautiful body inches beside him.

"Wait! I'll go first and turn my back, then follow me." He dove beneath the surface, wishing he could stay there where life was peaceful and there were no naked women to behold, all the while chastising himself for gazing at her so boldly. He dragged himself onto the sand and faced the jungle, listening to her splashes growing closer and trying desperately to focus on the chorus of birds, the hum of insects, the vines and leaves swaying in the wind—anything but the vision of water gliding over those curves.

When she bade him turn around, it was to her wearing only her chemise.

He averted his eyes. "I told you to get dressed."

"My clothes are wet. I dove in with them on when I first came upon this place. Surely I am covered enough." She gave him a coy look, then lowered to a rock and drew her dripping hair over her shoulder—slick strands of rich cocoa that made Savion lick his lips.

"If you were wrapped in sailcloth, I doubt you'd be covered enough." He cringed at words he shouldn't have spoken out loud.

Her smile proved him right.

Anger flamed. "Why are you out here swimming unclad for all to see?"

"Why did you burst unannounced into a lady's bathing pool?"

"Lady's bathing …" He growled. "I came looking for you. What did you think I would do?"

"I thought mayhap you would have reached your limit of the trouble I cause you." Water glistened on the skin of her neck and arms and pooled in her thick black lashes like diamonds. Savion grew warm again. He did not want to desire her. Any man could desire her. He wanted to help her.

"Besides," she added, "I am quite all right, as you can see."

More than all right, from his way of seeing things. He cleared his throat. "As I informed you, you cannot stay out here alone."

"I can do what I wish."

"You'll die of starvation or animal attack before another ship sails into the bay." He huffed. "That is, unless you *are* a mermaid and can swim away." He chuckled.

Perdita could sit in this spot for a thousand days and gaze upon this man before her. Standing there, the muscles of his chest rippling in the sunlight like the waves upon the pond, the lion tattoo on his bicep, his hands fisted firmly upon his hips, his breeches molded to his muscular thighs, wet hair slicked back, and those golden eyes—sparking with anger, yes, but also passion, care, hope—all jumbled up in an intense vision that drew Perdita in until she wished nothing more than to become a part of him.

Then why had she felt a surge of modesty when he saw her, a need to cover herself in his presence, even though the desire in his eyes was evident. Zost! She had missed her chance. She could have dove into the water, pretended to flounder, and he would have been forced to scoop her up in his arms. Wasn't that her plan? But instead she had felt dirty, unworthy beneath his stare.

Now, as he obviously fought to keep his eyes off her, she knew she could still have him. And with the prospect of a decade of torture looming before her, she had to try.

Rising, she slinked his way. "If I *were* a mermaid, I would have already swum away, don't you think?"

He studied her, gauging her movements as if she were a predator circling its prey. Stopping before him, she traced a finger over the lion tattoo on his firm bicep, longing to be held by such strength, to be cocooned by this man's power and love. She sensed a quiver run through him at her touch and he backed away.

"We could love each other, Savion—you and I, here in the sand, all alone. No one need know."

The woman smelled of gardenias and sunshine, and every cell in Savion's body longed to take her in his arms and make her his. But it wouldn't be right. She didn't need physical love. She needed something far deeper, far more lasting. Besides, he was saving himself for his bride—the pure, kind, honorable bride his father had promised him. Physical union outside of a lifelong commitment brought nothing but pain.

Perdita was but a test. Yet . . . so much more than that now. She was someone he wanted to help.

Bending over, he grabbed his shirt and tossed it over his head.

Disappointment shadowed her features.

"Why do you give yourself away so freely?" Savion plopped in the sand and drew up his knees.

At first he wondered if she would just storm away, angry at his rejection. Or worse, slip out of the chemise shielding her curves and make another attempt. But instead, she sighed, sat down beside him, and slid a finger in the sand.

"Doesn't King Abbas ask us to love each other? How can such an expression of love be wrong?"

"As I have said, love has nothing to do with a physical union."

"Of course it does! It has everything to do with it. You're just scared."

He raised his brows at her. "Woman, I would love nothing more than to accept your offer. You have no idea."

Her green eyes searched his. "Then do." No flirtation, just a pleading that nearly broke his heart.

"Physical union is the consummation of love. It is the seal upon a lifelong commitment. To share such a sacred union with someone who is not willing to enter into covenant with you, who will cast you off as soon as they grow weary of you, is to only cause yourself pain and cheapen the act."

She sat staring at the sand, a perplexed look on her face. "So, would you cast me off as well? When you grew weary of me?"

"Is that what men have done to you?" he asked gently.

She squirmed and dug her feet in the sand, and he got a feeling she was about to cry but struggled not to. A breeze tossed a strand of her hair across her cheek, and he longed to brush it aside.

"You can tell me, Perdita. I truly want to hear."

"No one has ever wanted to hear my story." She looked at the pond as a white bird dipped low over the water and caught a slippery fish with its feet.

"I do."

She lifted one side of her chemise and covered her shoulder in an act of modesty that warmed his heart. "Why?"

Because, despite his best efforts, he cared—he cared for her more than he wanted to admit. "It will comfort you to talk about it, and I'm a good listener."

She turned away and swallowed.

"I was in love once," she started, barely above a whisper. "Sir Ivan Moorehead, a knight of the kingly order of the Triden." She smiled sadly. "I was but a peasant girl, the youngest daughter of a shepherd, but Sir Ivan took note of me in the village. He would ride by on his dark steed adorned with golden tassels and clanging bells and look at me as if I were a precious flower, too beautiful to be plucked." She dug her toes deeper into the sand. "He would leave me gifts in secret places, jewels the likes of which I had never seen, perfumes from Araba, scarves of lace and satin." She glanced at Savion with such sorrow in her eyes, he felt tears prick his own. "He began to court me. Me?" She laughed. "I could hardly fathom it. Against his parents' wishes, of course. So we met in secret.

It was so romantic. Clandestine rendezvous in hidden alcoves of the town's cathedrals; trysts on mountaintops and forest floors; picnics in fields full of colorful flowers; swims in crystalline lakes much like this pond; riding behind him on his horse, my gown flowing behind me." She stopped, her gaze a million miles away in another time and place.

"Imagine *me*, a simple peasant girl, loved by a prince, a knight, who owned more lands than anyone in the realm. My father, of course, was thrilled at the match. He foretold that one day my beauty would bring fortune to the family. 'Twas the only thing I had to offer, or so he told me."

A breeze blew and she hugged herself.

Minutes passed. Savion's heart grew heavy. "What happened?"

"Forwin happened. Magician, warlock, town shaman. He loved me too. Wanted me for himself. He couldn't stand that I loved Ivan." She picked up a pebble and tossed it into the pond. Ripples spiraled out from the impact. "He … he … we made a bargain. A test to prove Sir Ivan's love." She swallowed. "As it turns out, Forwin was right. Sir Ivan didn't love me at all. At least not enough to risk his life for me."

Her jaw steeled, and she turned away from him.

He winced. *A test.* No wonder those words triggered pain in her. "I'm sorry, Perdita." He leaned over and gently brushed her now-dry hair behind her, then swung an arm over her and drew her close. She leaned her head on his shoulder as a sob rose in her throat.

"Go ahead and cry. You'll feel better."

But she didn't. She just gripped him as if she never wanted to let go. So, that is why she threw herself at men. She wanted to be loved. Not just loved, but loved unconditionally for who she was. Even her own father had only valued her beauty.

Savion kissed the top of her head. Yet didn't she seek what everyone wanted—to be special, valued, and loved no matter what? It was a rare thing to find in Erden. Most people settled for much less.

Savion was one of the fortunate ones, for he knew his father loved him that way.

Sunlight angled through the trees on its descent, bouncing off sparkling waters and transforming her skin into satin. He ran a finger over the bandage on her arm.

A tremble ran through her. She looked up at him, and he caressed the fading bruises on her cheek and eased a lock of hair from her forehead, drawing in her sweet scent. And before he knew it, he lowered his lips to hers.

CHAPTER 21

Perdita had known many kisses in her long life, but none as meaningful, none as powerful, as Savion's. She'd experienced passionate kisses, hungry ones, desperate ones, angry ones, and even some that hurt. She'd had kisses that were awkward and sloppy, others that were gentle— even hesitant—and others that drove her mad with desire. But Savion's kiss touched the deepest part of her. It touched her soul with a yearning so strong, it overpowered her physical need for him.

One arm behind her, he laid her gently on the bed of sand and caressed her face with the back of his hand while he deepened the kiss. Ah, sweet bliss! She had set out to seduce him with her enchanting skills, but he was the one who trapped her instead.

And what a trap! There, barricaded by his love and strength, all of Perdita's fears, all her sorrows, were swept away. She wrapped her arms around him and drew him close, welcoming him gladly, joyously, wondrously. His breath came fast, his body heated, and the thought that she pleased him made her heart soar.

But then he jerked up, a look of horror on his face. He sat back and shook his head as if trying to break an evil spell. "I'm sorry."

"Whatever for?" She rose on her elbows, her passions chilled.

Standing, he drew a deep breath and knelt by the water, splashing it onto his face and neck. "I shouldn't have done that."

Perdita's heart shrank. She had thought … the kiss had been so wonderful … she had thought he'd felt the connection, the love, too. She sat up and her chemise started to slip over her shoulder. She thought to allow it, if only to draw him back to her. But, oddly, she found she didn't want him on those terms. She covered herself.

"You took naught but what I offered." She heard the sorrow in her own voice. He must have too, for he glanced at her.

"You're so beautiful, Perdita. But then, you know that. You use your beauty as a weapon."

A tear escaped her eye, and she batted it away before he saw it. "Surely you felt the bond between us, Savion. There was so much more to that kiss than physical pleasure."

"I felt many things. Some of which should not be felt beyond the boundaries of marriage."

"I pity you if 'twas only your passion that was stirred." Pain and anger battled within her. "I felt love."

"Love?" He snorted. "In physical pleasure?"

"What else is there between man and woman?"

He walked back to her and looked her in the eyes. "So much more: friendship, admiration, respect, commitment, covenant, faithfulness, kindness."

It was her turn to snort. "You're a dreamer, Savion. Those things don't exist. At least not in strong enough measures to last beyond one's own selfishness."

"Then it is you who should be pitied. For what hope is left in this world if not for free and unselfish love?"

Indeed. What hope was there for her? A breeze fluttered the leaves around them. "You are the first man who has ever been able to resist me." She smiled, trying to lighten the mood.

"No easy task, I'll grant you." He returned her smile. "Yet there is so much more to you than your beauty."

His words touched her, softened the ache in her heart. But they couldn't be true. He was merely flattering her or trying to make her feel better. She tossed her head. "Lying does you no credit. Not a man like you. I've done naught but deceive you and try to seduce you." *And try to kill you, she'd add, if she were honest.*

"You give yourself away far too cheaply, Perdita. And I'm guessing to those who do not appreciate you, those who use you for their own pleasure."

She shrugged. "How else can we find love except by giving something to the other person? Something that will make them stay?"

"You can't buy love, Perdita. It must be given to you freely or it isn't love at all."

She frowned. "You make no sense. You hate beauty and are suspicious of women. What happened to make you this way?"

He laughed. "Neither are true. But if you get dressed, I'll tell you my story." He gestured toward her clothes hanging on the branch.

"Very well," she said as she rose and slipped behind the bush. After donning her bodice and skirts, she emerged and sat down beside him on the shore again, anxious to hear more about him and thankful when he didn't scoot away.

Instead, with the sweet chirp of birds and gurgle of water to serenade them and a breeze to keep them cool, he told her a tale of a glorious land where he was born—a land of beauty and peace with magnificent buildings made of marble, streets carved in gold, lush gardens, trees that bore fruit that healed diseases. And best of all, tales of a wonderful father who adored him and who taught him the value of wisdom and mercy and love. He spoke with such longing and joy, his face glowed, and it ignited a longing within her.

"Where is this place?" she asked. "For I wish to go there too."

"Far away, I'm afraid. And only accessed through a narrow bridge difficult to find."

"You wish to return there." The thought made her sad.

"With all my heart."

"Why would anyone ever leave such a place?"

"I fell in love. Like you, I chose unwisely. Lorelei was very beautiful, charming, intelligent, and kind. Or so I thought."

As she watched agony line his face, she felt pain in her own heart. "She betrayed you."

He nodded. "We were only married a year when I discovered she had lovers."

"Lovers?"

He flattened his lips. "Many. And apparently it had been going on for some time."

She touched his arm. "I'm so sorry, Savion." She had known rejection, but she had not known such betrayal.

The muscles in his jaw bunched.

She took his hand in hers. "I can't believe any woman lucky enough to be your wife would throw it all away. What did you do?"

"Divorced her, of course. My father insisted." He rubbed the back of his neck. "And then he sent me here to the Ancient Seas."

"As punishment?"

He shrugged. "To fight Natas. To learn a lesson. I don't know. He said it was to save someone." A breeze stirred the hair at his collar.

"Instead, you seem to save everyone." She smiled. "When can you return?"

"When my father summons me. Soon, I hope."

To a place Perdita could never go. Her breath escaped her. She would go back to the sea, and he would return home. And she'd never see him again. A red-and-blue parrot flew across the clearing, squawking, and landed on a branch above them. "'Tis no wonder you don't trust women."

He raised a brow. "Particularly beautiful ones."

"Then I'd give anything to be ugly." She squeezed his hand.

His gaze dropped to her lips. "At the moment, I wish you were too." He brushed a strand of her hair behind her ear.

His touch was like fire, heating every inch of her. His breath wafted over her cheek. She closed her eyes, longing for his kiss.

Instead, his voice was curt. "I cannot figure you out, Perdita. What is it you want from me?"

She opened her eyes. "I want you to love me, Savion."

"You don't even know what love is." He rose to his feet, brushed off his breeches, then sat on a rock and slipped on his boots.

"You could teach me." She struggled to rise on her sore feet, started to stumble and embellished it, hoping he'd come to her aid.

Instead, he grabbed his baldric and pistols. "My father will choose my next bride."

"Someone pure and good and perfect, no doubt. Not like me."

"What is that?" He slipped his baldric over his shoulder and knelt to pick up something in the sand by her feet. "A pearl." He held it up to the fading light.

Perdita's heart froze. She patted the outside of her pocket.

He noticed and raised incriminating brows her way. "Yours?"

"I found it on the ship." She lied and hated herself for it.

Suspicion rode in his voice. "First of all, there are no pearls on my ship. Secondly, were you planning on stealing it?"

"Nay." She tried to think. "I found it right before the battle and forgot to give it to you." Part of that was true.

He stood staring at her as if he were probing her spirit for the truth. She glanced at the pond and shifted her feet through the sand, trying her best to act casual.

"Why do you never cry?" he finally asked.

She gave a nervous laugh and faced him. "Surely you don't think I'm a mermaid? Of all the absurd things!" She continued her nervous prattling, knowing she should stop but unable to. "In good sooth, I'm simply not one of those women who cry easily. A mermaid! Preposterous!"

He heaved a sigh. "It grows dark. We should go." The earlier tender look in his eyes had been replaced by stern resolve. He grabbed his cutlass and slid it into its sheath, then turned and headed down the trail, gesturing for her to follow.

She'd rather melt into the sand at her feet. As her heart was doing at the moment. Through lies and deceit and seduction, she'd lured many men to fall in love with her, but because of those very things, she'd lost the one man she truly loved.

Knowing he would never allow her to stay in the jungle alone, she trudged after him, her anger rising with each step. She'd have no more chances with this man. This had been her best one. And still he had rejected her in favor of some prim and priggish prude his father would choose.

As the sun descended, shadows rose, forming monsters out of trees that were friends just moments before. The green thicket became a sweltering prison, and Savion tugged off his shirt, withdrew his sword, and hacked away at vines blocking their path. Perdita stewed in her anger as new sounds arose: the hum of night insects, the hoot of an owl, the low growl of ...

A cat—a very large cat.

Halting, Savion listened. The ominous throaty rumble sounded again. Louder. He grabbed Perdita and dove behind a bush.

"Shhh." He put a finger to his lips and peered through the leaves.

She settled beside him, hoping the animal would pass them by. But then a glorious idea occurred to her—a glorious, wonderful, *horrible* idea. Her pulse stormed through her. If she was going to do this, she had to act quickly or the chance would be lost.

She coughed. Not just coughed. She hacked and gasped for breath, and then coughed again. By the time Savion put his hand on her mouth, his eyes wide with panic, the damage was done.

The panther strolled down the path, lean muscles rolling across its back and shoulders as it moved—all grace and power. And large. The largest cat Perdita had ever seen. It stopped before their bush, sniffed the air, then growled and pawed the leaves. Finally, its jade-green eyes pierced them through the foliage.

And Savion did what she knew he would: he stood, sword extended, and stepped in front of her.

She rose behind him, unable to stop from trembling, yet all the while waiting for the pain, the itch, that would tell her the curse was lifting. It had to lift! If ever Savion risked his life for her, it was now. Regardless, she had already determined that she would not allow him to be hurt. If she remained a mermaid, she'd leap in front of Savion and be mauled instead. If not, and she became human, together they would fight off the beast. She scanned the jungle for the ever-present creatures of light, but saw none. No crew dashed to his aid. It was just him against the panther—a fierce, hungry-looking panther.

The cat moved closer and growled loudly, revealing sharp cutting fangs. The roar reverberated in her ears. It swiped a massive paw at Savion with claws as long as knives. Savion leapt back, shoving against her. Her knees went weak, and she stumbled.

One more swipe like that and Savion's leg would be torn in two. What had she done? The panther crouched, ready to pounce. And still Perdita had not changed. Zost! She was angry with Savion for his rejection, but she didn't want him to *actually* die. And her to be mauled afterward! Where were the creatures of light?

Savion's breath came hard; the muscles across his back and arms tightened. He gripped the medallion he always wore, while Perdita looked around for a rock, a stick, anything to help.

Then Savion did something she never would have guessed. He lowered his sword—dropped it, in fact—and held out his hand to the vicious cat that was about to eat them. The panther remained crouched, ready to pounce, but Savion gently knelt down and whispered to it.

Perdita couldn't move, couldn't breathe, her thoughts spinning.

An odd sound drifted to her ears. *Purring?* A loud, soothing rumble emanated from the panther as the cat blinked its eyes, rose on all fours, and quietly strolled away.

Perdita didn't remember the rest of the trek back to the beach, only that she felt as if she was worth nothing more than the mud clinging to the bottom of Savion's boots.

Two days later, standing at the helm of the *Scepter,* Savion waved good-bye to the crowd of stranded people on the beach before he turned and issued orders to weigh anchor and raise sails. Finally the repairs on his ship were completed, and it was time to leave. Since he only had room for fifty people on his small ship, he'd left two trapped boar and nets full of fish to feed the remaining people. Turned out, Petrok and Hona were good fishermen. They not only caught a barrel of grouper but had instructed several men to master the skill. The stranded people would be fine until Savion could get to the nearest port and send back rescue ships.

Sails snapped above, and the creak of yards and chime of tackle sounded as the ship veered to starboard and sped off into the blue sea. Wind whipped past his ears as he found Perdita standing at the main deck railing with several of the women they'd brought on board, her ebony hair blowing behind her. The woman beside her began to sob, her eyes focused on the retreating form of her husband on shore, and Perdita flung an arm around her and drew her close.

In truth, Savion was relieved to see the island growing smaller on the horizon. He'd almost failed the hardest test of all—he'd almost given in to Perdita's charms. Another poor choice based on outward appearance and not the heart. Yet, now there she was, kneeling to gather a small child in her arms. Lifting the babe, she kissed his filthy cheek and tickled him until both he and his mother laughed. What a dichotomy this woman was.

"Where to, Captain?" Petrok's question snapped Savion from his thoughts.

"Make for Mirkesh. It's the closest island."

There they could find enough ships to rescue the people. Plus, it had a large enough population where Perdita could find employment and make a life for herself. Perhaps she could find healing there in the arms of a decent man. Savion could not save her. It would have to be another. No, his bride would come from Nevaeh, a woman of his father's choosing. He could not afford to make another mistake. That's why, this time, *no matter what,* he must leave Perdita and never see her again.

CHAPTER 22

Savion abandoned her again. When she only had five days left as a human, he'd deposited her in the home of a friend—a cobbler and his wife—who lived above the shop they owned. Nice people. Quite aged. The man hard of hearing, the wife bent over in a feeble stance. But they owed Savion their lives and thus were willing to train Perdita in the art of cobbling shoes in return for food and lodging.

Now, as she stood in the stifling upstairs parlor, trying to ignore to the snores of Mr. Ackers in his rocking chair and the click-clack of Mrs. Ackers's knitting needles, Perdita felt as though she'd go mad. A cyclone of emotions whirled through her: anger, bitterness, fear, heartbreak.

Why was she in such turmoil? Isn't this what she wanted? To be free of the man whose words and actions constantly blasted through her heart like a cannon? Mayhap, but not like this. She had hoped for a sweet parting—one in which he, at the very least, professed a smidgen of affection for her. Instead, he'd not only ignored her on the ship for two days but no sooner had they dropped anchor, then he, along with several of his crew, had escorted her straight to the Ackers's home. She'd remained outside while he bargained with them in their front parlor as if she were some commodity to be haggled over.

Then, he'd smiled, wished her well, and told her to behave before turning and strolling out of her life as if she meant nothing to him at all.

Thank goodness the Ackers couldn't see very well, or they'd have wondered where all the pearls had come from.

With her sorrow long spent, fury now broiled within her. Savion thought he was so good, so righteous, so perfect! Humph. This was no way to treat another human being! Or part human being. Though it was only midafternoon, she excused herself by reason of exhaustion, went to her chamber, slipped out the window, and headed for the center of town, where most sailors assembled when they weren't on their ships. If Savion was anywhere, he would be among them making arrangements to rescue the stranded people.

Finding him turned out to be difficult. Yet, after an hour of slinking around peeking in windows, she was rewarded. He sat at a table in the Dry Desert Tavern flanked by his crew, talking to a group of Malum. *Malum?* How odd.

Backing away from the window, she scanned the street. Evening descended, reeling in the remaining light. Lanterns began to flicker from shops and street posts. Across from the tavern stood a small draper's shop. The owner had just lit a lantern in the window. Perfect.

'Twas a preposterous plan that probably wouldn't work, but it was all she could think of at the moment. Spurred on by her anger at Savion, her broken heart, and her desperation to try everything—anything—to lift the curse in her last two days on land, she tossed all concern aside for anything, save her mission. She would *not* slip back into the sea without a fight!

Pulling pins from her hair, she shook out the strands and allowed them to tumble down her back. Then stepping in front of the Dry Desert Tavern window, she lingered there long enough to ensure Savion spotted her. Once he did, she crossed the street and entered the draper's, smiling.

"We wish a word with you, young Savion."

The Malum's voice turned Savion's stomach before he even looked at the man—a lieutenant in Natas's army by the insignia on his arm and collar. He was flanked by two others of lesser rank: one short, one tall—both with empty eyes and sinister scowls.

Petrok rose to his feet beside Savion, hand on the hilt of his sword. Hona and Verrad did the same. Giving his men a cautious look, Savion also stood and crossed arms over his chest, studying the warrior.

Savion had just concluded making arrangements for five ships to return to the island and rescue the stranded people. Everything was going well. Perdita was settled in a good home—he ignored the pang in his heart at the thought—and his business here in Mirkesh was concluded. Good thing, because the city was overrun with Malum, which was another reason for him to leave posthaste. Besides, he had no sense of need here, and the sooner he put distance between he and Perdita, the better.

But now, this Malum lieutenant stood before him looking more smug and assured than normal, pricking Savion's nerves. Never had they requested an audience with him. Never had they directly attacked him.

Not until he'd met Perdita.

"I'm listening," Savion said.

"Sit. We have much to discuss."

Savion merely stared at him in return. A large man, as some of them were, the lieutenant stood at least a foot above Savion, the breadth of his shoulders reminding him of a sturdy yard on a mast. His dark ratty hair fell down his back. A tiny gold sword hung from his left ear. Candlelight glittered over the various metals hanging on his uniform, while a skull gaped at Savion from a pendant on the man's chest. His friends were shorter: one bald, whereas the other's red hair was pleated and tied behind him. The stink of the three of them made Savion's nose burn.

"Very well, we'll stand." The Malum sneered. He snapped his fingers at a passing maid. "Bring us some bread and wine," he ordered, then turned back to Savion. "You must be hungry after your long journey."

He was. Very hungry. It had been such a busy day, he'd forgotten to eat. "I will not eat bread with you, Malum."

"Hmm."

The woman brought a chunk of bread and a flagon of wine and left it on the table.

"We are done here." Savion started to leave, but the lieutenant stepped in front of him.

"Natas would like to make you an offer."

"What sort of offer?" Petrok burst out angrily.

Savion huffed. "Unless he is surrendering, I'm not interested."

All three Malum chuckled. The short one grabbed the flagon, took a swig, then wiped his mouth on his sleeve and stared at Savion and his friends as if they were cockroaches.

The lieutenant smiled. "Why would Natas surrender when he already rules Erden?"

"He doesn't rule *all* of Erden. And someday he will rule none of it." Savion said with authority. "Speak your offer. I grow weary waiting."

"He wishes to make you his second in command." The Malum's lip twitched. "Even above me."

"Not interested." Savion started to leave when a flash of black hair outside the window caught his gaze. *Perdita.* She crossed the street and entered the draper's. Against his will, his heart leapt in his chest. He hoped she was behaving herself and not getting into mischief.

But she was no longer his problem.

"Think of it," the Malum continued. "You will rule Erden. You will have more power than anyone. More wealth." He followed Savion's glance out the window to Perdita. "More women."

Savion's men were silent beside him as he studied the hideous man. Verrad cleared his throat, his eyes alight with interest. Petrok rubbed his chin as if he were pondering the implications. Did they wish him to take the offer? Were they that hungry for power that they would sell their souls to evil?

"I would rather be the lowliest servant in Nevaeh than rule with Natas," Savion returned.

Verrad moaned.

Shock crossed the Malum's eyes before they hardened again into steel. He spat on the ground. "I told him you were a fool."

Savion pushed the Malum aside and headed toward the door.

The crackle and spit of fire drew his attention across the street. The store Perdita had gone into was in flames!

The Malum lieutenant grabbed Savion's arm. "No need to risk yourself for the lady. She belongs to Natas. If you wish to put the fire out, do it from here—with but a word." He leaned toward him, dousing Savion with his putrid breath. "Prove who you really are," he whispered as his gaze landed on the medallion around Savion's neck.

Savion ripped from his grasp.

"Use the authority given you." The Malum reached for the medallion. Power crackled in the air between them. The amulet heated and sparks flew from it, striking the Malum's hand. Screeching, he snatched it back, his eyes seething hatred.

"I need prove nothing to you," Savion said. "Nor to your master. Now leave."

Then turning, Savion rushed toward the burning building, his men on his heels.

One glance over her shoulder told Perdita that Savion had spotted her. He stood just inside the tavern talking to three Malum, but his eyes were on her. Smiling, she slipped inside the draper's. Five minutes later, she had charmed the owner into believing there were some unsavory sorts behind his store who had attacked her, and grabbing his musket, he ran out to confront them. Biting her lip, she hesitated at the cruelty of her plan, but made a solemn vow to pay the man above and beyond any damage she inflicted. There was no other way. And she was running out of time. After ensuring there was no one else inside, she tipped over the lantern in the window and set the place ablaze.

Flames spread quickly over the bolts of fabric, hungrily consuming everything in their path and reaching for the wooden roof. The owner returned, glanced over his shop with horror, and tried to drag her out the back with him. After she defiantly resisted, he left shouting for help.

The crackle and roar of flames blared like thunder. Heat rose to sear her skin. She inched toward the back of the shop. Where was Savion? Surely he'd seen the fire! The thought that he would allow her to burn made her long to do just that—burn to ash and blow away in the wind. Surely the pain would be less than the one piercing her heart. Smoke filled her lungs. Hacking, she dropped to her knees seeking air. Another minute. She'd give him another minute.

He never came.

Fire reached for her legs, licking, devouring. She couldn't breathe. Ducking beneath the smoke, she crawled toward the back door, guided by a light from outside. She tumbled down the back steps, gasping for air, and landed in the arms of a man.

Savion!

He carried her away from the smoke and flames as the owner returned with a dozen men hoisting buckets of water. She coughed and hacked and gulped for air and clutched his arms. Ah, the feel of him … the strength of him … she could never get enough!

But he placed her on the ground. "What do you think you're doing?"

"What?" She gaped at him, shocked by the fury storming across his face. "What do you mean? Why didn't you come save me?"

Petrok, Hona, and Verrad ran toward them, breathless.

"I'll take her home," he said to his men. "Meet me back at the ship."

They nodded and left, scratching their heads and muttering amongst themselves.

Savion led her away from the line of people passing buckets of water to put out the fire. But it was already out. Smoke curled and sizzled from what was left of the shop as the owner fell to his knees and stared at the devastation in shock.

Grabbing Perdita's arm harshly, Savion pulled her around the buildings and down Main Street. "What were you doing at the draper's?"

Why was he so angry? "Purchasing calico for a new gown, what else?"

"And how were you going to purchase said fabric?"

"I was just looking." She tried to pull away, but Savion held her fast. For the first time, she actually feared what he would do to her.

He halted and spun her to face him. "*You* started the fire."

"Why would I do that?" She tried to sound innocent.

He glared at her. "Because you wanted me to risk my life for you yet again—to prove you are worthy of love."

"No, I didn't . . ." she started, but sighed as defeat stilled her tongue. "What does it matter? You didn't try to save me anyway." She tried to walk away, but he pulled her back.

"I knew it was one of your tricks and you'd eventually come out."

"What if I hadn't?" She fought back tears.

"Stop it, Perdita. Just this one time, please don't lie to me." Grabbing her arms, he shook her as if he could rattle it out of her. "Tell me the truth."

She lowered her chin, her insides wilting. "Yes, I did start the fire."

He released her with a huff. "Go back to the Ackers, Perdita. Get out of my life. And out of my head!" He stormed away.

"I'm sorry, Savion," she shouted after him. "You were so cruel when you left, dropping me off with your friends as if I was naught but a burden to you. You barely said good-bye."

He swung about, more angry than she'd ever seen him. "So you set a man's shop on fire, endanger lives for your own selfish vanity?" He growled. "What of this man's livelihood?"

"I'll repay him."

"How, Perdita?"

She had a feeling she'd cry a bucket of pearls tonight. But she couldn't tell him that. He wouldn't believe she was a mermaid. Nor could she tell him she didn't start the fire just to feel loved and valued. But to be free from her curse. Another thing she couldn't tell him—that she'd been trying to get him to die for her. Not exactly a story that engendered good will. Even if he believed any of it, would the truth make a difference to this honorable man? Or was there no excuse that would appease her selfish acts?

He slowly approached her, blowing out his anger like steam from a kettle. Moonlight cast him in a milky glow as he halted before her and rubbed the back of his neck.

"There is good in you, Perdita. Find it. And when you do, latch onto it and pray to King Abbas for it to grow."

For the first time in her long life, as she stared at this man, she felt ashamed—so very ashamed—of *all* the things she had done. Of all the lies and the tricks and pursuing her own selfish wants, especially at the cost of others' lives. She wanted to be better. Truly, she wanted to change.

"I don't know what to do. Please tell me what to do, Savion."

"Go back to the Ackers, learn a trade, be honorable, give to charity, look for ways to help others. Be good, Perdita." His tone was desperate. "Then you will find the love you seek."

But she wanted *his* love. Yet now, as she looked in his piercing gold eyes, she knew she would never deserve it. Some other woman would win his love. A lady with a pure heart.

"Can you do that for me, Perdita?" he asked.

"Yes." She swallowed down a burst of emotion. "Yes. I can. I will." For the first time, more than even wanting to break the curse, she wanted to be a better person. This man, Savion, had changed her.

"I promise," she added.

He brushed hair from her forehead and planted a kiss upon it. "Now, go with the favor of King Abbas." Releasing her, he took a step back.

A breeze stirred the hair at his collar and brought his scent to her nose. She breathed it in as if it were an elixir. "I won't see you again, will I?"

"No." He lifted her hand and kissed it. "Be good, Perdita." Then turning, he walked away.

She watched him until the shadows stole him from view, until she could no longer hear his footsteps. Then she dropped to the ground and cried.

Chapter 23

The next two days went by in a numbing haze. Still, Perdita kept her word to Savion. Though her heart was hopelessly broken, she spent her time helping the Ackers in their shop, running errands, and greeting customers. They were good people, who still loved each other after forty years of marriage. Watching them brought a smile to her face, but also pained her deeply, knowing she would never be loved like that—knowing she would never be worthy. Her only joy was in the great meals Mrs. Ackers provided: roasted goose with sage and onion dressing, boar's head, fresh oysters, yams, mince pie, and mango pudding. After two days, Perdita's gown grew tight, but soon enough she'd be subjected to meals of crab and seaweed.

Despite how difficult it was to spend her last days on land working, she found she rather enjoyed being good. The Ackers were a charitable couple who often sent Perdita out on errands of mercy to needy neighbors. 'Twas on such an errand to bring food and medicine to a starving family that Perdita experienced more joy then she could have imagined. She'd also been most pleased with herself when she'd given the owner of the draper's shop a pouch of pearls to pay for repairs. The expression on his face and his grateful exclamations would certainly bring her comfort through her upcoming decade of loneliness.

Now, as she walked down Main Street on her way to deliver a pair of mended shoes to a patron, she took a moment to close her eyes and soak in the warmth of the sun, feel the breeze dancing through her hair, and inhale the scents of salt and smoke and horses. And life—life above the waves. Horses clip-clopped past, people chattered, children laughed, wagons creaked, and bells rang from the harbor. She would miss it all.

She would miss Savion most of all. How she wished he could see that she'd kept her promise. That she was being charitable and good and doing honorable work. But he had probably already set sail. She hadn't ventured down to the wharves to look for his ship, fearing she wouldn't be able to control her tears when she found it gone.

Now, pushing through the doors of the tavern where the patron was staying, she surveyed the tables spread across the dining area to her left. Serving maids doled out steaming plates of corn fritters and smoked pork for the noon meal. Her stomach grumbled. Mayhap she'd stay after her business was concluded and enjoy a meal. All around her people chatted and laughed, enjoying their afternoon as a cool breeze blew in through the windows.

Whistles flew at her from a dark corner to her right where men were served drinks, but she ignored them and inquired of a man standing behind a desk where she might find a Mr. Garnet.

The tall man with a thin mustache pointed to a lone older gentleman eating his meal at a table near the window.

Hoisting her sack, she started toward him, when a hand clamped around her arm. She spun around, intending to give the man his comeuppance for daring to touch her, but a familiar face swayed before her.

Verrad.

"Well, if it isn't the mers…maid?" He slurred, then stumbled, catching himself on a nearby table. The reek of spirits assailed her.

Heart in her throat, she turned to leave, but he tugged her back.

"Let me go this instant!" she shouted for all to hear, hoping someone would come to her rescue. All it did was draw all eyes her way.

Verrad lifted his chin and blinked as if trying to focus. "I have an announcessment to make. This woman is a mersmaid." He hiccupped.

Laughter tumbled through the room.

Horrified, Perdita struggled against his grip. Pain etched up her arm. She swung the bag of shoes at his head, but he grabbed them from her. "Tsk, tsk, tsk, mersmaid."

"Please, help me!" She appealed to those around her. One man, who was as wide as he was tall, rose from his chair and sauntered toward her, licking his lips.

"I's can prove it." Verrad continued. He yanked her closer, grabbed the lacing of her bodice and ripped them open.

Perdita shrieked. "How dare you!"

Tightening his grip, he tore the fabric down her left side, exposing skin at her waist. Women gasped. Husbands hurried wives and children from the tavern. Men stared. Anger and embarrassment stormed through Perdita until she was sure her face was as red as a lobster. Furious, she attempted to hold the sides of her gown together, but Verrad held them open and leaned over to peer at her waist. "Hmm." He grunted and almost fell over, then ripped the fabric even more. "Where are they?"

Were there no gentlemen in this place? Perdita wanted to cry. She couldn't. So she screamed and slugged him across the jaw.

Blinking, he stumbled back, rubbing his cheek. "Where's your gills, mersmaid?"

"You're mad! Get away from me!" She surveyed what was left of the crowd. Most simply stared at her, smiling as if she were the afternoon entertainment. A few of the serving maids gaped at her in horror. Finally the thin man from behind the desk appeared, pistol in hand, and pointed it straight at Verrad. "Lay off her, you besotted oaf, or I'll put one through your skull."

Eye twitching, Verrad gave a disgruntled huff and slunk back into the shadows. The owner lowered his weapon and turned away. Relieved, Perdita scanned the floor for the sack of shoes, when the portly man who resembled a puffer fish grabbed her arm.

"I'll save ye. Come on to Bernie, littl' darlin'." He plopped down at a nearby table and pulled her into his lap.

Just as Savion charged into the tavern.

His eyes shifted from her ripped gown and her bared skin to the lecherous grin of the man who clutched her. Her heart raced at the sight of him, then plummeted at the disgust on his face. She was about to appeal for his help when he shook his head. "You promised, Perdita." With that, he marched out of the tavern.

Perdita kicked the obese clod in the shin over and over. Yelping, he shoved her to the ground and limped away, mumbling. "Taint no woman worth that."

She longed to run after Savion and explain what had happened. She longed to tell him how good she had been. Instead, she crumpled to the floor and watched two cockroaches devour a meal of spilt ale.

What would be the sense? He wouldn't believe her anyway.

After a few minutes, an elderly woman with curls poking from within a white mobcap—who Perdita assumed was the owner's wife—wrapped a cloak around Perdita and led her away. But what did it matter? Savion would forever think she was nothing but a tramp.

"Come join us for a drink," a voice beckoned Verrad from the dark corner. He wouldn't have gone except he thought he heard something about a drink. Stumbling, he dropped into a chair and peered through the shadows at a man dressed in fine silk with Caestrian lace bubbling from his neck and cuffs. The waning candlelight revealed dark hair streaked in gray, a cultured beard, and jewel-laden fingers, along with a pretentious grin. Two large well-armed men sat on either side of him.

"Rum," Verrad shouted to a passing wench.

She slammed a sloshing mug in front of him and held out her hand. The finely-dressed man flipped her a coin.

Verrad took a sip. "I thank you for your hospitality, Mr. Gund."

"So, you know me." Pride etched the man's voice.

"Everyone knows the second most powerful man in Erden." Now, if only the man would stop spinning in Verrad's vision.

"I couldn't help but notice we have a common interest." Damien took a puff of his cigar and blew the smoke over Verrad.

He batted it away. "We do?"

"The mermaid, you fatwit."

"I knew it!" Verrad slammed his fist on the table, drawing glances his way.

"Quiet, you fool!" Damien hissed.

"When I saw you in Kadon, I knew Perdita had to be the mersmaid you were looking for." Verrad slumped back in his chair and rubbed his eyes. "But I don't think so anymore. I tossssed water on her and no tail appeared. I tried to make her cry and no pearls. And now, theres were no gills on her side where they were supposed to be."

"Seems you've done your homework on mermaids."

"Of course." Verrad gulped his rum. "She plans harm to my captain. It's my duty to protect him."

"That do-gooder Savion?" Damien snorted and his men chuckled.

Verrad set his mug down and leaned forward. “He’s a great man.”

“He keeps getting in my way. Showing up to save her when I am about to finally capture her.”

Verrad belched. “I’ll agree with you on that. He won’t listen to reason when it comes to the wench.”

Damien puffed on his cigar, the ruby on his hand twinkling in the candlelight. “So, what is it you want with her?”

“Nothing. I wish to protect my captain.” The chair wobbled, or was it the room?

Damien chuckled. “It has nothing to do with those pearls you spoke of earlier, I suppose.”

Verrad grinned. “Perhaps.” He tried to focus on the man. If only Savion had agreed to Natas’s offer, he would be even more powerful and wealthier than this bloated fool. Why had he turned it down? He constantly proclaimed that his purpose was to help others and do good. Think of the good he could do with all that power!

Damien slapped Verrad on the back, nearly toppling him. “How fortuitous that your captain brought both you and the mermaid here to me.”

“And why’s that?”

“I propose a deal, my new friend.”

Friend? Friend to one of the most powerful men in Erden! Things were looking up for Verrad. “What deal?”

“The mermaid knows you. You can lure her into my trap.”

Verrad snorted. “As you saw, she doesn’t trust me.”

“But she trusts your captain, does she not?”

Verrad sipped his rum, forcing his numb mind to think. The wench *did* trust Savion. She would do anything he asked. “What do I get?”

“What is it you want?”

No one had ever asked Verrad that before. He took another sip and allowed the pungent liquor to warm his throat. What *did* he truly want? Riches, yes. Power, of course. Women always. But most of all, Verrad wanted Savion to rule. The man was destined for it. Verrad wouldn't even mind being his second-in-command. Yet repeatedly, Savion resisted accepting the power that was his due. Why? It was beyond infuriating. No, Savion was far too humble to ever take his rightful place. All he needed was a little push from Verrad.

CHAPTER 24

Through all the heartbreaks Perdita had suffered, through all the pain of rejection, this final one by Savion was the worst of all. The look of disappointment and disgust on his face would forever be imprinted on her mind. No doubt it would haunt her in the endless years to come, reminding her she would never be good enough. Even when she tried. And she *had* tried. She'd tried so hard to be good. But her past, her curse, and her lies had all caught up with her. Surely, her crumbling heart didn't have the will to keep beating much longer. If only death would find her—set her free! But she knew it wouldn't. She would live with this pain forever. Until it drove her completely mad.

Her feet as heavy as bricks, she plodded down the street, hugging herself. The tavern owner's wife had been kind enough to provide Perdita with a new gown, albeit a rather large gown that even now dragged in the dirt. No matter. She had nowhere to go. In fact, she had no idea where she was heading, save out of town and away from people. She couldn't face the Ackers's scorn when she told them she'd lost the shoes. One more look of disapproval would be the end of her. Instead, she would search for a pleasant spot in the hills bordering the town where she could spend her last two days in peace. Perchance King Abbas would grant her at least that.

Scattered rain drops fell. Lightly at first. Then it seemed the skies unleashed whips of rain to punish her.

Zost! Clutching her skirts, she slogged through the mud forming on the street.

A splash sounded behind her. Whirling around, she wiped water from her eyes. Verrad's tall dripping form appeared out of the torrent. She backed away. "Stay away! I warn you!"

He held out hands of surrender. "Don't fear me. I came to apologize."

"Yes, I've heard your apology before."

"I don't blame you for not believing me. Or trusting me." The rain lessened to thick droplets that plopped into puddles around them. "I thought you were a mermaid and would hurt Savion. I know now I was wrong."

She took another step back. "Please, just go."

Standing there, dripping wet, with his dark hair flattened on his head and his eyes no longer filled with spite, he looked like a little boy who'd somehow lost his way. "He's hurt," he continued. "A loose tackle fell and struck him in the leg. Haddeus says it's broken, so he sent me."

"Savion?" Alarm sped through her.

"Yes. I explained to him what I did, that what he saw in the tavern wasn't your fault, and he wants to apologize."

She eyed him suspiciously. "Why didn't he send Petrok or Hona? He knows I won't come with you."

"They are readying the ship to sail. Remember, I'm only a deck hand now." One side of his lips lifted.

"He's finally leaving town, then." She swallowed down the pain.

"Tonight."

This was her last chance to see Savion. To explain everything and mayhap see approval—even affection—beam from his eyes. She had no hope of anything more than that, but at least she would take good memories with her to sea.

"Very well."

Verrad smiled and gestured back toward town. "Follow me."

Savion couldn't get away from Mirkesh fast enough. Too many Malum roamed the streets, he sensed no need here that required his help, and he couldn't get Perdita—barely clad in the arms of that sailor—out of his mind. She had said she loved him, just as Lorelei had done. Lies! All of them lies. How could any woman love one man and then turn around and give herself to another—many others? Though his heart felt like mashed yams, Savion was glad he'd entered that tavern when he did. Now he knew without a doubt he'd made the right decision.

Pacing in his cabin, he reached the bulkhead and spun around. Still, why did it hurt so much? Perhaps once he was back out to sea and on to his next mission, thoughts of Perdita would fade, and he would find peace once again.

He longed for her to turn away from the mess she'd made of her life through her selfishness, vanity, and lies and find the abundant life offered through being honest, kind, charitable, and moral. But he knew now that his hopes would never be realized.

She would never change.

Which was why he must get as far away from her as he could.

If only he could get some sleep and be rested for the morning's travels. Instead, he found himself pacing endlessly through the night. Sometime in the dark hours, he fell into a chair, head in hands, but couldn't shake his emotions. He tried to feel the power in the medallion, to hear what his next step should be, to remember the words of his father, but there was nothing.

As sunlight speared the stern windows, the expected change to his dour mood never came. Instead, a headache grew and he started pacing again. Finally, a knock sounded on his door.

Hona, Nuto, and Petrok stood before him.

"Verrad hasn't shown up?"

"No, Captain."

Verrad. Did the sot have to go drinking and carousing in every port town? His wayward purser was the reason Savion ran into Perdita in the first place.

"We won't wait for him," Savion said. "It's dawn and we must be away. Have you loaded the goods on board?"

Hona nodded. "We should make a decent wage transporting them to Jamak."

"Good. We need the money. Let's get—"

Verrad burst into the cabin, his shirt unbuttoned, his breeches stained, and his hair out of place. "It's Perdita."

Though his heart clenched, Savion held up his hand. "I don't want to hear it. Petrok, weigh anchor and make all sail."

"Aye, Captain." Petrok shot Verrad a look of disdain in passing.

"But, Captain—" Verrad urged.

Savion turned to his quartermaster. "Hona, set a course north-by-northeast for Jamak."

"Aye." He started for the door.

"What you think you saw in that tavern wasn't true, Captain." Verrad's voice held an unusual panic.

Hona halted and turned. Savion marched to his desk. "I *said* I didn't want to hear it."

"It's Damien Gund. He's the one who ripped her dress. He shoved her into the arms of that sailor. She was only there delivering shoes for the cobblers you placed her with."

Savion studied Verrad with suspicion. "How do you know this?"

Verrad sighed and rubbed his temples as if they pained him. "Because I was there. I was sitting at a table in the shadows—quite drunk I might add."

Savion drew close. The stench of stale alcohol permeated his clothes. That much seemed true. As for the rest of it …

"It's true, Captain." Verrad shifted blood-shot eyes between Savion's. "I swear."

"Why help a woman you tortured when you thought her a mermaid?"

Verrad released a heavy sigh. "Because I regret my foolishness. I was wrong, and this is one way I can make it up to her."

Conflicting emotions tromped through Savion. "What is that to me? As long as she's back safe with the Ackers, she'll be all right."

"That's just it, Captain. She's been kidnapped by Damien Gund. He captured her last night and sailed away on his ship, the *White Crypt*."

CHAPTER 25

The ship canted and the irons yanked Perdita's wrists, scraping her skin raw. Creaks and groans of wood rose to join the slosh of water in the barrel she stood in. An ache wrenched down her arms and across her shoulders from being chained to the hull above her head. A continual throb pulsated across her back from being slammed against the edge of the barrel. But it was the wound in her heart that would be her undoing.

The ship righted itself as the purl of the sea joined the rats squealing and scampering about the hold. It had been a day—a long, torturous day—and she'd long since gotten used to the stench and the darkness. But not the rats.

Nor the incessant itching from her drowned legs.

She should tell them they didn't have to soak her legs in water in order for her to transform into a mermaid. That would happen tomorrow all on its own. Then Damien would have his proof.

And his revenge.

No doubt he had plans on how best to enact that revenge: using her as a carnival exhibit, mining her for tears, forcing her to heal his wounds until she had no strength left. And when he was satisfied, he could always give her to the Malum to torment endlessly.

But the worst part was, she couldn't even release the tears heaping up behind her eyes. She *wouldn't* allow herself to cry and give Damien the pearls he sought.

Lantern light on the ladder preceded the clomp of boots, and Perdita braced herself for more of Damien's gloating tirades. Did he never tire of punishing her? For a man of such power and wealth, she assumed he'd send down one of his lackeys to spit on her and strike her face. But apparently she was special enough to warrant the derision of the man himself.

"Hello, my pretty mermaid." His voice was caustic as he held up the lantern to inspect her. "What? No tail yet? And here I thought you were at the end of your time on land." He stopped and studied her. "Oh yes, I see you are surprised that I know about that." He tapped his head as if a massive brain protruded from it. "I've spent many years trying to figure out how you could have spent so much time on land with my father." He hung the lantern on a hook and studied her. "And I've talked to the relatives of some of your victims—Geeden Tyne's son, for one."

Perdita flinched at the name.

He sneered. "You do remember Geeden Jr., don't you? You tried to bury him alive in a cave."

Perdita wanted to tell him that Geeden was a horker and wasn't man enough to rescue his cat from a tree. "I don't know who you are talking about nor why you have me in this water. You're clearly mad."

The strike came hard and swift. The force of it shoved her head to the left as pain radiated across her cheek and down her jaw.

He shook his hand. "Then, there was my father, of course. Raynar Gund. You do remember him?"

Perdita swallowed the sudden shame that clogged her throat. Sails thundered overhead and the deck tilted. Damien leaned on a post for support while the irons bit at Perdita's skin. Of course she remembered Raynar. Ivan twenty-eight. Though it had happened twenty years ago, the memory was as fresh as if it was yesterday.

Thankfully, he'd been much more attractive than his son. But what had happened to him, what she'd caused … She shook her head and shriveled at the hatred seething on

Damien's face, made all the more hideous by the shifting lantern light. Mayhap she should tell him her side of things. Mayhap he would see reason.

"You didn't mean to leave him in the middle of the sea?" he asked.

"Nay. Nor did I know he would dive in after me."

"Finally you admit *what* you are." He took up a pace, bristling and fuming like a caged bull.

She had tried more than once to get Raynar to sacrifice himself for her. She'd leapt in the path of a charging wild boar, forced herself to trip and fall down two flights of stairs, "happened" upon a nest of killer ants. But each time he either pretended not to notice the threat or bumbled so much in his rescue attempt that he never risked his life. They were heading to Simar to get married, but a storm delayed their progress. Perdita knew her time as a human was at an end, so she slipped into the sea at night, hoping Raynar would give up looking for her. Of course he would. He had more than proven he was not the courageous type. How was she to know he would spot her in the distance and dive in after her?

"I didn't ask him to come after me. I didn't want him to—"

"You little vixen!" Damien slapped her again. She spit out blood. "Do you know what was left of him when his crew finally hauled him aboard?"

She didn't want to know. She had smelled the blood from a mile away.

"One leg and part of his torso."

Nausea rose in her throat. She'd seen the shark approach but couldn't get to him in time. If only Raynar had risked himself an hour before. Just an hour earlier and she would have become human again. But she hated herself for even thinking that now.

Damien struck her again. This time blood spurted from her nose.

"You will pay, mermaid! You will pay." And with that, he grabbed the lantern and marched up the stairs, taking the light with him.

A rat approached, stopping on its hind legs to stare at her, but then skittered away as if climbing the barrel to get to her wasn't worth the trouble.

Hours passed in endless misery until finally the slosh of bilge in the hold softened along with the rush of water against the hull. No doubt night had descended. Hungry, thirsty, and devoid of all hope, Perdita's head lobbed back and forth with the sway of the ship as she fell into a semiconscious state of exhaustion.

Pain faded … hunger and thirst satiated … her irons fell … her rags transformed into a snowy wedding gown embedded with crystals. She stood in a magnificent church with rows and rows of onlookers extending behind her to massive white doors. Before her, a golden altar glittered in the light of several candles, while a choir dressed in white robes sang the most beautiful song she'd ever heard. Their faces held such joy and peace, she could hardly pull her eyes away. Stained glass rose behind them to the ceiling, depicting a land of such beauty, it made Erden look like a slum.

A being made of light approached and stopped before her. To her right, Savion, dressed in a fine suit of black camlet and a purple robe trimmed in gold, looked like a prince. His hair was groomed and slicked behind him, and when his piercing golden eyes met hers, she wanted nothing more than to be with him. He slid his hand in hers as the man of light began reciting from a book.

She was marrying Savion? Had he broken the curse? She shifted her legs and found them sturdy and wonderfully human, and her heart swelled to near bursting.

Thunder bellowed outside the window. The choir stopped and murmurs spread through the crowd. Perdita's wedding dress shriveled into filthy rags, stained and torn. Her hair became as dry as straw. She shrieked as Savion's hand slipped from hers, then turned to see Raynar Gund standing beside her instead. He rubbed his finely-groomed goatee and smiled. Out of all the Ivans, he had professed his love most ardently. He had not only showered expensive gifts upon her, he'd spent every second of the entire month with her, groveling at her feet, loving her with his body.

"What are you doing here, Raynar?"

His gaze dropped to her rags. His smile turned into a smirk. "I never loved you, Perdita. I thought I did. I loved the idea of you, the passion and romance. And of course your beauty. But that is gone now." He looked away in disgust. "And so am I."

His body folded in on itself and fell in a heap to the floor, a bloody mass of flesh.

Vomit rose in her throat, and she turned away, breath heaving.

Savion appeared at the side of the altar. She reached for him, but he shook his head in disappointment and left through a door in the back. Her glance took in the white robes of the choir, the golden altar, the light beyond the colorful glass and then down at her stained rags and filthy skin.

"I am undone. I am unworthy." She dropped to her knees. "Please let me die."

The man in light grabbed a pair of tongs and plucked a coal from the altar, bringing it to her.

"You must choose the light," he said, then lowered the searing coal to her lips.

She awoke slumped against the barrel in the ship, weak and sick. The man's words echoed through the hold.

You must choose the light. But darkness surrounded her. The gush of water against the hull had ceased, and she could hear a sail flapping in the wind and footsteps far above. A mighty chain rattled before the anchor splashed into the sea.

They had reached their destination.

Perdita's lips burned.

Savion stood at the taffrail gazing over the ebony sea. A full moon draped strips of silver atop select waves as the *Scepter* rose and plunged through the waters on its way to rescue Perdita. *Yet again.* Only, this time, Savion wasn't entirely sure it was her doing. Not if what Verrad said was true. The ship tumbled down the trough of a swell, and Savion braced his boots further apart on the deck. Salty mist sprayed over him, dampening his skin and hair.

If what Verrad said was true, Perdita was in real trouble. Damien Gund was not a man who dealt kindly with others. For years, Savion had suspected that he'd formed an unholy alliance with Natas. His methods of acquiring wealth not only preyed on the less fortunate but forced them into cruel subjugation to Natas's interests. Either way, Savion could not allow the fiend to follow through with whatever evil plans he had for Perdita.

The ship bucked again, and Savion gripped the moist railing and stared at the foam climbing the bow of the ship as if it were trying to drag him to the depths. It would never succeed. Not until he completed his mission. And only if King Abbas willed.

He glanced over his shoulder at the men on watch and those tending sails. They'd been surprised to see him come above while it was still dark—especially Hona, who was now manning the helm. But Savion couldn't sleep. How could he, when he had no clue what Perdita was enduring, whether she was hurt, being ravished … or worse.

"Father, what is this woman to me?" Wind gusted over him, and he struck the railing with his fist. "I cannot seem to rid myself of her, either physically or emotionally. Are you still testing me? Or perhaps"—the word reminded him of Perdita's archaic speech—"*mayhap* she is more than that. Perhaps *she* is the one I am to save?"

No answer came, but Savion swore the amulet around his neck warmed. Which meant he was on the right path.

A band of gray formed on the horizon, faintly separating sky and sea. Within minutes, it transformed into gold and coral, announcing the arrival of the sun's reign and forcing the moon to retreat. Slicking the moisture back through his hair, Savion drew a deep breath and asked his father for strength and wisdom for whatever lay ahead. Peace swelled in his heart, and he finally felt the turmoil of the past days vanish. Wheeling, he marched to the main deck to issue orders to raise all sails to the wind.

Two hours later, with the sun beating down on them and the deck heaving beneath them, Savion stood at the main rail, Petrok on his right, Verrad on his left.

"Aye, that's the island, Captain." Verrad lowered the telescope and handed it to Savion. The slight shift of Verrad's eyes spun a thread of distrust through Savion. Shrugging it off, he lifted the glass to his eye and brought the island into focus.

Skull Island. At least that's what he thought it was called. Uninhabited, except for a few peaceful natives, and with no decent harbor and not enough land for farming, it wasn't even marked on most maps. And at the moment, it appeared no ships were in sight.

"What possible motive could Damien have for coming here?" Savion lowered the glass and shook his head. "Are you sure this is the place?"

"Yes," Verrad replied, staring off into the distance. "Skull Island. That's what he said."

Petrok scratched his dark head. "Perhaps Damien needs food and water."

Savion frowned. "Unlikely. He's only been at sea for two days. Besides, there were plenty of other ports along the way with far more enticing entertainments. No." Savion slapped the scope against his palm. "What does he want *here* with Perdita?"

Verrad gripped the railing. "Sell her to the natives?"

The thought had occurred to Savion. But it didn't make sense. Natives had nothing of value Damien wanted. Why not just sell her as a slave to one of the wealthy overlords as Savion heard Damien was prone to do with women who displeased him? A woman like Perdita would bring quite a fortune.

"Lower sail and bring us in easy, Petrok," Savion ordered, sending his first mate barreling down to the main deck, braying orders.

"Lay aloft! Furl main-and-fore sails! In spanker and jib!"

"Maybe his ship needs careening or other repairs," Nuto offered.

Unease flooded Savion. If Damien had set sail before Savion, why wasn't he here already? Savion scanned the small inlet on the lee side of the island, the most logical place to anchor. Yet he could see nothing but turquoise waters and a sandy beach framed with palms and palmettos.

Wind raked through his hair, sending a chill down his back.

"Bring us within thirty yards of that inlet," Savion ordered Hona. "But no closer." Not until he made sure Damien wasn't around. After that, he could go about setting a trap for the scoundrel.

With all but topsails lowered and the ship veering slightly to port, the *Scepter* eased alongside Skull Island—

aptly named because when it had first been discovered, the beaches were lined with skulls. Apparently the original inhabitants had been cannibals.

Sweat streamed down Savion's back as he studied every cliff, rock, beach, and cove that gave the island its jagged appearance. "Looks like they aren't here yet."

Verrad shrugged.

Petrok appeared beside him. "Orders, Captain."

"Bring us into that inlet ahead. Slow and easy." Savion glanced at the two lookouts he'd stationed above. Spyglasses to their eyes, they perused the island as he'd instructed them. Surely they would see anything suspicious before Savion did.

Then why did he feel so unsettled? Verrad shifted nervously beside Savion.

So his friend felt it too. "What's got you all jittery, Verrad?"

Verrad barely looked his way before turning back to the island, but what Savion saw in those dark eyes made his mouth suddenly dry.

Boom!

Savion had no time to react before the chain shot sped overhead with an eerie whine and struck the mainmast above the course. "Battle stations!" He stormed across the deck.

Off their stern, a ship, its white sails filling with wind, emerged from a hidden alcove and sped toward them.

The ominous crack of splitting wood etched terror down Savion's spine as the mainmast split.

"Look out below!" Petrok yelled. Men scrambled for cover as the mast, complete with yards, sails, lines, and tackles, came tumbling down to the deck in a tangled web of destruction.

The *Scepter* staggered beneath the jolt. Howls punched the air. Two men dropped to the deck, injured.

After ordering them brought below to Haddeus, the sound of gushing water drew Savion to lean over the railing. Smoke curled from a hole in the hull that was half below the waterline.

A sailor poked his head through a hatch on deck. "We're taking on water, Captain."

"Nathan, Tund—man the pumps!" Savion pointed to two men, then turned to Bart. "Take Simeon and Matias and try to patch that hole." All the men sped off, fear on their faces.

Bilging fast, without a mainmast, and with a list to starboard, they'd lost both speed and maneuverability. And if they couldn't patch that hole, they'd sink within the hour. Savion glanced at the *White Crypt,* fast approaching on their starboard quarter. A few more well-placed shots from them, and it would be all over.

"If we drift into the cove we'll be trapped!" Petrok shouted. Yet the winds and current were driving them to do just that.

"Nuto, ready the guns. Run them out on my order." Savion would not go down without a fight. The master gunner sped off and dropped below, his commands to the gun crew echoing above.

Savion turned to find Verrad, grabbed his shirt, and flung him against the bulwarks. "You knew this was a trap! Why? Why would you betray us?"

Verrad clutched Savion's choking hands, his eyes filled with rage. And something else—desperation. "I did it for *you*. You can defeat Damien! I know you can. I've sailed with you long enough to see what you can do. Your powers are like no other. He is Natas's top man—if you kill him, you can take his place. Think of the good you can do!"

"Good?" Savion flung his arms up. "You don't care about doing *good,* Verrad. You only care about power."

Verrad wiped sweat from his forehead and stepped up. "How long must we sail with you before you take what is rightfully yours?"

Savion shook his head angrily. "I am not here to rule, but to serve. When are you going to understand that, Verrad? Leave. Swim to your master." He glanced at the *White Crypt* veering to block the entrance to the inlet and trap them within. "I haven't time to deal with you now."

Savion turned and bellowed, "Drop the anchor, Petrok, before we ground the keel."

The first mate nodded and ordered the crew to task. Most of them stood frozen in place, shock and despair on their faces as they watched their enemy positioning to fire a broadside upon them. Their glances sped to Savion, longing for his assurance, hoping he had a plan.

But he had no plan. He fingered his medallion, seeking wisdom, peace, anything. He'd been foolish to trust Verrad. His love for Perdita—his desperation to rescue her—had muffled the voice within that had warned him. Now, he would once again pay the price for loving a woman. And trusting a friend.

The *White Crypt* lowered sails and glided into the inlet just twenty yards off the *Scepter*'s beam. Her anchor splashed to the seabed, and Damien himself, all silk and lace and glittering gold, swaggered to stand amidships and raised a cone to his lips.

"Surrender at once or face the full force of my broadside!"

No doubt he wanted whatever goods Savion had on board, including his ship, or he'd have already blasted them to bits. Savion drew a deep breath and gripped the railing, gazing at the colorful fish swimming about the hull. *Father, I need your help.* He closed his eyes and waited, listening to the lap of water, creak of wood, and whistle of wind through the rigging.

And then it came.

Despite the dire predicament, despite their impending death, peace bubbled up within Savion like nothing he'd ever experienced. His medallion warmed against his chest, and he knew he could never surrender. He *would* never surrender.

Petrok and Hona appeared beside him, fear tightening their features.

Savion grinned. "Let's give the man our answer, shall we?"

Chapter 26

Perdita's bones shook. The irons around her wrists rattled. The hull trembled. The blast of the cannon thundered in her ears—over and over, ringing terror through her soul. Footsteps thudded above her. Muffled shouts drifted to her ears. Even the rats sped for cover. Who had they fired upon? Was she now to be in a sea battle? Chained and defenseless?

Sails snapped and wood creaked as the ship swerved and the deck tilted. Slimy bilge water gushed toward her filled with rats struggling to stay afloat. It slapped against the hull and splashed over her face and arms. She spit it away, nearly retching as the ship teetered in the other direction, drawing the water and rats with it. Water spilled from her barrel. Her legs began to itch.

Zost! Not now. The itch intensified. Of all the times to turn back into a mermaid. Without the ability to walk, she'd be trapped for sure. The itching turned to pain until she thought she'd go mad if she didn't scratch. Her feet snapped together. Scales formed, binding her skin, wrapping around her legs, marching up her thighs to claim her waist.

A cannon roared. The hull shuddered. Perdita's ears nearly burst. Shouts of victory blared from above. She pitied the poor fool Damien was attacking. Whoever it was, she longed for them to return fire, blast holes through the ship, or better yet, blow it to bits. She may end up in agonizing pain for several months, but at least she'd be free of Damien Gund.

Her lungs started to collapse. If she didn't get beneath the water soon, she'd suffer tremendous pain as she suffocated over and over. It had happened to her once before when she'd lost track of time and transformed an hour from shore.

The purl of the water against the hull softened, the anchor released, and the ship jerked to a stop. The squawking of birds told her they were near land. Her hopes lifted.

But Damien's graveling voice crushed them as he ordered his foe to surrender.

Struggling against her chains, she tried to lower her head into the barrel, gasping for a breath of water, but it only reached her belly.

She strained to hear anything that would clue her in to what was happening. She was rewarded by the sound of several distant cannons. *Boom! Boom! Boom! Boom!*

Shouts clamored from above.

The hull exploded. Seawater gushed in through a hole just a foot above Perdita's head. Dazed, she gulped in the liquid, filling her lungs and reviving her body. The force of it shoved her across the hold. Across the hold? The blast had broken her chains!

Dare she hope? Had the stars shone down upon her?

Fighting the current, she swam to the hole. Seawater slammed her. She clutched the jagged edges and struggled to pull herself through. Voices sounded behind her, muffled in the water. They were coming to inspect the damage! The hole wasn't big enough for her.

Thunder roared through the ship. The rising water quivered beneath what had to be Damien firing a broadside.

She glanced back at the ladder. Lantern light trickled down it. A boot appeared. Thrusting herself into the opening, she sucked in her stomach and chest and pushed herself through. Sharp spikes cut her skin. Ignoring the pain, she popped out the other side, fully expecting someone to grab her tail and pull her back in. When no one did, she swam to the seabed just a few feet below the keel of the ship and glanced up. No one came after her!

She was free!

Elated, she flapped her tail and sped off into the deep, away from the island, away from Damien, and away from the hideous battle.

Speeding quickly through the water, she watched as the corals disappeared and the seabed dropped out of view. Her wrists stung where her chains had been, and she stopped to seek out some seaweed with which to bind them. The muted sound of a distant boom traveled over her in a wave, and she peered through the murky sea toward the island. Why was she in such a hurry? She had nothing to look forward to but a broken heart, an empty cave she called home, and ten years of loneliness.

She broke the surface and looked back, curious to see who Damien was firing upon. Mayhap she could give them some help.

The *Scepter*! Smoke poured from the ship's hull where Damien's broadside had taken out her guns. Her mainmast fell in a heap of spikes and netting. Her crew lined the railing awaiting their fate. Perdita's heart sank to the seabed.

Had Savion come for her? Nay. He couldn't have known where she was. Had he sensed her distress? Why wasn't he winning as he always did?

She couldn't leave him. She *wouldn't* leave him at the mercy of that monster.

Shouts from the *White Crypt* indicated they'd discovered her missing. Damien's angry cursing confirmed it as he slugged one man across the jaw and marched toward the railing. Grabbing his scope, he scanned the seas.

On the other side of his ship, sharpshooters sped to the top while culverins were being loaded to attack Savion and his men. Both would do more damage to humans than the ship.

She couldn't allow that.

There wasn't much she could do to stop Damien save distracting him. If she could keep his focus on her rather than blowing Savion from the water, maybe that would buy Savion some time.

Diving, she hurried back into the inlet. The seabed rose rapidly until she had but ten yards of water in which to maneuver. Positioning herself between Damien's ship and an outcropping of rocky cliffs, she popped her head above water and shouted, "Damien! I've escaped you yet again!"

Damien lowered his scope and gaped at her, jaw dropped.

Just as she expected, he ordered a boat lowered and filled it with men. Two boats, in fact—one headed for shore and the other one Damien climbed into before it started in her direction.

She spun, headed toward the cliffs, and squeezed between two rock walls. Several narrow pathways between rocks and boulders spread out in all directions. Good. She dove and found the underwater passages widened and opened into deep pools. She could easily lose Damien's men in here, and then dive beneath the water whenever she wished to avoid them.

This would keep him occupied for hours—enough time for Savion to slip away. Afterward, she would find an outlet and escape out to sea. Yet, after Perdita explored several narrow passages, she found they were all dead ends. Even beneath the water there was no opening through which she could leave. Finally, swimming down one final shaft, she entered a cave that was half underwater, half above, just like her home. Surely there was a way out. But after close examination, naught but rock surrounded her.

She was trapped.

CHAPTER 27

"Have they forgotten about us?" Petrok asked, brandishing his sword as if he could slice the incoming cannon balls in half.

"Unlikely." Savion stared in confusion. The men who were preparing to fire upon them from the *White Crypt* had suddenly stopped and rushed over to the opposite side of the ship, while Damien marched across the deck, huffing and puffing like a smokestack.

"Verrad's dead." Haddeus's tortured voice turned Savion about to see that the doctor's hands, face, and clothes were stained with blood, his eyes numb with horror.

Savion gasped. "How?"

"He was on the gun deck when that last broadside hit. Shot got him right in the gut. Ripped him in two."

Petrok sank back to lean on the railing, his breath coming hard. Hona groaned and spun to face the sea.

Sorrow clamped Savion's heart. "Anyone else injured?"

"Just him, Captain."

Visions of Verrad flooded Savion's mind: sharing meals amid laughter and singing, fighting Malum hoards side by side, late-night chats when neither could sleep. Emotion burned in Savion's throat both at his death and his betrayal. "Wrap what's left of him in sail cloth. We'll bury him later."

"Isn't that Perdita?" Hona's shocked voice instantly brought Savion around.

Savion grabbed the scope and lifted it to his eye. There, beyond Damien's ship, a woman clung to a boulder before an outcropping of jagged cliffs, waving. *Waving?* Black hair spiraled over her chest in streams of ink. Perdita! What was she doing? She must have escaped from Damien's ship. But why in the name of Erden wasn't she hiding?

"By all the powers that be, it's her!" Petrok exclaimed.

"What is she doing?" Hona squinted to see her.

Movement caught Savion's eye, and he shifted the scope to see two boats leave the *White Crypt*—one headed for shore, the other toward Perdita. He focused on the second boat, and Damien's stern, angry face came into view.

"Vak! He's going after her!" Savion slammed the scope shut and punched the railing.

Petrok grabbed his shoulder. "She lured them toward her to save us, Captain."

Shock and realization filtered over Savion, stunned at the woman's selfless act to save them.

"She disappeared into the rock cliff!" Hona exclaimed.

Savion whipped around to see the sharpshooters idle in the *White Crypt*'s tops and the remaining men leaning haphazardly against railings, chatting excitedly amongst themselves.

"Seems we have a moment's reprieve!" He turned to Petrok. "Check on the progress below and assign more men to pump out the water, then"—Savion glanced across the pile of broken yards, tackles, and rope—"clean up this mess, fix the foresail, and make sure the rest of the lines are taut and secure. I want every able man set to task. Let's take advantage of this gift from King Abbas."

Savion found Nuto at the stern managing the repair of one of their swivel guns.

"Nuto," Savion shouted, bringing the man's gaze to his. "How many of those charges do you have left?"

"Ten, Captain."

"Get them."

With a nod, Nuto darted across the deck and dropped below.

"Hona, ready your musket and climb to the tops."

Petrok rubbed his chin. "What are you thinking, Captain?"

Savion smiled and glanced at the *White Crypt*. "I'm going to destroy our enemy and rescue Perdita, what else?"

Petrok shook his head, though a smile appeared on his lips.

Moments later, Nuto reluctantly handed Savion the oilskin sack containing the ten charges. "It's a fool's errand—you'll be killed for sure."

Tying the sack around his neck, Savion flipped it onto his back, then grabbed Nuto's shoulder. "Ever the optimist, Nuto." He swung a leg over the railing and grinned at his men who were hovering around him, keeping him out of sight. Not just his men—his friends.

"For once I agree with Nuto, Captain," Petrok said. "The woman has been nothing but trouble. Let's patch the ship as best we can and slip away before Damien returns to finish us off."

Hona approached, musket loaded and ready, and a pouch of gunpowder hanging from his belt. Suddenly he looked so young, so innocent. But the man was the best sharpshooter Savion had. "What say you, Hona? Do you think me a fool as well?"

"I know you must do this, Captain. But I fear for you like the others."

"I will return. I promise." Savion nodded and slipped over the side, the warm water lulling him to believe his own words—even though the mission ahead was the most risky he'd ever attempted. For one thing, the unstable charges on his back could blow at any minute. Even now as he swam deeply to avoid detection, he felt them shift across his back. Or they could explode when he positioned them on the *White Crypt*'s hull before Hona had a chance to set them off with his musket shot.

Then there was Perdita. Finding her in the middle of what he assumed to be dark caverns and passageways, all while Damien and his men—armed to the teeth—searched for her as well seemed impossible. How would Savion avoid detection? Would he get there in time? And if he did manage to find her, how would he bring her out without getting them both killed? So many questions, so many unknowns. Impossible odds. Yet that peace—that marvelous, abiding peace—still burned within him like a torch on a dark night, guiding him, leading him ... assuring him.

He surfaced and gulped in air as quietly as he could. The *White Crypt* rose before him like a tombstone toward a gray sky. The stench of sodden wood filled his nose as creaks and groans met his ears, accompanied by a sailor's ditty from above. Good. They hadn't seen him. Opening his sack, he pulled out the first charge and fixed it to the hull with the fasteners. Then, gliding down the side of the ship, he carefully placed the other charges in points where he knew they'd do the most damage. He thanked his father when all were set and none had blown.

Now to rescue Perdita. Diving back to the bottom of the bay, he swam to the edge of the rocky cliffs and surfaced behind a large boulder. As he caught his breath, he heard the crunch of feet and cursing of Damien and his men as they searched the outlying rocks for any sign of Perdita. Good, they hadn't entered the maze of cliffs yet.

Taking a deep breath, Savion dove and wove among boulders stuck in the seabed. Crashing waves jostled him to and fro, delaying his progress, but finally, a narrow opening in the cliff wall came into focus. He eased his face above water and tried to peer inside, but a wave shoved him through the opening, bashing him against jagged walls on either side. Blood stained the water as pain spiked through his side and back. The swell carried him into a small cave, where he gripped the edge of a rock as the water sloshed back out.

He glanced around. No sign of Perdita. Men's voices echoed through the maze. Damien's crew wasn't far behind.

Savion dove into an opening at the edge of the cave and waded through waist-high water down a long channel. Water dripped off walls, *plop-plop* echoing over the rock ceiling. His bare feet landed on something sharp. More pain. More blood pinking the water. The roar of another wave warned him to hang on. A wall of foam slammed into him. He tumbled forward. Sharp rocks scraped his arms, legs, face, and back.

The gush deposited him on a bed of sand in a narrow shaft and rushed out the way it had come. Blood seeped from multiple gashes. His head hurt. He spat salt and blood from his mouth and glanced around, gasping for breath. If he didn't find Perdita soon, nothing but scraps of flesh would be left to mark his attempt to save her.

He no longer heard voices. No doubt Damien and his men had assessed the danger and retreated to surround the cliffs instead. That's what Savion would do in their shoes. But he wasn't in their shoes. He didn't want to hurt Perdita, to use her, to abuse her. He wanted to save her.

Because he loved her.

Mission or not, Perdita was not a means to an end. She *was* the end. He realized that now. And the more the revelation sank in, the more peace he felt, the more resolve to keep going.

Struggling to rise, he started down the narrow channel, seeking direction from within. The medallion warmed his shivering body, guiding him, empowering him to go on despite the pain and fears racking through him. Water roared behind him. The tunnel filled with churning foam, dashing toward him, twisting and turning like steam from a dragon's mouth, ready to swallow him whole. Heart crashing against his chest, he dove into a small opening in the cliff wall just in time before the frothing talons reached him. Scrambling backward in the water, he fell into a wide pool.

He rose to stand in waist-high water and glanced above, where an opening in the cliff allowed streams of sunlight to pour into the small cave. A loud gasp brought him around. Perdita sat on a rock, covering her breasts with her hands, a kelp-forest of black hair falling over them, her green eyes wide with terror, her lips apart.

He started toward her. "Perdita, thank Abbas! Where are your clothes—"

A movement beneath the water caught his eye. The tail of some type of fish—a beautiful, multicolored luminescent tail. Mesmerized, Savion stared at it, following it up … up … up … until it melded into Perdita.

A single tear slipped down her cheek, glistening in a ray of sunlight. Slowly it took shape and form, no longer transparent, but milky white with a hint of pink. It fell from her jaw and plopped into the water.

A pearl.

CHAPTER 28

Perdita wished she could melt into the sea and disappear. She heard Savion gasp in horror. She heard the thump of his heart echoing through the cave, the heaving of his breath. But she could not look at him.

"I … I can't believe my eyes." He heaved. "It's true. You're a … you're a"—his voice faltered—"a … mermaid." Water splashed, and Perdita looked up to see him stumbling backward. Blood slithered through the water around him from dozens of slashes marring his body.

"You're hurt!" She slid off the rock and swam to him. "Let me help you."

"Don't come near me!" He spat.

Those four little words speared her insides, ripping through what was left of her soul. She dove beneath the water to breathe and to hide the tears that now gushed from her eyes. As pearls dropped to the sand, she collected herself. Slowly she eased her head above the surface.

Standing in swirling water up to his waist, Savion stared off into the cave, fury and shock hardening his expression. Still, he remained. He did not run away in horror. He did not abandon her. And that alone gave her hope.

She cringed at the deep cuts she saw through his torn clothing. "I can help you. I can heal your wounds, Savion."

She waited, her heart braced for his rejection.

He mumbled, "I thought there were no … no … mer—"

"I'm the only one."

Waves slammed against the outside of the cliffs. Or was it thunder?

"It was *you*." He faced her, shock and realization blinking from his eyes. "You were the one who saved me. When I fell overboard during that storm a month ago. You left me on that island." He rubbed his temples. "I remembered you … in my dreams. I thought I only imagined …"

"I have saved many sailors from the sea."

He continued staring at her. Rushing water roared outside the narrow entrance. A foamy swell pushed up behind him, but he braced himself against the rocky edge. "Of course. That's what Damien wants with you. He hopes to use you for gain."

The water rushed back out as a spear of sunlight landed on him from above, glittering through his hair and casting him in a golden glow, confirming to Perdita that he did not belong among the evil in Erden—that he did not belong with her.

But then the light was gone, swallowed up by a dark cloud.

Savion placed both hands on a flat rock beside him and hauled himself up to sit. He winced, and Perdita longed to go to him, to take away his pain. Bloodied water streamed from his torn shirt and breeches. He slicked back his wet hair and took deep breaths as if making sure he was awake and not dreaming. She could almost see his mind spinning, trying to put the pieces together.

"Why did you come for me?" she asked. "I was trying to distract them so you could escape." She dared to swim closer.

He looked up, studying her with concern as he used to do, but then he saw the rest of her beneath the water and snapped his eyes away. He lifted his wet shirt over his head, wincing, and tossed it to her. "Put this on."

She obeyed, glad for the covering, and climbed onto a rock close to him, thrilled when he didn't shrink back. She pulled her tail from the water. His breath heightened again as his eyes drifted between her face and tail as if he still couldn't believe what he was seeing.

The itching began … the tingling … writhing up and down her body as scales faded and fell away and skin turned creamy and smooth. She tugged the ends of his shirt to cover her knees and then stretched out her feet and wiggled her toes.

"See? It's still me, Savion. I'm still Perdita."

But he didn't seem convinced. Cuts lined his chest where muscles flexed as if he were preparing to either flee or do battle. Agony wrenched through her at the thought she'd never lay her head on the strength of that chest again or feel those arms barricade her in safety and love.

"Can you change at will?" he asked.

"Yes, but only for twenty minutes. Then I must go in the water again."

"But you were with me for …" He sighed and squeezed the bridge of his nose. "I don't understand."

"That was a special time. I only had a month on land."

His brow wrinkled. "Why a month?"

Should she tell him? Would he understand? She hugged herself, her heart wilting, her throat clogging. She couldn't do it.

Yes, when she glanced back at him, his eyes clouded with unshed tears. Why? Because he'd discovered she lied to him? He'd caught her in lies before. Mayhap 'twas that he'd risked his life for naught but a mermaid—in fact, still risked his life now. Regardless, she had hurt him in so many different ways. And that bothered her most of all.

They sat in silence. Water lapped the edge of the rocks they sat upon as another rumble of thunder shook the cave. Shadows descended and Perdita looked up. A storm arrived. One to match the tempest brewing within this tiny cave.

She was tired of the lies. So very tired.

"Every ten years I am allowed to spend a month on land as a human. During that time, and *only* during that time, I can break the curse."

Water beaded on his chest, sliding over wounds and dripping from the amulet hanging about his neck. It seemed to glow as if sunlight were striking it, but the sun had disappeared behind a gray mist that turned the moist walls into silver. She gulped, but he said nothing.

"I wasn't always like this, Savion. I used to be human." She watched him intently as she told him the full story of Forwin and her banishment to the Ancient Seas. A myriad of emotions drifted across his face while she spoke: unbelief, anger, sorrow, despair. And finally pity.

But she didn't want his pity.

She wanted his love.

"So you expect me to believe you've been alive for three hundred years?"

"'Tis the truth, whether you believe it or not. You can plainly see I'm a mermaid. Why is it so hard to believe I was cursed with immortality?"

She lowered her eyes to the lion tattoo on his bicep. It turned to face her. Nay. It couldn't have. She was seeing things. Perdita rubbed her eyes.

"If that's true"—he finally broke the silence—"then you spend decades without human companionship."

Perdita would have said yes, save for the knot of emotion stuck in her throat.

"How incredibly lonely," he added.

Her eyes burned, and she fought back tears and turned aside. If only he knew. Nay, she wouldn't want him to know, to ever experience the agony of such loneliness.

Lightning etched across the sky in the opening above them as a cream-topped swell charged into the cave, then backed out quickly.

Savion shifted on the rock and dangled his feet in the water. "During your month on land, how do you break this curse?"

Savion waited for her answer, his mind still reeling from everything that had happened, everything she had told him. How was any sane man supposed to believe her crazy story? Evil warlocks and curses? It was the stuff of fables and myths."Zost!" she exclaimed as she slipped back into the water. Had it been twenty minutes already?

Savion breathed a sigh of relief. He was having trouble keeping his eyes off her legs. At least he'd worn a shirt that was thick enough to shield her curves from view. Though the rips and tears in the fabric offered him enough glimpses.

Beneath the surface, her tail formed again. She was indeed a mermaid. And he was not insane. That much he knew.

After a few minutes, her head emerged, water sliding back off her silky hair and skin. Green eyes—filled with shame—slowly met his. She started to talk, hesitated, then started again, her chin lowering. "To break the curse, I must find a man who loves me enough to die for me."

Thunder growled, closer this time.

Her words, though simple enough, muddled in his mind. Finally, when their meaning sank in, fury lit in his belly.

"You followed me." He started, slowly … methodically … so he could keep his temper in check. "After you saved me, you followed me, pretended to be accosted on the beach so I would carry you aboard my ship. That's why I couldn't get rid of you!" His breath came hot. His pulse pounded. "You jumped overboard in the storm. You stole the major's money in Kadon! You wanted me to die for you! Didn't you?" His roar echoed through the cave, matching the thunder outside.

She slid backward in the water. "At first, yes."

"It makes sense now. Why you seemed disappointed when I lived!" Savion pushed off the rock into the swirling water, his face heating. "You jumped off a cliff so I would follow you!"

"Nay." She shook her head pleading. "I didn't mean to do that."

"The panther. You made noise so he'd attack us!"

"I was angry and hopeless. You rejected me." Agony poured in her voice.

Trying to control his fury, he grabbed the medallion for help. *Father, what is going on? What do I do now?* There was no answer, save Perdita's pleading.

"'Tis true that I started out trying to get you to die for me, but after ... after... I came to care for you, I couldn't do it anymore. I couldn't stand the thought of hurting you." Her eyes begged him to believe her.

"Care? What do you know about caring for anyone but yourself? So many lies! So much deception! All to save *yourself*. No matter the cost to others."

Tears slipped down her cheeks, turning into pearls as they dropped in the water. Sniffing, she wiped the back of her hand over her face. "When I escaped Damien's ship, I could have swum far away. But I came back to distract him, so *you* could be safe." Her lips trembled. "Doesn't that count for anything?"

"How do I know you didn't return so I'd risk my life for you again?"

"Because it's too late now. My month is up. I'm trapped for another ten years." Black hair floated around her face like an ebony halo.

Savion turned from her and leaned back against the rock. "This entire past month, you've done nothing but lie to me about who you are, where you come from, and what you were doing with me—nothing but lies and more lies."

"I just wanted you to love me," she whispered.

He was too angry to respond. "So, every ten years you come on land, chose some fool, and throw yourself at him. Just like you did with me. I'd wager most of them fell for it too."

"All but you," she said, her voice cracking. "I … I never wanted to hurt anyone. I just wanted to be free."

Another rush of water spilled into the cave and swept over her. She turned her back to him as sobs racked her body.

Savion swallowed. His anger faded. Yes, she'd done horrible things—to him and many others—yet he could never imagine the pain of her curse. The loneliness, the despair, the heartache.

She spoke through sobs. "Each professed his love, but none meant it. Nobody loved me. Not Sir Ivan of Moorehead and not any of the men since then. In truth, I am not worthy of love."

Thunder rumbled and the cave darkened even more. She became but a gray blur in the distance, her weeping a song tugging on the chords of his heart. Regardless of all she had done—her lies, her immoral behavior, her selfishness—he still loved her.

"Come here," he said gently, holding out his hand.

His soft tone turned her around. Blinking back tears, she swam toward him.

He took her hand in his. "Didn't I tell you that love is so much more than physical joining? True love is caring more about the one you love than for yourself."

She nodded. "I see that now. Because of you. Do you forgive me, Savion? Please say you forgive me."

Placing a finger beneath her chin, he raised her eyes to his. "I do. I don't know why, but I do."

A half sob-half laugh emerged from her lips. "You are too good to me, Savion. Too good, too kind, too merciful for the likes of me." She shook her head. "Why did you come? You could have escaped, and now you are at great risk."

"I will always come for you." He caressed her cheek.

She leaned her head in his palm and closed her eyes.

"I love you, Perdita."

Her eyes opened and she stared at him. "You love *me?*"

Smiling, he eased a lock of wet hair behind her ear. "Surprising, isn't it?"

"But …" Her eyes filled with tears. "I've done naught to earn your love. Quite the opposite in fact."

"True." He kissed her forehead. "Love is not based on performance—it's a choice of the heart. I don't know how it happened exactly, but I *do* love you, dear, sweet Perdita."

"I love you too, Savion. Mayhap my love isn't as pure as yours, but it's strong. It's so strong." A tear slid down her cheek, transforming into a pearl. He caught it and held it up in the fading light.

"You may keep it," she said. "To remember me by."

"It is a treasure of great price."

She looked down. "It is nothing. I have many more where that came from."

"But this one"—he kissed it and slid it into the pocket of his breeches—"was a tear of true love."

She snuggled against him, and he wrapped his arms around her and held her tight as another foamy wave tumbled through the opening around them. "I will never forget you, Savion."

"I don't believe I'll allow you to." He lifted her head up again, a warm smile on his face.

She shook her head and pulled away. "I won't subject you to the pain of my curse. You must be free to love another—a *real* woman."

"How boring." He chuckled.

"You tease me, sir."

"We'll discuss it later. At the moment, we have bigger problems." Savion studied the cave. "We need to find a way out of here. Damien and his men guard the front."

"There is no other way. I went through the entire maze of cliffs before I ended up here."

He pulled her close again. "Then we will have to go out the way we came in."

"But they'll kill you and trap me."

"I won't let them do either. Besides, I have a plan in place. Hona awaits my signal." He kissed her forehead. "Do you trust me?" He held out his hand.

Despite the terror in her eyes, she nodded, took his hand, and allowed him to lead her from the cave.

CHAPTER 29

Perdita's mind and emotions spun in a whirlwind as Savion led her from the cave down the water-logged channels of the cliffs. *He loved her*! She could hardly believe it. Finally, someone truly loved her. Not just anyone, but the most honorable, kind, generous, noble man she'd ever known. It was too much for her heart to absorb. Even now as he forged through the undulating surf, he stopped to throw his body over hers, protecting her from incoming waves and taking the brunt of the torrent himself—adding even more cuts to his body from the sharp walls.

No man had willingly taken wounds that were her due, nor risked his life when she was the one who deserved to die for the things she'd done. Finally, she understood the real meaning of true love.

Finally, after several minutes of constant bashing, they emerged through a jagged opening to a dark, seething sky and a band of men waiting with muskets and knives.

Savion dragged her behind a boulder.

But it was too late. They'd been seen.

"Come out, Savion! And bring the mermaid with you," Damien shouted over the crash of waves.

Savion's breath wafted over her cheek as he crouched beside her in the water, his eyes scanning the scene, assessing their predicament.

"Wait, I can take you under ..." Perdita frantically searched for an opening where she could slip beneath the waves and drag Savion safely into the deep. But they were caged in by boulders, and the water was too shallow for them to swim away unseen.

"It will be all right." Savion's eyes met hers, confidence brimming in their golden depths.

"How can you say that?"

"You got ten seconds!" Damien's shout was followed by the cock of several pistols.

Lightning flashed. A wave tumbled around a boulder, bathing them in bubbling foam. It rose on Savion's chest, then retreated. But he never took his eyes off her.

The amulet around his neck glowed. He eased his thumb over her cheek. "Will you marry me, Perdita?"

She laughed even as her heart swelled. "You ask me this now? When we are about to die?"

Smiling, he brushed hair from her face and leaned to kiss her—a gentle, tender kiss of promise that almost made her believe all would be well. *Almost.*

The sound of a pistol shot separated them.

But it did naught to erase the smile from Savion's face. "Your answer, milady?"

"You're mad." She ran a finger over the bristle on his chin. "Of course I will marry you."

He kissed her again, then extended his hand for hers. "Then let's get this over with, shall we?"

"Nay. They want me, not you. Let me go to them." She gripped his hand and pulled him closer. "After they take me away, you and your men can leave. Please, Savion. I don't want you hurt."

He smiled at her with such awe and approval, her heart nearly burst. Another wave sent foam dancing around them as he leaned over and kissed her cheek. "Damien will not let me go. He serves Natas, and Natas wants me dead."

"Then I've all but killed you." Tears welled in her eyes. "I cannot bear it."

"It was my choice, and my choice alone, to come save you. I love you, Perdita. I'm not going to leave you. Ever."

She didn't know whether to cry or shout for joy, push him away or fall into his arms. Instead, she merely stared into his eyes so filled with love. "Promise?"

He stood. "Forever." And extended his hand once again.

Drawing a deep breath, she nodded and followed him as he waded through waist-high water around boulders and beds of coral. The water grew shallow, and Savion helped Perdita along while she propelled herself forward by shoving her tail against the sand. All the while her heart seemed to sink into that very sand. She glanced out to sea, seeking an escape—any escape—but there was no way out save through Damien's men.

When they emerged from the maze of rocks, Damien and ten of his men waited, waves swirling about their knees, guns leveled at Savion and Perdita.

A maniacal grin twisted Damien's lips. "You thought you could escape, *mermaid*. But you are mine! And so is your gallant hero." He eyed Savion with disdain and then shook his head. "I heard you were smart, Savion Ryne, but now I see you're nothing but a fool." He spit to the side and chuckled. "Natas will reward me greatly for your capture." He turned to a man beside him. "Take her."

A large black man approached.

Savion blocked his path. "You will not touch her."

The man lifted the handle of his musket, no doubt to strike Savion, but Savion blocked the blow with his arm and then slugged him across the jaw. The man's head spun, arms flailing, as he tumbled backward into the water with a mighty splash. His head struck a rock—hard—and he slumped over, gun still in his grip.

A pistol fired. Perdita felt the shot whiz in the small space between her and Savion.

"No, imbecile! I want them both alive!" Damien bellowed.

Unfazed, Savion crossed arms over his bare chest—cut and bruised and bulging with strength. "Then we are at a standstill, Mr. Gund, for you are not taking either of us."

Perdita's heart twisted. She could not see how they would get out of this alive. At least not Savion. Yet, there he stood with all the confidence of a prince, his eyes shifting over his enemy and then curiously over to his ship.

She hefted herself onto a nearby rock, dragging her tail through the sand. The fallen man's musket lay atop the boulder he'd struck—just outside her reach. "Let him go, Damien!" she shouted. "And his ship, and I'll come with you peacefully."

Savion gave her a stern look. "No, Perdita. We discussed this." He followed her gaze to the pistol and shook his head.

Damien growled and ordered two more men to grab her.

Thunder bellowed so loud it seemed the sky would crack. A white spire of lightning brought the men's glances up—and off Perdita. She leapt for the gun. Cocking it, she leveled it at Damien. "I will kill you where you stand, Damien Gund. Order your men to back away and toss their weapons into the water." She tilted her head toward the island. "The men on the beach too."

"No, Perdita." Savion moaned.

Foam whirled around Damien's legs as he grinned and fingered his goatee. "You won't shoot me."

"You know I will." She narrowed her eyes. "You—of all people—know what I am capable of."

His smile faded. A momentary flash of fear crossed his eyes.

"Do it now!" she shouted, ignoring Savion's commands to lower the weapon.

Damien snorted. "You have but one shot, and I doubt your aim is very good."

"Shall we find out?" She closed one eye and brought the gun up for better aim.

Beyond Damien, Perdita spotted one of his men on the beach raise his musket toward her.

After that, everything became a blur—a slow, agonizing blur.

She heard Savion's "No!" and saw him leap in front of her.

The crack of a musket whipped the dark sky. Perdita dropped her weapon. It sank into the water. Savion's body jerked in the air. He tumbled backward and landed with a splash. Blood gushed from a hole in his chest, spilling out in an advancing pool across the water.

"No!" She heard herself scream, but it came out hollow and distant as if she were watching the events unfold and wasn't part of them. Gripping Savion's shoulders, she drew him out of the water and laid him across the rock. Fear like she'd never known spiked through her, numbing her senses. She pressed her hand on the wound. "Savion, Savion!"

Darkness as thick as tar descended.

Boom! Boom! Boom! Boom! Explosions rocked the bay, trembling the water and shooting wood and fire into the sky. Perdita covered Savion's body with her own as flaming spikes rained down on them. When she glanced up, Damien's ship was ablaze. Sails lit like candles. Flames reached for the sky. Black smoke poured from jagged holes in the hull. Bodies and debris floated in the water. What? How?

Men emerged from the jungle framing the shore—Savion's crew—muskets and swords in hand. They must have circled around the island. But Damien didn't see them yet. His attention was on what once was his ship, his face white, his jaw hanging.

Gunshots peppered the dark sky. Damien spun to face the beach, weapon at the ready, but the barrels of a dozen pistols greeted him. Savion's crew had subdued his men and had them surrounded.

But Perdita didn't care. All she cared about was Savion.

"Savion! Savion!" Blood gurgled up between her fingers as she pressed her hand on the bullet hole. With her other hand, she felt for a pulse.

Nothing.

He can't be gone. Not to save someone like her. Where were his guardians? The men of light who protected him? She frantically glanced about, but they were nowhere to be seen. Finally, she lay on top of him, sobbing.

A strange sensation spiraled around her tail and rose upward toward her waist. Not the itching she always felt when she transformed into a human, nor was it the pain she felt when she changed back into a mermaid. This was a pleasant feeling: a warmth, a tingling, a lightness—as if an enormous weight were being lifted from her. Mayhap she was dying. She hoped so.

She didn't want to live without Savion.

She laid her head back on his chest, tears spilling down her cheeks. The amulet warmed beneath her skin, and she rose and studied it. A strong wind swirled about her, and the amulet lifted off Savion and floated toward her as if it were drawn to her somehow. But that wasn't possible. She tried to press it down, but it rose toward her again. Tears still trickling down her cheeks, she relented and eased it over Savion's head. Then, laying a gentle kiss upon it, she slipped it around her neck and tucked it beneath her shirt—his shirt. She pressed it and felt its warmth through the wet fabric. It would be a reminder of him. One she would cherish forever. She hung her head and sobbed, then swiped tears from her face.

Wait. Her hand was moist. No pearls littered the rock around Savion.

Shouts, curses, and water sloshing sounded behind her. A pistol fired. The chime of a blade rang in the wind. Fire crackled, and wood creaked and sizzled as it fell into the sea. But she would not take her eyes off Savion. A wave crashed over her, nearly pushing her from him, and she drew up her legs for a better grip.

Legs.

She had transformed into a human. But how could that be? She'd been in the water. She took Savion's hand in hers. True, he had died for her, but it was past ephemeral redemption. Oh, what did it matter? She cared not whether she was human or mermaid or a sea slug. She just wanted Savion back.

"Savion." She kissed his hand and drenched it with her tears. "Savion, please come back to me."

Petrok, Nuto, and three others from Savion's crew sloshed toward her. Haddeus dropped before his captain and took his pulse. His baleful groan filled the air.

"What have you done?" Agony screamed in Petrok's voice. "You've killed him!" He fell beside his captain while Nuto merely stood there, horrified.

"He died saving me." Perdita wept, her words coming out muffled and hollow.

Petrok's face reddened. Tears filled his eyes. He shoved her aside and enlisted the others to help carry Savion to the beach. Perdita trudged after them, barely able to move for the guilt and sorrow weighing her down.

They laid their master gently on the sand. Hona came running up the beach and fell on his captain and wailed, his cries stabbing Perdita's heart. The others kneeled around him weeping, moaning, staring in shock at the man they had all loved. How long they all sat there, Perdita couldn't say. Long enough for the wind to blow the clouds away, long enough for the sun to make an appearance before it sank listless and dull toward the horizon as if it, too, mourned the loss of a great man.

Wind blew Savion's hair into his face, and she gently brushed it away.

"We should go." Petrok finally said, his voice empty.

The words crushed her.

"Where?" Hona asked.

"Home. We will take him to his home."

The men nodded and each rose to their feet.

Perdita's heart turned to stone. She tried to stand, but her legs kept folding beneath her. Nuto assisted her up. Her insides collapsed, knowing she'd never see Savion again, never hear his voice, see him smile, see the light and wisdom and care in his eyes.

"Come along." Petrok motioned for her to join them.

She stepped back. "I can't."

"Listen, I know I was angry—*am* angry—with you. But Savion would want us to look out after you."

Hona gripped her arm. "Do come with us, Perdita."

But she couldn't. She'd done enough damage. These men hated her and for good reason. In truth, she hated herself. "Nay. Please go. I'll be all right here."

It would seem Petrok had no fight left within him for he simply nodded. She watched as Savion's men reverently carried him to a boat and rowed him to the *Scepter*. She watched as they gently lifted him up the ladder and hoisted him over the railing.

She watched until she saw him no more.

But her now-human body would be a constant reminder of his love. The one true love who had been willing to die for her.

Chapter 30

Seven months later

Perdita balanced her boots on the foredeck of the *Victory* as the ship crested a wave and then crashed down the other side. Spray came sweeping aft, cooling her skin and depositing liquid diamonds on her waistcoat and breeches. Above her, sails filled to near bursting while a sky spanned the sea in a bowl of star-twinkling black.

"Where to, Captain?" Her first mate, Jard, slid beside her and scanned the horizon.

She gripped the amulet—Savion's amulet—hanging around her neck. It began to heat as it always did when she was needed on an important mission—just as she and her crew had done yesterday in Renok. Rescuing a town from an incoming tsunami hadn't been the hard part. 'Twas fighting off the influx of Natas's forces who'd been waiting to infiltrate after the damage was done. But she'd chosen her crew well. Strong, brave men who were more than willing to serve a female captain as long as they got to fight Natas's hordes and extend the kingdom for King Abbas.

Then again, she'd learned from the best.

Her first mate shifted his stance, awaiting her answer. But although the amulet warmed, no direction came from within. There was the usual peace and, oddly, a bit of rising excitement. But no guidance. "I don't know," she answered. "Keep heading east. We shall see what awaits us there."

He touched his hat with the tip of his finger and sped off.

A golden glow rose on the horizon, announcing a new day—a new day of adventure and purpose, a new day that would take her to places she'd never been, to help others she'd never met. Grunts and groans brought her around to see her crew emerging from hatches, rubbing their eyes, and shuffling to their daily duties. She faced forward again and smiled, still not believing that a once-cursed mermaid was captain of a ship full of warriors! Warriors who fought on the side of good.

She gripped the hilt of the cutlass at her side. Thus far, they had done much good as they scoured the Ancient Seas, following where the amulet led. They set captives free, healed the sick, fed the hungry and thirsty, brought hope to the hopeless, sheltered the homeless, comforted the despondent, and defeated Natas's hordes wherever they found them.

'Twas all so incredible, this grand adventure she was on, and one she did not deserve.

After Savion died, she had wallowed in self-pity and despair for more than a month, not eating, barely drinking, and longing for a death that would soon come now that she was mortal. But Savion called to her on the wind, in the crash of the waves, the beauty of the sunset. She would not allow his death to be for naught. She would not. She would follow in his footsteps, do the good that he had done. Pick up the mission where he left off.

How could she do any less after he had given his life for her?

The sun peered above the horizon in an arc of gold, spreading ribbons over the sea in every color of the rainbow.

Perdita squinted against its brilliance and closed her eyes, allowing its warmth to wash away the chill of night.

"A sail! A sail!" one of her top men yelled from above. "Straight off the bow."

Plucking the telescope from her belt, Perdita focused it toward the sun. Out of the brilliant glow, the stark outline of masts and sails appeared, growing larger and larger.

Jard and Aiden appeared beside her. "Who is she?"

Perdita shook her head, trying to focus on the ensign flapping from her mainmast. "I don't know." She lowered the scope. "Ready the guns just in case, Mr. Aiden."

"Aye, Captain."

"She's coming fast!" Her first mate whistled. "It's like she's flying over the water."

Indeed, she was. Yet Perdita felt no fear, no trepidation. She curled fingers around the amulet, felt its warmth, saw its glow, but still naught but excitement burned within her.

The *Victory* lurched to starboard. Wood creaked and blocks rattled as sails snapped above. Creamy foam bubbled over the bow onto the deck. Balancing, Perdita raised the scope again. A stiff breeze gripped the ensign of the oncoming ship and flattened it for a moment. The flash of a lion with a scepter in its hand crossed her vision.

The *Scepter*! Her heart leapt. She shifted the glass to the deck. A bush of dark curly hair flopped in the breeze. Petrok? She adjusted the scope for a clearer view. It *was* Petrok! And Hona stood beside him.

"She signals for a parlay, Captain," Jard said.

"Signal her back that we are happy to comply!" Perdita laughed and leapt down the foredeck ladder onto the main deck. "Lay aloft and furl tops and mains! Tack aweather! Bring us alongside our guests."

Her crew scrambled to do her bidding, some leaping into the ratlines, others retrieving slack lines as sails were lowered. Soon the two ships slowed and heaved-to just yards apart. Lines were tossed, and both crews tugged until the ships thudded together.

Perdita could hardly contain herself. She leapt onto the bulwarks and flew over the railing of the *Scepter,* landing on the deck with a firm thud. This was Savion's ship. His presence was still so strong, she could feel him, sense him, as if he still walked her decks. It did her heart good. It also did her good to see his crew.

Without waiting for permission, she flew into Petrok's arms, not caring if he was still angry. Thankfully, he embraced her as if he were meeting an old friend. Elated, she withdrew and hugged Hona and Nuto and several others of the crew—all who seemed happy to see her.

Petrok smiled. "Perdita, you look well."

"I am more than well. I am changed. I am doing Savion's work now."

At the mention of his name she expected sorrow to claim Petrok's expression, but he only smiled wider, his eyes twinkling as if he knew a grand secret.

"You should join me!" She nearly burst with the idea. "The *Scepter* and the *Victory,* side by side, defeating Natas together! Won't that be wonderful?"

"We *will* do that," Hona said, snapping hair from his face. "Soon. But first there is something else you must do."

Dread crept through Perdita. Despite their smiles—or mayhap because of them—she wondered if they intended to punish her for past sins. Make her walk the plank, keelhaul her, tie her to the mast, flog her, or mayhap all. She certainly deserved it. And more. She stepped forward, heart in her throat. "I'll do whatever you require to atone for—"

"For what?" A voice interrupted Perdita from the companionway. It flowed past her ears like the dulcet tones of a cello. She *knew* that voice. But it couldn't be.

Light hair appeared, then his glorious face, and then the fullness of him as he walked toward her in his tan breeches and white open shirt with his sun-kissed hair blowing behind him. She blinked. Nay! Savion was dead. This was just a vision, a dream conjured by her longing, her need for him.

She kept staring, taking in all the details she remembered, knowing that soon he would fade away or transform into one of the *Scepter*'s sailors.

But he didn't. He stopped before her, gazing at her with those piercing gold eyes of his that always spoke more than words could say. Now they were saying love, hope, joy, peace … all the things she wanted her heart to embrace, but feared to because she didn't deserve them.

"It's me, Perdita. Never fear." He brought her hand to his for a kiss.

She stumbled backward, and he put an arm around her waist.

"You're alive? But … how? I saw you die." Blood rushed from her head. His kiss, his touch— they felt so real.

"You best get her some water before she faints," Savion said to Hona as he led her to sit atop a barrel. "My crew brought me home, where my father healed me. He has power over death."

"Home?" Perdita rubbed her temples.

"Nevaeh."

She gaped at him. Now she *knew* she was dreaming. "No one knows how to get to Nevaeh."

"I know the way." He smiled and glanced over his crew. "Besides, my father is the king."

Breath fled her lungs, and she gripped the edges of the barrel. "You are the son of King Abbas? You are the prince of Nevaeh?"

"I am."

Perdita dropped to her knees, her mind whirling with all the horrible things she'd done to this man—the prince!

She'd used him, lied to him. Zost! She'd tried to seduce him! More than once she'd tried to get him killed.

Finally she did just that, when it was the last thing she wanted.

Would he now sentence her to death and worse—send her to some horrible dungeon? Trembling, she bowed her head. "My lord and my king."

"And you, Perdita, are my princess. Rise." He took her hand and helped her to her feet. Baffled, she stared at him. *Princess?* This couldn't be happening. Dreams didn't come true for women like her. She rubbed her eyes, trying to settle her whirling thoughts and emotions.

But when she focused on him again, he smiled and gently kissed her cheek, his eyes sparkling with delight. "I believe you owe me a wedding."

EPILOGUE

If you combined all the fables and stories and descriptions of Nevaeh and then enhanced them a hundredfold, it would never come close to how glorious it truly was. Everywhere Perdita turned, there was a new delight to discover. A melodious song. Food that sent her taste buds into ecstasy. A waterfall, lake, forest, canyon, or field of flowers that surpassed those in Erden a thousand times over. Colors she'd never seen before bursting vibrantly as though they were alive. Palatial buildings constructed entirely of gemstones that climbed upward toward a sky that was the most luminous blue she'd ever seen.

And best of all there was peace. The peace she had always longed for. There was love. The love that she'd always yearned for. Companionship. Every person in Nevaeh was kind and generous and good. She felt loved—and cherished. They all welcomed her as if she were royalty.

Now on her second evening there, as she stood before the altar in a massive cathedral, she realized she would truly *become* royalty. She would be a princess in a land she had never thought to see, let alone inhabit—and rule over.

She wore a shimmering white gown that flowed behind her in a magnificent train that stretched for yards. Silver embroidery adorned the lace at her neckline, sleeves, and hem. Tiny pearls were embedded in every inch of the silken fabric, making her shimmer in the candlelight.

A flock of gleeful women had curled her long hair, then entwined it with threads of rubies and diamonds, allowing it to flow down her back to her waist.

Savion stood beside her, more handsome than she'd ever seen him in his white doublet trimmed in gold braid covering a black cambric shirt. A purple cape hung from his shoulders to his knees, where white breeches retreated into golden boots. His jaw was strong, his hair slicked back, his eyes alight with love. He turned toward her and touched one of the pearls on her dress and smiled. He had told her that each one represented a tear she had shed in Erden. None had gone unnoticed and none had been wasted, for they now adorned her wedding gown.

Before her, a golden altar rose, and beyond it, a stained-glass window reached for the sky. A rainbow of colors arched across the glass with a single white dove above it. Beneath the window, Guardians of Nevaeh, decked in white and gold, stood in formation in full armor—the creatures of light she'd seen protecting Savion in Erden.

Behind Perdita, thousands upon thousands of joyful people filled the massive church, dressed in shimmering gowns and suits, their excited murmurs echoing like chimes in the domed ceiling.

More candles than Perdita could count flickered from golden lampstands standing on either side of the altar and from sconces lining the walls. Sweet incense filled the room.

Savion's father appeared before them. Upon her arrival, King Abbas had welcomed her into his family with open arms and brought her into his home for a grand party. It had only taken Perdita two days in his presence to realize he was the wisest, kindest man she'd ever met. Now, he smiled at her, his eyes twinkling.

Vows were spoken. Promises made. And when Savion kissed her, the crowd cheered and music swirled through the room. As was the custom in Nevaeh, the wedding feast lasted for seven days, filled with more merriment, joy, laughter, and delicacies than Perdita thought possible.

When all the festivities were concluded and the guests had gone home, Perdita and Savion retreated to their wedding lair, where they spent three glorious days alone. Now, they sat on the balcony overlooking a lake that was so pure and clear, it looked like glass. Wind blew the fragrance of sweet flowers over them.

Perdita leaned her head on Savion's shoulder. "It's so beautiful and peaceful here. I never want to leave Nevaeh."

"I know, my love. I feel the same." He stroked her hair. "But we have work to do. There are still many people in Erden suffering under the hand of Natas's rule. We must go back and destroy Natas forever. We must set things right—the way my father intended. It is our destiny."

She smiled. "Of course. You are right. How can I enjoy my happiness when so many suffer?"

He kissed her forehead. "Soon all suffering will end."

She gazed up at him. "And I will be by your side forever."

"Forever and ever and ever." He leaned over and kissed her.

And so the adventure begins ...

The End

For God did not send His Son into the world to condemn the world, but that the world through Him might be saved.

John 3:17

ABOUT THE AUTHOR

Christy Award nominee and best-selling author MaryLu Tyndall describes herself as an introvert, neighborhood cat-lady, tall ship enthusiast, friend of pirates and mermaids, obsessive compulsive control freak, hopeless romantic, and a sword-wielding princess-warrior of the King of Kings. Her books are filled with adventure and romance guaranteed to touch your heart! Her hope is that readers will not only be entertained but will be brought closer to the Creator who loves them beyond measure. In a culture that accepts the occult, wizards, zombies, and vampires without batting an eye, MaryLu hopes to show the awesome present and powerful acts of God in a dying world. She has published over fourteen novels and currently lives in California with her husband, six kids, and several cats.

If you enjoyed this book, one of the nicest ways to say "thank you" to an author and enable them to continue writing is to leave a favorable review on Amazon, Barnes and Noble, and elsewhere! I would appreciate it if you would take a moment to do so. Thanks so much!

Comments? Questions? I love hearing from my readers! Feel free to contact me via my website:

http://www.marylutyndall.com

Or email me at:

Marylu_tyndall@yahoo.com

Join my Facebook Fan Page

https://www.facebook.com/groups/221955524678618/

Twitter:

https://twitter,com/MaryLuTyndall

Blog:

http://crossandcutlass.blogspot.com

Pinterest:

http://www.pinterest.com/mltyndall

To receive news about special prices and new releases, please sign up for my newsletter on my website or blog!

Other Books By MaryLu

Legacy of the King's Pirates

The Redemption, The Reliance, The Restitution,
The Ransom

The Falcon and the Sparrow

Charles Towne Belles Series

The Red Siren, The Blue Enchantress,
The Raven Saint

Surrender to Destiny Series

Surrender the Heart, Surrender the Night
Surrender the Dawn

Veil of Pearls

Escape to Paradise Series

Forsaken Dreams, Elusive Hope
Abandoned Memories

Westward Christmas Bride Collection

Made in the USA
San Bernardino, CA
14 November 2014